How to Kill a
ROCK
STAR

How to Kill a
ROCK STAR

Becky Ann Bartness

iUniverse, Inc.
Bloomington

How to Kill a Rock Star

Copyright © 2012 Becky Ann Bartness

This is a work of fiction. All of the characters, names, incidents, organizations, and dialogue in this novel are either the products of the author's imagination or are used fictitiously.

iUniverse books may be ordered through booksellers or by contacting:

iUniverse
1663 Liberty Drive
Bloomington, IN 47403
www.iuniverse.com
1-800-Authors (1-800-288-4677)

Because of the dynamic nature of the Internet, any Web addresses or links contained in this book may have changed since publication and may no longer be valid. The views expressed in this work are solely those of the author and do not necessarily reflect the views of the publisher, and the publisher hereby disclaims any responsibility for them.

Any people depicted in stock imagery provided by Thinkstock are models, and such images are being used for illustrative purposes only.

Certain stock imagery © Thinkstock.

ISBN: 978-1-4759-6421-9 (sc)
ISBN: 978-1-4759-6422-6 (e)

Library of Congress Control Number: 2012922318

Printed in the United States of America

iUniverse rev. date: 1/14/2013

Chapter One

August was the wrong month to start my jogging program. Even at five thirty in the morning, the temperature was in the nineties and the mercury was rising fast. I'd taken Ralph, my large dog of indeterminate breed, with me, thinking that he would be thrilled with the opportunity to run, sniff, pee, and poop along the two-mile jogging path next to the canal. We had made it only a quarter mile, though, when he plopped down under a palo verde and refused to take another step. I told him I'd stop by for him on my way back. I'm not sure he understood, but I'm fairly sure he didn't care: he was asleep before I made it ten feet down the trail.

As I ran along the gravel path beside the canal, sweat dripped into my eyes and soaked my tank top and running shorts. Normally, what they say is true: Arizona has a dry heat. But August is monsoon season, and the humidity is unusually high for us. In other words, there is no redeeming value whatsoever to Phoenix in August.

I was on a quest to lose weight, though. So, unbearable heat notwithstanding, I was jogging when I should have been asleep in bed.

The shade of graceful willows and eucalyptus trees lining the canal as it wandered through the grounds of the Biltmore Hotel provided a bit of respite from the heat. I rounded a gentle curve and saw what looked like a heap of glittery red fabric lying on a grassy berm. As I got closer, I realized that there was more to the heap than fabric.

I knelt beside the woman and saw right away that CPR was going to be a waste of time. Red ants had discovered the body and streamed into her vacant blue eyes and slightly open mouth in search of whatever it is ants find intriguing. Her white-blonde hair spread around her as if arranged. Heavy white makeup covered her face, interrupted by a gash of dark red lipstick staining her lips.

I started to brush the ants from her face with a shaky hand but caught myself. The woman had obviously not died of natural causes, and I could be disturbing evidence.

I scrambled to my feet and frantically searched my fanny pack for my cell phone. You would think finding a cell in something as small as a fanny pack would be a piece of cake, but phones have shrunk in size, and I had crammed so much into my pack that locating and unwedging individual items was a challenge.

My fingers closed around the phone, and I pried it out, dragging a packet of Kleenex, a tube of ChapStick, and a small can of breath spray with it. I punched 9-1-1, although in light of how my life had been going lately, I probably could have hit redial. When the dispatcher picked up, I rattled off the description and location of my discovery and my name and phone number. (As they say, practice makes perfect.) I listened while the dispatcher called in the report and came back on the line.

"Kate," she said. "It's me, Dolores."

Dolores was a former employee of Pole Polishers. Pole Polishers is a major client of my law firm and is managed by my best friend, Tuwanda Jones. We'd met and hit it off when I was investigating the disappearance of the previous manager of Pole Polishers. To put it bluntly, Pole Polishers offers sex for hire, although the company's brochure euphemistically describes its business as "providing opportunities for clients to fully express themselves in a caring environment."

After finishing her training at the police academy, Dolores had left her position at Pole Polishers (or maybe I should say positions—double entendres are hard to avoid in this area) and was now a dispatcher in the 9-1-1 division.

"Hey, Dolores," I said weakly.

"Look, Kate, I don' mean to be critical, but you got a nasty habit of findin' bodies."

There was really nothing I could say in defense. It was true. Even if I locked myself in my condo, one would be tossed through a window so I could meet whatever body-discovery quota was assigned to me as part of the cosmos.

"You doin' okay, Kate?" asked Dolores, apparently attributing my silence to shock rather than resigned acceptance.

"I'm doing better than the victim," I quipped in an attempt at *Law & Order* humor.

"Well, hang in there. Our guys are on the way."

Even as she said it, I could hear the sound of approaching sirens.

I ended the call and, having done my civic duty, suddenly felt weak. I moved away from the body and sat on a boulder that, from the smell of it, primarily served as a doggy pit stop.

The shock that prevents people from responding to horror *with* horror was wearing off, and I felt nauseous. The smell of dog urine didn't help. I began to wretch and after a couple of stomach convulsions upchucked my morning coffee and orange juice on the already abused and beleaguered boulder.

Mid-upchuck, I saw two squad cars screech to a halt on the frontage road adjacent to the canal, and a cadre of police officers emerged.

"Are you Miss Williams?" inquired the first officer to reach me.

"Ms.," I automatically corrected. I pointed at the body lying in the grass. "There."

One of the officers started making calls while the others placed crime tape in a wide circumference around the body. They were the first of the CSI responders; the detectives would follow.

A young, fresh-faced officer approached me. "Would you like a blanket, ma'am?" he asked.

I stared at him in disbelief. It had to be over a hundred by now. "Why don't you bring me some cocoa and make a fire too?" I rasped. But he looked so dismayed that I took pity on him. "Actually, a bottle of water would be wonderful."

"I'll get one from the car for you, ma'am," he said. He hesitated before trotting off on his mission of mercy. "The publicity's gonna be bad on this one because … well, you know, because of who she is … was."

"Who—" I started to ask, but at that moment his captain called him. After shrugging apologetically, he rushed off.

I bet he would forget my water; damn chain of command.

I had no idea who the victim was or what the officer meant about the publicity being bad.

A Crown Vic pulled up and parked behind a couple of squad cars. A familiar figure emerged from the driver's side, the early morning sun glinting off his ever-expanding bald spot. He wore his standard uniform—a brown polyester suit with the pant hems hitting his ankles just above the flood-line, giving everyone a fine view of his white cotton socks. His shoes were black, his shirt was yellow, and his tie was red, white, and blue, which, upon closer inspection, would likely evidence a multitude of stains, some of which, I knew, had historical significance.

Detective Webber and I had a love/hate relationship. Actually, a better description would be a dislike/hate relationship. We had worked, depending on your point of view, either together or against one other on several high-profile cases. In fact, Webber had been the chief detective on so many of my cases that I had a sneaking suspicion he'd been permanently assigned to the Division of Kate Williams, Esq.–Related Cases, no doubt one of the busiest divisions in the department.

Webber walked directly to the body and shouted orders to the tech team, which had arrived seconds after him. The team quickly established a search grid. Cameras clicked and flashed, and every bit of possible evidence was collected and labeled. (They were being thorough; the Biltmore would have to resod the entire area.) The crowd was soon joined by the reps from the coroner's office and the EMTs, the job of the latter being to stand around and download iPhone applications until the morgue van arrived and they were dismissed.

According to my watch, it was six thirty; too early to

call my office. Beth, my secretary, who was usually the first one to roll in, didn't show up until eight. My other staff members, MJ, my paralegal, and Sam, my investigator, came in at nine. Tuwanda, however, would be getting off work about now. I dialed Pole Polishers' number, and Marge, Tuwanda's uber-efficient office manager, answered on the first ring.

"Pole Polishers; we can lick anyone," she announced.

"New motto?"

"Hi, Kate. No, we're just trying out different catchphrases for our marketing program. You want to talk to Tuwanda?"

"Yes, please."

I waited as Marge yelled into the intercom. Both Beth and Marge had never accepted the fact that an intercom meant you didn't have to raise your voice to yodeling volume to be heard in another room.

"Damn," said Tuwanda, getting on the line.

"Good morning to you too," I replied.

"I'm gonna rip that intercom right out of the wall," she said for the umpteen-millionth time. "It's like livin' in a bus station with a damn loud speaker blarin' all the time."

"Tough night?"

"Ain't they all? If you ain't goin' crazy over bein' busy, you goin' crazy worrying that you ain't busy. Las' night was a crazy-over-bein'-busy night."

Tuwanda had recently taken off time to rethink her

career path as a successful madam but was now back on track after she realized that she wasn't qualified for any other work until she finished her education. She had recently gotten her GED and was now pursuing her favorite pastime—taking random classes at the local community college—but this time with an eye toward obtaining a premed degree. In the meantime, bills needed to be paid.

"You callin' about meetin' for breakfast? Ain't this kinda early in the day for you?" she asked.

I gave her a quick rundown of what had happened.

After a few beats of silence, she said, "Thas jus' sad. This makes the third dead body you foun' in six months. An' then there's a whole other group of folks that died in your vicinity."

I didn't say anything, because again, there really wasn't anything I *could* say.

"They takin' you down to the station on this one?" she asked.

"I don't know. The detective hasn't gotten around to talking to me yet."

"I'm jus' guessin' in light a' your pas' history an' unb'lievable bad luck that that would be Webber you referrin' to?"

"Yes," I said.

A few more beats of silence.

"You jus' tell me where you want me to pick you up, an' I'll be there in a jiffy," she said, her voice softening.

"An' you hold up, girl. Ain't none a' this your fault. You jus' at the wrong place at the wrong time … again."

We both knew that I had some seriously bad karma. Maybe I was Genghis Khan or Jack the Ripper in a former life and the next few iterations of me had to suffer the karmic payback.

"Thanks, Tuwanda. I'll give you a call as soon as I know where I'll be. If it gets too late, don't wait up for me (this was technically Tuwanda's bedtime, after all). In fact, if you haven't heard from me by eight, call my office and ask Beth to pick me up."

Tuwanda was all for coming over right away to at least lend moral support, but I insisted that she wait until she heard from me again, because, among other things, parking at the scene of the crime was scarce and access was limited. The jogging path, side street, and grassy berm between the path and the canal had been steadily filling with more police vehicles and an entourage of news station vans and reporters' cars. The media had pulled out all the stops. In addition to the vans and cars, helicopters from Channel 12, Channel 3, and Channel 15 circled over the crime site. The NPR guys would likely arrive on their bicycles any minute.

Chapter Two

As I ended the call with Tuwanda, something wet touched my leg. I jerked my leg away and prepared to defend against an assault by some icky desert creature. But it was only Ralph, who must have gotten tired of waiting and came to find me.

"Good boy, Ralph," I said, praising his tracking ability. Ralph was more interested in sniffing the boulder than basking in glory though.

"Don't let that mutt contaminate the crime scene," ordered Webber, who had come up (or snuck up, depending on your perspective) behind us.

"If you're concerned about this rock, it's already been contaminated by decades of dog pee and, most recently, regurgitated coffee and juice."

"What were you doing out here at five in the morning?" he asked, ignoring my boulder input.

"Jogging."

"You? You don't jog, and *no* one jogs in Phoenix in August."

"I decided to get in better shape," I said sulkily. I wanted to add *which is something you should consider doing too*. Instead, I settled for staring pointedly at his bulging gut.

"Trying to get that boyfriend of yours back?" he chuckled.

Ouch. Bryan Turner, acting Maricopa County sheriff, and I had been an item until recently. Last month Bryan decided to toss his hat into the ring and run for sheriff in the fall election. Although he would never admit it, I think the major cause of our breakup was that someone such as I—a highly publicized (never in a good way) defense attorney—was a liability to a candidate running on a law-and-order platform. While Bryan remained polite and aloof whenever we met in public, his campaign manager, Dave Sneadly, made a finger-cross and backed away whenever he ran into me.

Webber must have seen the wounded look in my eyes and either taken pity on me or, more likely, decided to save the Bryan weapon for later. In any event, he dropped the subject.

"Are you okay to give a statement now or do you want to come downtown, get a Diet Coke, and give me your statement in an air-conditioned room?"

The air-conditioned room part was tempting, but I knew that if we stayed here the interview would take less time. One hundred degree heat inspires verbal efficiency.

"I'll give it now," I said.

"Can we at least go sit in an air-conditioned van?"

Sweat ran down his face and stained his collar.

I agreed to the compromise, reasoning that maybe dealing with a hot, cranky Webber was not such a good idea, regardless of the efficiencies. I followed Webber, and Ralph trailed behind. He panted loudly—Webber, not Ralph—as he led us to a white evidence van where the noisy whir of a generator gave promise of a cool interior. He swung one of the van's back doors open and gestured for us to climb in.

"We sure would like some water," I said. "One of your officers promised to bring me a bottle some time ago."

Guilt was usually an ineffective weapon against Webber, but I think he was thirsty too. He ordered an officer standing near the van to bring three bottles of water.

"And a bowl if you have one," I added. Ralph had many talents, but drinking out of a bottle was not one of them.

After we got settled in the van with our drinks (Ralph drinking from a motorcycle helmet), Webber took a pen, a small writing tablet, and a cigarette lighter–sized recorder out of his pocket. The van had no windows and was lit by a single dome-light, triggering childhood memories of backyard tent sleep-outs. I half expected Webber to shine a flashlight under his chin and tell a ghost story.

Webber balanced his butt on the narrow, built-in metal bench, turned on the recorder, and then stated the date, time, and location, stumbling over the description of our exact whereabouts.

He asked me to state my name and address, which I did, and then he led me through the usual list of questions.

After I finished my brief statement (I came, I saw, I barfed), Webber clicked off the recorder and sat back.

"You have no idea who she is, do you?" he said.

"You mean the victim? No, I've never seen her before."

"Do you recognize the name Queen Ta Ta?"

I stifled a guffaw prompted by the memory of a word we used in junior high to refer to women parts.

"No," I said, shaking my head both for emphasis and to squelch the giggle urge.

"Have you been living in a cave?"

I looked around the van's tiny space. "Not until now."

"Ha ha. Very funny. Let me ask you this: why do you think so many reporters, news vans, and helicopters are here?"

I shrugged. "Slow news day?"

"Queen Ta Ta is—or was—a pop star. Every one of her songs is a hit. If she whistled 'Yankee-Doodle' it would be number one on the charts the next day."

"Are you a fan of hers?" I asked.

"No. I have a fourteen-year-old daughter, remember? She's downloaded every Queen Ta Ta song onto her iPod and plays them in a continuous loop. She has a poster of Queen Ta Ta in her room, a Queen Ta Ta T-shirt, and a Queen Ta Ta cell phone cover."

Webber was the father of an incredibly cool kid named Emily. The connection between the father part and the incredible kid part was hard for me to fathom. I guess we'll never understand the interplay between genetics and environment.

"Are you sure that's who it is?" I asked. "It seems to me that bleached blonde hair and club clothes are de rigueur these days."

"Spider tattoos on asses are not," he said.

"Silly me. I should have looked there first."

He sighed. "One of our officers made the initial ID. The confirmation came from her manager. They're staying at the Biltmore Hotel. She had a performance at the Comerica Theater tonight. Be prepared for a lot of media hype on this one, Kate. They're gonna be in your face for weeks."

Webber's unexpected advice surprised me, and I groaned aloud at the thought of the media. I hated the media. Every time I got involved with them it turned out poorly—for me. Among the published pictures of me were images of me running naked from a house fire carrying a Chihuahua that was too small to cover much of anything, one of me standing, sopping wet, in a fountain at the mall with a fast-food wrapper stuck to the side of my head, and another of my butt taken from an unflattering angle as I knelt to look into a hole in the floor of Sam's office where a child's skeleton was found.

"I don't think they've gotten any pictures of me this time around," I said hopefully.

Webber put that fantasy to rest. "Think again. You've been on live feed since the helicopters got here. We all have."

I hate technology.

Chapter Three

Panic set in. "How am I going to get out of here without the press spotting me?"

"If you have someone who can pick you up, I'll tell the traffic control officers to let them through and we can try to slip you out."

I looked at him gratefully. "Thank you," I said. "Tuwanda offered to pick me up. I just need to call her and let her know when."

"Tuwanda?" he said in a near shout. "She drives a pink convertible El Dorado with spinners. We might as well bring in a limo with *Witness Transportation* printed in gold and surrounded by marquis lights on both sides. It would draw less attention."

"You've got one of those?"

Webber rubbed his temples. "Ask Tuwanda to find something more understated to pick you up in," he said.

He stood to leave, bumped his head on the low ceiling, and exited the van among a stream of curses.

I patted Ralph on the head as I called Tuwanda.

"Apparently the body I found is that of someone named Queen Ta Ta," I said without preface. "Do you know who that is?"

"Hell, yeah. She another white girl makin' money offa' black people's moves an' black people's music. Can't white people think a' nothin' on they own?

"An' you din't have to tell me who it was neither. You been on Channel 12 off an' on all morning. They showed you sittin' on a rock with the police millin' aroun' lookin' for stuff. They been showin' Queen Ta Ta's music videos an' interviewin' people too. It's like when Michael Jackson died. Everybody expressin' opinions without knowin' what the hell really happened, an' the police not sayin' anythin' to anyone."

"How did the press find out she was the victim?"

"Cops called the hotel where she was stayin' an' talked to her manager. Then the manager e-mailed every news outlet in the world an' let 'em know.

"Did you know Michael Jackson was in big debt before he died an' now he's made enough money to pay it all off plus add another ten mil to his back account?"

Tuwanda was not big on segues.

"Michael must be pleased," I commented.

Tuwanda missed my sarcasm. "Bein' dead, I doubt he

gives a damn. But his family an' all them attorneys they got on the payroll sure is pleased."

Leaving the subject of Michael Jackson's postmortem career success, I asked if she could come get me and explained about the police escort and the need for her to drive an understated vehicle.

"Where's the POS parked?"

POS, an acronym for piece of shit, was Tuwanda's nickname for my Honda Hybrid. We disagreed on this point. I thought my environment-friendly little car was pretty spiffy.

"It's in my condo building's garage. Ralph and I walked here."

"You leave the keys on your kitchen counter as usual?"

"Yes."

"I'll swing by an' switch cars."

Tuwanda had a key to my condo, although she didn't need one. Everyone seemed to be able to get into my condo without a key except me.

"You gonna take me to brea'fast in appreciation of my efforts," she added.

"You'd better pick up my purse, too, then. I didn't bring any money with me."

"Is it on the coffee table where you usually leave it?"

"Yes." Was I that predictable? "But I've got Ralph with me. We'll have to drop him off at the condo if we're going to a restaurant."

"Got it. Let's do this!" she said.

I ended the call and gave Ralph some quality tummy-rubbing time as I waited. Outside I heard a series of siren blips, probably made by the coroner's van as it worked its way through the crowd of reporters and cameramen.

A little over twenty minutes later, I heard another series of siren blips. Within seconds after they stopped, the van's back door opened. Ralph and I blinked in the sudden sunlight.

Tuwanda motioned for me to follow her. As soon as Ralph and I stepped out of the van we were surrounded by a protective cadre of police officers, who escorted us to my car and made sure we got in without interference. I attributed the officers' helpfulness to Tuwanda's resemblance to a black Angelina Jolie.

Ralph and I got down on the floor in the back, which required a fair amount of wedging (Ralph), sucking in of body parts (me), and whining (both of us). I ended up in a fetal position with my head smashed up against Ralph's rear end. Ralph was trying to keep a positive attitude, but his tail-wagging wasn't helping.

Tuwanda threw Ralph's travel blanket over us and, in furtherance of the deception, put our purses on top.

"Ouch," I muttered. "What do you have in that thing, Tuwanda?"

"Tha's your purse, and you know damn well you got enough provisions for a two-week campin' trip in there.

Which reminds me, what the hell you need a can of Sterno for?"

"Macy (my elderly neighbor) told me I needed to buy one for the chafing dish."

"You don't got a chafin' dish, an' I doubt you know what one is," scoffed Tuwanda.

She was right. I didn't, and I didn't.

"Now keep quiet. Talkin' is inconsistent with the properties of an inert object."

Tuwanda was taking a chemistry course and had been throwing around terms like "inert," "immiscible," "solubility"— you get the picture.

Tuwanda hailed a police officer, and I listened as they plotted our escape. He suggested that she meander to the other side of the crime scene. (I didn't know how you'd meander cross-country in a Honda sedan in the absence of a meandering, paved road, but I left the details to them.) Then she could take the cart path to Thirty-Second Street, observing all golf course rules of courtesy en route (except, of the course, the rule where you aren't supposed to drive cars on the golf path). According to the officer, Thirty-Second Street mostly served as a back lot for the press while all the real action was at the Biltmore and along Twenty-Fourth Street. Once we were on Thirty-Second we'd be home free.

After what seemed like an eternity, Tuwanda started the engine. She fiddled with the radio until she found a station she liked before we got moving.

"It's hot back here, you know," I complained.

"Tha's 'cuz your POS got crappy air-conditioning. You want good air-conditioning you gotta buy American. Americans got low tolerance for extreme temperatures. People in Europe jus' take off their jacket an' open the window when it's hot an' do the opposite when it's cold. Here we roll up all the windows an' change the climate."

The car went over a huge bump and rocked wildly.

"What was that?" I asked nervously.

Tuwanda chuckled. "I jus' ran over Webber. That man makes for one hell of a mound."

"You did not!"

"It was a rock. You gotta have more trust in the process, girl. Now shush. We gettin' into enemy territory."

Tuwanda turned up the radio, and Etta James's voice vibrated through me. Even with the loud music I could hear shouting outside. Tuwanda shouted back without rolling down the window. "I'm a damn cleanin' lady jus' tryin' to get to work cleanin' white people's bathrooms while you out there writin' shit only white people's gonna read."

Tuwanda was far too glamorous for anyone to believe she was on her way to clean toilets, but when she morphed into her Malcolm X persona, people were afraid to point out any inconsistencies in her monologues.

The shouting lessened and then disappeared altogether after the car made a hard right turn and accelerated.

Tuwanda gave Ralph and me the all-clear, and I crawled out from under the blanket, picking dog hairs off my tongue.

We swung by my condo to drop off Ralph, and within a short time were sitting in a booth at the Lamplight Inn, an all-night diner that catered to night-shift workers.

I was still feeling queasy over my discovery of the late Queen Ta Ta, so I stuck to cereal and orange juice. Tuwanda ordered a triple stack of pancakes, a cheese and ham omelet, bacon, toast, and a yogurt parfait. She had an enviable metabolism. No matter what or how much she ate, she remained a trim size two. I comforted myself with the thought that in the event of worldwide food shortage, Tuwanda would starve before me because I had fat reserves she did not. This stretch of logic prevented lapses into periods of jealous pouting.

Our breakfast was served in record time, prompted no doubt by management's desire to get the lady in the smelly jogging shorts and tank top out of there as soon as possible. Even the Lamplight Inn had its standards.

Tuwanda downed her breakfast without pausing for conversation or even to breathe, from what I could see. I was still picking at my cereal when she pushed her empty plates away and said, "I'm worried about you, Kate. You been through a bad breakup, you workin' your ass off bein' a lawyer, an' every time you so much as step outside you find dead people. Hell, you don' even need to step outside. You found a body under your own damned floor once."

"It was a skeleton, and it was under Sam's office floor, not mine," I corrected, as if that made it better. A couple of months ago, we'd discovered the remains of a young girl under the floor of the bungalow that serves as my office building. We'd found her murderer but still had a resident ghost whose occasionally disruptive behavior interfered with business as usual from time to time.

I studied the sodden piece of Special K floating in my spoon. "It's not like I have control over any of this," I continued defensively. "Stuff just happens."

"The discoverin' dead people part maybe, but overworkin' an' havin' no social life is somethin' you can and *need* to change."

"Maybe so, but now doesn't seem to be a good time. The reporters are bound to track me down eventually and will make my life, temporarily at least, more miserable than usual."

I felt a stab of guilt as soon as these words were out of my mouth. A young woman was dead with all indications pointing to murder, and I was worried that my pathetic life was going to be interrupted because of it.

"I'm sorry. I shouldn't have said that," I added.

"It's a fact, though. You need a plan for handlin' things. Did you give more thought to hirin' a PR person?"

Tuwanda had raised this possibility after the fountain and fast-food wrapper incident. I had yet to act on it, though, because I was sure nothing that embarrassing could ever happen again. Now, two embarrassing events later, it was time to consider the idea.

My cell phone rang, and I answered it when I saw my office number on the screen.

"Hi, Beth," I said.

"You're on Channel 12," she announced, skipping the how-are-yous. "The news anchor said you were the one who discovered Queen Ta Ta's body, and they're showing a sky-cam shot of you sitting on some rock with Ralph lying next to you."

"Yes. I found the body early this morning. Tuwanda picked me up after I finished talking to the police. I'm with her now."

"You doing okay?" she asked, a bit belatedly, I thought.

"A lot better than Queen Ta Ta," I quipped again, sounding just as lame as the first time. "Has anyone from the press called the office?"

"I think the only station or newspaper that hasn't called is KNRT."

KNRT is a local Christian radio station catering to the religious right.

"They probably think it's an act of God intended as a warning to immoral women, so interviewing mortals is a waste of time," I muttered.

Remembering, too late, that Beth is a hardcore

Baptist and a loyal listener of KNRT, I quickly changed the subject.

"Are any members of the media outside?" I asked.

"Uh-uh. Not yet. They're still at the murder scene interviewing neighbors and hotel employees. A spokesman for the police department said the head of police was going to make a statement to the press in about an hour. Once that's over, I expect our office will be one of the press's first stops.

"If it's all the same to you, Kate, I'm going home to change into my navy blue suit. We want to make a good impression on the public."

Since I had already appeared on TV with no makeup, stringy, sweaty hair, and perspiration-stained shorts and shirt, makeup, a comb-through, and a change of clothes wouldn't fool anyone. Still, Beth had a point. I, too, should at least try to look presentable before confronting the press.

"Do MJ and Sam know what's going on?" I asked.

"Neither of them has come in yet, but they called just before I called you. They both know what's going on and say they'll be here in about a half an hour. They want to talk to you, of course, so I scheduled a staff meeting at ten."

Beth was keeper of the sacred appointment book and would schedule my bathroom breaks if I let her. Once something was written in the appointment book it became an inviolable duty.

"Okay. I'll be there." Like I had a choice. "By the way, Beth, it's been a tough morning and I know this is a sensitive subject, but I could really use some cookie power."

Beth had cut off my cookie supply pending a weigh-in.

"They're already in the oven," said Beth. (The office had a kitchen with all the accoutrements necessary for cookie baking.) "I'm trying a new low-sugar, low-fat recipe."

This was not good news, but I tried to look on the bright side by reasoning that it was a step in the right direction. I'd be back to the primo drugs—chocolate chip and macadamia nut made out of real butter, sugar, and flour—in no time.

I thanked her enthusiastically in much the same way I praised Ralph for coming close to doing something I wanted him to do. (For example, last week I feigned ecstasy when he didn't eat the ball during a game of fetch. He didn't fetch it, mind you, but this was the closest he'd come.)

I signed off with Beth and told Tuwanda we should go. I had to get ready for work and a press confrontation.

"An' I gotta get some sleep," she said, placing her napkin on the table with finality.

I picked up the tab, and as we drove to my condo, Tuwanda again suggested that I find public relations help, at least until the whole Ta Ta thing blew over.

The idea of getting a temporary PR agent had new

and immediate appeal to me. I saw my sweaty, post-test visage on the TV behind the bar as we left the restaurant, and when Tuwanda started the car, the radio came on full blast in the middle of a news update about the murder. (Tuwanda insisted on driving, provided I agreed to jump behind the wheel in the event of an accident so she wouldn't be "found dead behin' the wheel of the POS.")

"Do you know anyone locally in the PR business?" I asked.

Tuwanda grew up in Phoenix, and the people she didn't meet growing up she knew through her business. As Tuwanda once said, "I meet 'em all one way or another."

"Max Demple's real good. He used to handle Governor Mecham's stuff, an' you know what a challenge he musta' bin."

Evan Mecham had been the governor of Arizona in the mid-eighties, and although this was way before my arrival in Phoenix, stories about Mecham still abounded. He was a home-grown good ol' boy who, prior to taking office, was the owner of a local car dealership. Mecham's definition of plain-speak was to say whatever was on his mind no matter how stupid. This resulted in some legendary gaffes, including canceling Martin Luther King Jr. day, attributing high divorce rates to women taking jobs outside the home, and defending his use of the word "pickaninny" in describing African-American children. He was the only governor to simultaneously face removal by impeachment, a scheduled recall election, and a felony indictment. The fact that he wasn't tarred and feathered and ridden out of town on a rail is a testament to Demple's talent.

"How old is Demple now?" I asked. I remember seeing photos of him taken in 1987, and he looked old then.

"He's gotta be in his eighties, but he still runs a PR firm with his children, an' he's got more contacts with the media than anyone else in town. If I was you, I'd give him a call pronto."

I nodded in agreement. "I think I will. I'm too tired to deal with this mess on my own. And you're right: I need to start building a life outside of work and impromptu murder investigations. I'll call Demple as soon as I get to my office." I sounded a lot more determined than I felt, though.

"Why don' you call now on your mobile? It ain't too early."

"Because," I explained. "When I'm in my office dressed in business clothes I feel professional and focused. I do not feel that way now; I feel as if I need a shower."

"You smell like you need one too," said Tuwanda.

I punched her arm in feigned indignation.

Chapter Four

I went all out in the image category. After an intense shower, I dried and styled my hair, carefully applied makeup, and dressed in a white linen suit and a pastel pink silk shirt. The only thing I couldn't do was bring myself to put on panty hose. Wearing panty hose in Phoenix in the summer is like wearing rubber trousers in a sauna. Before the local courts eased up on the rule that female attorneys were required to wear hose in court, Phoenix was a major profit center for Monostat sales.

I donned a pair of beige Manolo Blahniks and checked myself in the mirror. I thought I looked darn good; kind of Christie Brinkley-ish. I'd like to think Ralph approved, because he wagged his tail manically, but I knew I would get the same tail-wagging treatment if I was wearing sweats and hadn't seen a hairbrush in weeks.

I drove uptown and turned onto Third Street. I saw several vehicles with radio and TV call letters plastered on their sides parked in front of my office building. Since one of them was blocking the driveway and several more lined the street, I had to park around the block.

I prepared myself mentally by repeating the mantra, "Remember the three Cs: calm, classy, and clam up." I couldn't be misquoted if I didn't say anything, right?

I got out of my car and strode down the sidewalk, affecting a confidence I did not feel. My mouth was dry, and my lips stuck to my teeth as I affixed a sad smile on my face, attempting to exude a combination of sorrow and competence.

A short young man with a largish nose and curly black hair intercepted me as soon as I rounded the corner.

"Miss Williams, Miss Williams," he called out to get my attention even though he'd already accomplished this by blocking my path.

Upon hearing my name, more reporters leaped out of their air-conditioned vehicles and rushed toward me, recorders and microphones at the ready.

The questions came thick and fast: "Did you know Queen Ta Ta?" "Why were you out looking for her?" "Did you see her killer?" "Did *you* kill her?"

My resolve to say nothing disappeared, especially when a red-haired reporter with buckteeth and what had to be fake boobs spilling out of her low-cut top asked, "Why did you kill her? Were you jealous?"

"I was out jogging …" I started to say.

"In August? C'mon. Why were you really out there?" prodded the fake-breasted lady.

"I was with my dog …"

"You took your dog out in this heat? That's animal abuse. Did Queen Ta Ta catch you at it? Is that why you killed her?" Big Nose chimed in.

My teeth stuck to my lips, making it hard for me to talk. I reached in my bag and felt around for the tube of ChapStick I always carried with me. Miraculously my fingers quickly closed around it despite my purse's crowded interior. Without taking my eyes off the growing crowd of reporters, I generously applied ChapStick on and around my lips. When I finished I recapped the tube and threw it back into my handbag. Thus prepared, I waved my hands for silence and then noticed that everyone had already quieted down. The tempo of the whirs and flashes of digital cameras had increased, however.

I decided to take advantage of the lull in questioning and make my escape. Pushing my way through the reporters, many of whom were surprisingly cooperative and stepped nervously out of my way, I made it to the small front porch of my office. The front door opened, and Sam's arm snaked out, grabbed my wrist and hauled me inside.

Beth and MJ were sitting in the reception area. The former had a stricken look on her face, and the latter was laughing hysterically. Sam locked the door and guided me toward a decorative mirror hanging over the couch. Without saying anything, he handed me a box of Kleenexes.

Ronald McDonald stared back at me from the mirror. What I thought was ChapStick was a tube of lipstick in a shade known as Voluptuous Rouge. As I recall, the saleswoman told me it was "perfect for after-work cocktail parties." I bought it because a part of me believed I'd go to a cocktail party at some point, and when I did, I needed to be ready.

"God, no," I whispered hoarsely.

"Now, now," said Sam, patting my shoulder. "You've done worse things."

I did not find this comforting.

The first few swipes with the Kleenex had little effect. Apparently Voluptuous Rouge had the same properties as a Magic Marker.

Beth came up softly behind me and handed me a jar of cold cream. After a minute or two of scrubbing, it looked no worse than if I'd had a glass of red Kool-Aid with my animal crackers that morning.

Trying to regain what professional aplomb I could, I straightened my jacket and told everyone to meet me in my office for our ten o'clock meeting.

I went to the kitchen and poured a cup of coffee. A plate of Beth's low-sugar, nonfat cookies lay on the counter. I took four instead of the two I normally snagged, reasoning that the caloric intake was negligible, so no harm done.

Beth, MJ, and Sam were already in my office when I strode in.

MJ, my fortyish paralegal, had gone all out for the benefit of the press. She was wearing a short, red plaid kilt and a black T-shirt with "I have no private parts" printed in neon orange on the front. Both the kilt and the shirt were, as usual, a couple of sizes too small. MJ relied on the elastic properties of spandex to accommodate the difference. Spandex can do only so much, though, and MJ's hips pushed out the pleats so her skirt looked more like a plaid tutu than a kilt.

Her black nail polish matched the black shirt and knit cap she had pulled down over her hair, the visible tips of which indicated that her hair color de jure was black with red stripes. A pair of Doc Martens worn without socks completed the ensemble. I should also add that MJ had multiple tattoos and piercings, but I'd gotten so used to them I barely noticed them unless she got a new one, and she had: down her left arm was a rainbow-colored tattoo picture of the scales of justice, under which was written *Play Fair or Die.*

Sam, my investigator, was at the other end of the fashion continuum. He looked like an ad for Brooks Brothers, foregoing his usual Armani and Hugo Boss suits for a Brooks Brothers suit. He had even donned a pair of black wingtips in place of his usual in-office footwear: strappy Manolo Blahnik or Jimmy Choo sandals. (The higher the heel the better.) Sam sat with his legs crossed at the knee, and the way he nervously bounced his top leg indicated that he'd rather be wearing high heels.

I absently munched a cookie and sipped coffee while I briefed them on what had happened and told them of my plan to retain Max Demple's firm to provide public relations support for us during the media blitz attendant to Queen Ta Ta's death.

Sam muttered, "A little late for that."

"Didn't Demple handle the Ed Mecham fiasco?" asked Beth.

"The one and the same," I confirmed.

"He's gotta be old. I mean real old; as in 'he prepares for meetings by checking for his pulse' old," said MJ.

"According to Tuwanda, he's in his eighties but is still active in his profession and has more media contacts than anyone else in town. I figured we should give him a try."

MJ shrugged. "It's your money. It *is* your money, right? This isn't affecting our salaries, is it?"

MJ asked this question whenever I made a decision that required a cost expenditure we could not pass through to a client. She's as predictable as the kid in high school who always asks, "Is this going to be on the test?"

"It will not affect your salaries," I said wearily. "Now, unless anyone has anything else to say, this meeting is over. Just remember: say nothing to the press until we get direction from Demple's firm."

As soon as Beth, MJ, and Sam cleared out of my office, I picked up the phone and punched in 4-1-1. The recorded voice, which for some reason had a British accent, gave me Demple's number, and I was automatically connected to his office.

While I was on hold listening to country western music, I grabbed another cookie. The low-sugar, nonfat version was to the traditional cookie what a communion wafer was to a Twinkie. I would need to find a supplier outside the office if I was going to survive the next few weeks. I wondered if Paradise Bakery made deliveries.

"Demple Public Relations," announced an efficient, female voice midway through Jo Dee Messina's "My Give a Damn's Busted." "What can we do for you?"

I gave her my name, said I was referred to the firm by Ms. Tuwanda Jones, and explained that I needed help dealing with the press in connection with a recent, high-profile matter.

"Mr. Demple is currently unavailable, but if you wish, I can put you through to Max Demple."

This temporarily threw me. Then I remembered Tuwanda mentioned that Max Demple worked with his children.

"Umm, Demple Junior?" I hazarded.

"Yes, ma'am."

"Yes, please. I would be happy to talk to Max."

I was placed on hold again. Garth Brooks was singing "I've Got Friends in Low Places." It occurred to me that this would make a great theme song if a movie of my life was made, which was doubtful.

"Max Demple," announced a low, gravelly voice.

I introduced myself again and repeated what I had told the receptionist except that I added more detailed information as to why I was seeking representation.

I took a deep breath before saying, "I would like to discuss retaining your firm to troubleshoot and run interference with the press for us."

"And manage damage control," he said. "I'm watching your impromptu press conference as we speak."

In the background I could hear a man speaking and what sounded like someone choking.

"Was that thing with the lipstick an accident?" he asked.

"Yes. What's that noise in the background?"

"That's the TV announcer speaking."

"No, it sounds like someone choking; or coughing maybe."

"Oh, that's the weather girl, Jenna Perkins. She's laughing. Oh boy is she laughing. I think they're gonna need someone else to do the weather."

Max was doing a very poor job of stifling some chuckles of his own.

"Would there be a better time for me to call you?" I asked coldly.

"No, no. But it might make more sense for us to set up a meeting rather than try to do this over the phone. I'll put together an outline of our services and some suggestions for strategy. After you hear my presentation, you can decide whether you want to retain us."

I was still a little miffed, but I agreed to a one o'clock meeting at his office. He was blowing his nose when I hung up, but I was fairly sure he didn't have a cold.

I worked on my oral argument for a motion scheduled in Judge Wiener's court tomorrow morning. Normally Wiener calendared motions for Mondays or Fridays, but he was going on vacation, so everything had been moved up a couple of days. Lawyers have little or no say over these things. Regardless of the level of disruption to your plans, the only appropriate response is, "Yes, Your Honor, [fill in the blank; e.g., 'My daughter can get married any day'; 'I guess my grandfather doesn't *have* to be buried within twenty-four hours'; or 'I can reschedule the operation. How fast can cancer metastasize anyway?' You get the idea]."

Beth picked up a sandwich for me at Subway since I didn't feel like further exposing myself to my adoring public so soon after what was now referred to by my staff as "Lipstick-gate." Sam went so far as to suggest that all cosmetics be removed from my reach for the safety of me and others, whereupon I whipped a mascara wand out of my purse and threatened to lengthen and curl if he didn't lay off.

Chapter Five

At twelve forty-five I snuck through the back door into the alley where Sam had parked his obsessively clean Volvo for my undercover departure, with the proviso that I pay for detailing if I so much as left a fingerprint on the steering wheel. He had thoughtfully provided a fresh packet of sanitary wipes in the event of accidental skin/fine leather contact. I saw him in the rearview mirror watching me, or rather his car, drive away with the expression of a mother watching her only child head to war.

In deference to Julia's sensitivity to ultraviolet rays (Julia being the appellation Sam assigned to the Volvo), I parked in the underground garage at Demple's high-rise office building.

I checked the directory posted next to the elevator door and saw with a sinking feeling that Demple was on the twenty-second floor.

Very few people know this about me, but I'm scared

to death of heights. When I stay at hotels I insist on a room no higher than the third floor. I even turned down a lucrative job offer by a Chicago law firm solely because its offices were located in a high-rise.

Since you cannot avoid all high buildings in today's world, when I am forced to visit one, I edge along its inner walls and do not ever, ever look out the windows.

I stepped in the elevator with trepidation and pushed the button for the twenty-second floor. I noticed the buttons started with the parking garage and then the ground floor and then skipped to the fifteenth floor, which meant it was a high-speed elevator that only served tenants on the top levels.

At ground level it stopped to pick up a horde of workers returning from lunch and then launched itself into space like a Disneyland ride. Milliseconds later it stopped abruptly on the twenty-second floor.

I pried my fingers from the waist-high metal railing running across the back of the elevator. The horde parted like the Red Sea before Moses to let me out. Their extraordinary politeness was likely induced by my green complexion and the retching noises I was making in the back of my throat.

I panicked when I saw the floor-to-ceiling windows. An elegant blonde sitting behind a reception desk watched dispassionately as I edged toward her with my face to the wall.

Once I was close enough to speak without having

to raise my voice to cover the distance, I stopped, introduced myself, and explained that I had a one o'clock appointment.

"Max or Max?" she inquired politely.

"The younger one."

"Max is currently on the phone. Why don't you take a seat for a bit? Would you like some coffee?"

I envisioned plummeting twenty-two floors to the sidewalk and considered asking for a parachute and a Dramamine and passing on the coffee. Instead I shook my head no and pressed into the wall.

"Do all the offices have this, er, great view?" I asked.

Her lips stretched into a thin smile. "Why, yes. In fact, you can see all the way to Camelback Mountain from Max's office."

"Great," I said unenthusiastically.

She looked at me speculatively. "Do you have that—whatsicallit—the thing where you're afraid of heights?"

"Acrophobia," I provided.

"Isn't that the one where you're afraid of going outside?"

"No. That's agoraphobia."

"I'm afraid of snakes and stuff like that. What's that called?"

"Herpetophobia."

"Wow. Are you like a psychiatrist or something?"

"No. I'm neurotic."

She wrinkled her brow in what she probably considered

deep thought but most would consider a light brush with consciousness. The buzz of an intercom interrupted her before she could decide if I was a threat.

"Is Mrs. Williams here yet, Debby?" boomed a voice I recognized as Demple Junior's.

"Ms.," I corrected.

"She says its Ms., not Mrs.," responded Debby, pronouncing Ms. like "mizzzzzzzz," making me sound like a stinging insect.

"Well, send herrrrrrrr on in," said Demple.

What a card.

Debby popped up and said, "Please follow me, Mizzzz Williams."

Debby reminded me of that children's card game where the goal is to get cards that match to create a person or animal that makes sense. Debby was what you end up with after the first deal: the top half of a ballerina and the lower half of a hippopotamus. If not for my quick reflexes, her hips would have taken out a vase and a candy dish.

At the end of the hall she opened a door, waved me into an office larger than most Eastern European countries, and retreated.

Demple stood when I entered, and I was surprised to see that Max was a she. She was of medium height and had a zaftig figure that was not disguised by the severe black business suit she wore. Her brown, gray-streaked hair was styled in a pageboy. Her facial features were unremarkable except for large, brown puppy-dog eyes. She wore no makeup or nail polish.

I guesstimated her to be in her midsixties.

"Kate? Max. Short for Maxine." She must have picked up on my initial confusion. "I'm pleased to meet you," she said in the same low, gravelly voice I'd heard on the phone. "Here, let me take that vase and candy dish so we can do a proper handshake."

I handed her the breakables without explanation, figuring that she was used to seeing this sort of thing with her more agile clients.

Then the handshake came, and it was a knuckle-breaker. I had to fight back tears.

"Guess you've had a pretty rough day," she commented, misreading the agony in my eyes.

"It has been an interesting day," I said through gritted teeth.

"Please, have a seat," she said, gesturing to a leather wingback chair in the vicinity of Kiev.

I dutifully sat, still nursing my wounded hand. She took a seat in her comfy-looking upholstered desk chair.

"I've reviewed all the media reports on your current, er, situation," she said in the same tone used to announce the death of a loved one. "I've also read several articles relating to other situations in which you've been involved."

"I have bad karma," I said defensively.

"I don't know about that, but my job will be to present Kate Williams's best side to the public."

"I'm not sure my best side is that much better than my worst side."

"You tend to be hard on yourself, don't you? Don't be. Sometimes very bright people have a difficult time dealing with members of the media. They're a tough, relentless crowd. Reason and appeals to conscience don't work on them.

"Here's how I think we should approach the current situation."

She placed her hands on top of her desk, boosted herself up, and leaned toward me, bringing her face within inches of mine. I smelled cigarettes, which might have explained her low voice.

"I will handle all media contacts. If anyone from the media calls or confronts you or a member of your staff in person, give them my name and phone number and say nothing more."

It was an attractive proposition. I didn't like dealing with the media, and more importantly, I sucked at it. Despite these compelling considerations, I held back from jumping at Demple's proposal.

"Could you give me an idea of how your firm would respond to questions from reporters? For example, what would you say if asked why I was jogging in August, which seems to bother a lot of people?"

Max straightened her back, her mouth relaxed into a half smile, her brow smoothed, and her eyes widened.

"Ms. Williams is a conscientious athlete. She doesn't

let weather stand in the way of her exercise routine. In the summer she moves up her schedule to avoid the worst of the heat." Her delivery was comforting, in the manner of the shared confidence of a favorite elderly aunt.

She was totally believable. So much so that it took me a few beats to spot the defect in her hypothetical response.

"But that's not true. That was my first attempt at jogging in over ten years. I don't have an exercise schedule, unless you count walking my dog to his pooping spot twice a day."

Demple sat back in her chair and morphed into my third-grade teacher, a woman whose narrow interpretation of the multiplication tables is responsible for my aversion to math.

"You *intended* to be rigorous in your new program, then. Ms. Williams, I don't mean to sound critical— I'm only saying this for your own good, but you lack both creativity and the ability to appreciate creativity in others."

I wondered how she distinguished creativity from lying.

Interpreting my silence as confusion, she proceeded to elucidate. "My job is to put the best face on your situation."

I thought this was an unfortunate choice of words in light of the lipstick incident.

She went on to say, "You, like most in your profession,

are left-brained and unable to express yourself outside the parameters of reason and logic."

And truth, I silently added.

"I, on the other hand, can take a set of facts and from them extrapolate a kinder reality. Because the truth is: in your case, there's no good way to factually clarify your behavior without a little creative spin."

What? This time my confusion was real.

"Let me give you another example," said Max. She pushed a black button on her desk, and floor-to-ceiling red velvet drapes hanging on a side wall slid open to reveal a large TV screen. She hit two more buttons, and Ron Gaines, the Channel 3 anchor, appeared. A box at the top of the screen showed my naked-woman-holding-a-Chihuahua photo.

Kate Williams, a local attorney who in the past has been associated with several high-profile murder cases, reportedly discovered the body of Queen Ta Ta this morning when she was jogging. [He said "jogging" in a sarcasm-laden "yeah, right" kind of way.] *Our own Scott Nelson was able to catch Miss Williams this morning as she pushed through reporters to get to her office.*

My image filled the screen. I said something unintelligible in response to the reporters' shouted questions and then stuck my hand into my purse. I closed my eyes for the rest of it.

"Well, Scott, what's your take on Miss Williams's behavior?" asked Gaines, addressing a weasely little man

I recognized as the reporter who accused me of dog abuse.

"Ron, this is a woman on whom the discovery of a bloodied body less than four hours earlier had so little emotional impact that she could still go to work and, worse, make a joke of it all by drawing a clown's mouth on her face when asked about the tragic incident."

"She wasn't bloodied," I mumbled.

The camera then went to Jenna Perkins for the weather, but Jenna, who was fighting to control hysterical laughter, could only get out, "Gonna be hot," which, quite honestly, is the only thing a Phoenix weather person *needs* to say in August.

The segment ended, and neither of us spoke while I massaged my temples.

"How much do you charge?" I asked, breaking the silence.

She explained the firm's billing rates and retainer requirements. What it boiled down to was that I would be working for the sole purpose of paying her bill.

"I don't think I can—" I began.

"I have a proposition," she interrupted.

Every time I heard that phrase I got the short end of the stick. This happened so often that my staff, in a meeting to which I was not invited, decided that all financial decisions affecting the firm would be handled by Beth, who had a firm grasp on economics along with the ability to utter the words "No" and "Hell no."

But then Demple hit "replay," and I panicked.

"What is your proposal?"

She hit "pause."

"We barter. I will represent you as your PR agent at a discounted rate if you allow us to use your case as part of my firm's advertising campaign once your matter is resolved."

"What if everything goes sideways and you want nothing to do with me or my case?"

Max smiled and said, "It won't go sideways."

I saw no rational basis for her optimism, but it warmed my heart nonetheless.

Still, I hesitated.

"You realize, of course, that you are likely to be not only a suspect in this case, but *the* suspect," she said.

"*What*?" I yelped.

"No one is going to believe you were out jogging in this heat."

"But you just said I have an exercise compulsion." And even if I didn't, darn it, taking a stab at jogging on a hot August morning made sense in Kate-world. One of my hallmark behaviors is starting activities without any planning or forethought, secure in the knowledge that I will give up after the first try. "Besides, what motive would I have? Until the police told me, I had no idea who Queen Ta Ta was."

"Even if you're not officially charged, you know how good reporters are at innuendo. They'll recycle that old chestnut about the recently rejected middle-aged woman who stalks and kills the young, beautiful singer."

"Recently rejected?" I asked, leaving the middle-aged characterization alone for now.

"I was referring to your breakup with Sheriff Turner."

"How do you know about that? More importantly, what makes you think he broke up with me and not the other way around?"

"As for the former, it's is my job to know everything about my clients and prospective clients. As to the latter, Turner is running for sheriff on a law-and-order platform, so any public or private connection with you would be … stupid."

"How do you get your information?" I asked suspiciously, envisioning Watergate-like late night break-ins into my office and apartment.

"Google, Facebook."

My stomach lurched. Information on the Internet has the half-life of uranium; thousands of years from now people will still be able to pull up the Kate-Williams-running-naked-from-a-fire photo.

"Rumor control is your job," I said.

She emitted a short bark of laughter. "Now you're getting it. Don't worry. By the time we're finished we'll have you looking better than Lady Di."

"She's dead."

"Yes, but the public still adores her."

Apparently for folks in this profession image was numero uno and breathing was farther down the list.

The idea of someone else handling the media was an attractive option, and I reasoned that I could include an at-will termination clause in Max's contract in case her efforts weren't successful. Besides, no matter what she did, it couldn't be worse than what I'd done to myself.

I nodded slowly and told her to send an agreement over for me to take a look at. I stood to leave, but Max held up her hand in the "wait" position.

"Welcome to the Demple and Sons family," she said cheerily.

"Subject to my approval of a written agreement," I said. (I chose to neither comment on my adoption nor the confusing reference to "Sons" in her firm's name.)

"Subject to contract approval," confirmed Max.

Chapter Six

I decided against going back to my office and went to Biltmore Fashion Park for some retail therapy instead. Sam would no doubt object to Julia's part in my shopping plans, but necessity overrode my concern for his feelings.

I called Beth from the car. She sounded tense when she answered.

"Has it been rough over there?" I asked sympathetically.

"Brutal. The phone hasn't stopped ringing, and the vultures are still waiting outside for you. I caught one of them trying to sneak in the back door. I smacked his hands with a spatula, and … let's just say he'll have to dictate his yellow journalism for a while."

"Then this should be good news for you." I outlined the terms of my verbal agreement with Demple and Sons, told her to check the written agreement to make sure it tracked with my understanding, and dictated a unilateral right to terminate for her to insert into the contract. If she approved the financial arrangement, she was to sign on my behalf. (It's not forgery if you authorize the person signing for you, and Beth signed my name better than I did.)

When I got to Twenty-Fourth and Camelback, I spotted news vans and reporters clustered around the entrance to my condo building. (The Biltmore Fashion Park is either conveniently or inconveniently located, depending on your budget or your ability to ignore your budget, across the street from where I live.)

I pulled into the mall's rear parking lot and, as casually as my code-red panic level permitted, walked into the first-floor cosmetics department of Saks. I stopped next to the Estee Lauder counter and took a couple of deep breaths to calm myself.

"It's her! It's the lipstick lady," screamed a model-thin blonde standing behind the Estee Lauder counter.

One expects more subtlety from Saks employees.

"Omigod! She's the one who found the body!" said Clerk No. 2, who had been restocking shelves before Clerk No. 1 announced my arrival.

Although I had found more than one body in my time, I had no doubt which one she was referring to.

Clerk No. 2 vaulted over a Clinique display, made a two-point landing despite six-inch heels, and trotted over to me. "What did she look like? Was it gross?" she asked in that urgent half whisper that people use when they're excited about something that's in bad taste to be excited about.

Clerk No. 1 skidded up next, panting. She was young and blonde like Clerk No. 2 but looked like she'd been hitting the Godiva chocolates a little too hard.

"Queen Ta Ta, she means," provided Clerk No. 2 helpfully.

"Thanks for the clarification," I said drily.

My sense of irony was lost on Lady Godiva, who continued to press. "Was it awful? Was there blood? The guy on the news said there was blood."

A third clerk, an older woman wearing a name tag that read, "I'm Carol; ask me about your free makeover," made her way toward me, weaving around displays and counters with more dignity than that exhibited by her younger associates.

Extending her hand in greeting, she said, "Hi, I'm Carol, your local Maximum representative. You're Kate, right? You must have had a rough day. Would you like me to do your makeup? We have a new product I know you'll love. It's called Transformation."

"Do I get to decide what I'm transformed into?" I asked, smiling weakly.

She smiled graciously. "Certainly. Come to my station, and I'll take care of you."

Every woman knows that she should never get a makeover during times of emotional turmoil. Every woman also knows this is the first thing she does during times of emotional turmoil. I had gotten some seriously bad haircuts and made regrettable fashion choices while in the throes of crisis.

So of course I followed Carol to her station and obediently sat in the barbershop-style chair.

She hit a lever at the base of the chair, and I flew back. "Now you relax and let ol' Carol here make you gorgeous."

After tying a pink plastic bib around my neck, she got down to work. She talked softly, explaining each step and product as she removed my makeup and then applied a layer of spackle (my word, not hers) to smooth out the wrinkles.

"Do you exfoliate?" she asked. Her tone implied that clearly I did not, which was true.

"Not as much as I should," I said sheepishly. "It's hard to find the time."

"Exfoliation is extremely important. You must exfoliate at least three times a week. Otherwise the dead skin cells accumulate and your complexion becomes dull and uninteresting."

"Better my skin than my life," I smirked.

Carol overenthusiastically swiped my face with an abrasive cloth.

Don't joke with an aesthetician about exfoliation; you will, quite literally, go away red-faced.

"Ouch. That stings," I protested.

"Yes, but now those dead cells are gone and the living cells can breathe."

And scream, I thought.

I opened one eye and saw that a small crowd of sales clerks had collected around my chair.

"Just think. Queen Ta Ta was in that chair yesterday," said Clerk No. 2 reverently.

"Really?" I asked, suddenly feeling creepy.

"Yeah. Carol sold her story about it to *Star Stalker* magazine, so she can't talk about it," continued Clerk No. 2. "We all saw her, but Carol was the only one who talked to her and touched her."

I detected jealousy in her tone.

"Well," said Carol, "the magazine only told me I couldn't talk to other members of the media, so I guess it'd be okay if I talked to you guys. Especially since Kate here has a connection to the murder."

"I don't have a connection to the *murder*," I protested, half rising out of the chair. "I only had the bad luck to find the body."

Carol gently pushed me back. "Of course, dear," she said soothingly. "I remember now; they said on the news that you were out jogging at the time."

Her tone implied that jogging in August excused me by reason of insanity.

Maybe I'm paranoid, but I thought I heard a snicker ripple through the group of onlookers.

"This lotion is specially made to plump your skin

cells," she continued, massaging a delicious-smelling cream into my neck and face. It felt good and I relaxed in spite of myself.

"As Teri here was saying," Carol continued, "Miss Dorfman—"

"Who's that?" I interrupted.

"Queen Ta Ta's real name is Gladys Dorfman," Carol explained patiently. "What kind of parents would name their child Queen Ta Ta?"

What kind of parents would name their child Gladys?

"Anyway, as I was saying, Miss Dorfman came in yesterday about three in the afternoon with some Guido."

"What's a Guido?" I interrupted again.

"It's, like, a guy-type, you know?" chimed in Teri. "Like the ones on *Jersey Shore.*"

"Still not getting it," I said.

"Gelled hair, a diamond earring, designer jeans, and look like they spend most days working out and tanning," provided Clerk No. 2, a.k.a. Teri.

Ah yes. You saw packs of them standing outside Scottsdale bars Saturday nights trying to look cool and, in my opinion, failing. The women checking them out were usually heavily made up, fake-boobed blondes dressed like hookers. Actually, the latter description fit Queen Ta Ta to a T, except maybe for the fake-boob part; I hadn't checked.

"So she comes in with this Guido," Carol began again,

sounding irked, probably because the conversational spotlight had momentarily shifted away from her, "and they're arguing about something. She called him a bitch; I remember that.

"Then she sees the Maximum counter and comes over. I asked her if she wanted me to freshen up her makeup, because she had about a ton of it on, but it looked like it was melting. People visiting Phoenix in the summer come unprepared. They don't realize you have to reapply makeup a lot here because the sweat floats it off."

The other clerks murmured in acknowledgment of the wisdom of this statement.

"Well, she was all for it, but the guy with her grabbed her arm and said they had to leave. She pulled it back and said she wanted to get freshened. He said he didn't have time to arrange a photo op, and she snaps back that 'not everything has to be a photo op,' which I thought was a real human thing for her to say."

I agreed. The Guido sounded like a jerk, though.

"So then he says, 'Your attitude is gonna make you yesterday's news,' and stomps off."

"I saw him stop and buy a couple of shirts and some shorts on his way out," said Teri. "He didn't even look at the prices or try 'em on. He just grabbed 'em off the rack and threw 'em on the counter. And they were expensive too. Paul Smith, I think. Even a pair of his socks cost like a hundred dollars."

"Queen Ta Ta was real nice, though," said Carol. "She

apologized for the guy and said he was an asshole. I took all her makeup off and reconditioned her skin like I did yours. Performers' skin's got a hard life, having to breathe under all that makeup and deal with the hot lights and all."

Carol talked about skin as if it was a separate being with lungs, senses, and emotions. I felt new respect for what I had taken for granted as nothing more than a covering that kept my internal organs from drying out.

"She seemed kind of down. She didn't ask many questions about the products I was using and kept sighing-like. I didn't want to pry, but I did ask her if she was feeling okay, because how a person feels has a big effect on their complexion.

"She looks me in the eye and then says, 'What does it all mean?' I thought at first maybe she was talking about the product descriptions—they can get pretty technical and tough for laypeople to understand—so I asked her for particulars. She just closes her eyes, kinda smiles, and asks, 'Do you think there's life beyond all this crap when it's over?'

"That really threw me. You ask me a question about something I've got in-depth training in, like lip plumper, and I can go on all day. But a question about the hereafter? You gotta ask a Harvard grad if you want an answer to that one."

Like a Harvard grad would know.

"What did you say to her?" I asked.

Carol shrugged elaborately. "I told her I didn't think it mattered and she should condition her eyelashes with vitamin E oil."

"So you're a nihilist," I commented.

"Not really. I mean, I can do nails, but that's really not my specialty."

Carol's revelations were not especially enlightening. Depressed people are not more likely to be murdered than happy people, although they may not mind as much.

"Don't pinch your eyes shut, dear," Carol instructed. "I can't apply the shadow evenly when you do that. Just relax."

"Shadow?"

"Yes. I noticed when you were on the TV news that you like bright lipstick. You need a little color on your eyes for balance; otherwise your eyes disappear and all you see is the lipstick."

"Relax, dear. You're scrunching your eyes again."

I'm not scrunching. I'm clenching. The motives for scrunching and clenching are different.

"Did Queen Ta Ta say anything else?" I asked, trying to keep my voice even.

"Nothing of much interest. She said that she and her significant other were going out to dinner and then to a party that night. She asked for the name of a good restaurant. I told her about Nasties in Scottsdale. Then she offered me free tickets for her concert tomorrow night."

Carol dabbed a makeup brush over my eye-lids and then worked the area carefully with a smaller brush.

"You can wear this color both to work and, after a little touch up, on a night on the town."

"I don't have nights on the town," I said, stifling a sneeze.

"You wear this makeup and you will," Carol asserted confidently.

She finished with my eyes, and I started to get out of the chair.

"Not through yet, dear. The blush and the blending come next."

"Um, Carol?" interrupted Teri. "Some people walked in, and I think they might be reporters."

I bolted upright. "Where?"

A scattering of camera flashes went off as I gaped in surprise at the group of reporters and cameramen.

"Wait!" shrieked Carol. "I have to blend and soften!"

Chapter Seven

I pushed out of the chair and ran for the exit, nearly blinded by the camera flashes. I didn't get far.

A bespectacled young man in shirtsleeves blocked the door. Panicking, I remembered some advice Tuwanda gave me should I be accosted. "You jes' gotta act crazier than they is. No one wants to mess with a crazy woman."

I stopped short and intoned, "They wasted, o'er a scorching flame the marrow of his bones; but the miller us'd him worst of all, for he crush'd him between two stones."

Startled, he froze. Then his eyes narrowed and his shoulders relaxed. "Robert Burns? You're quoting Robert Burns?"

Darn. Just my luck; he was an English major. I continued down this destructive path, however.

"You mean *Rabbie* Burns, young bairn." Striking a menacing stance (not an easy trick when you're wearing a pink plastic bib), I dove into the abyss. "Forbye some new, uncommon weapons, urinus spiritus of capons."

"Wow. Your accent is really good," he said, sounding genuinely impressed.

I could hear his colleagues thundering down the aisles as well as the reiterations of a determined sales clerk asking each person charging by if they would like to try a sample of a new fragrance called "Spite."

I looked around frantically for an escape route. Seeing none, I appealed to the English major. "Help me get out of here and I'll give you a …" The word eluded me. I knew it had something to do with serving ware. Spoon? Ladle? No wait; ice cream, it had to do with ice cream.

"Scoop?" he provided helpfully.

"Yes. That's it."

"I think the Bobby Burns rant is pretty good all by itself."

In the heat of the moment, I stomped down on his foot.

He yelped and pulled back, losing his balance. I pushed him aside and took off.

I know the layout of the outdoor mall like the back of my hand, so I ran with purpose and direction. (Of course my previous visits were shopping outings and involved an entirely different strategy.)

I ran into an often overlooked covered walkway and wove through a warren of administrative offices and janitors' closets. I lost most of my pursuers when I circled around Human Resources instead of going to the parking lot. I jogged around the loading docks and then headed for my planned destination: Macy's men's department.

Once inside Macy's, I slipped into a dressing room in the back of the Ralph Lauren section. As I'd hoped, this section of the store was empty of both customers and sales clerks. It's not that Ralph Lauren is not popular in Phoenix; it's just that Ralph starts to show his fall and winter clothing lines in August and, even with the store's air-conditioning system turned down to fifty, people aren't interested.

The dressing rooms at Macy's were also a good choice because they had full-size doors and locks instead of flimsy curtains that never close completely. The changing room I chose was a three-mirrored affair with a platform in the middle used for alterations. I plopped down on an upholstered bench and, since there was nothing else to look at, stared at the three images of me.

Carol was right: I needed blending and softening.

I removed the pink bib and scrubbed it over my face, which didn't so much blend and soften as it did redistribute.

I found my mobile and called Sam, who knew more about the shopping mall than I did.

"Sam! It's Kate," I whispered when he answered. "I'm in the men's dressing room at Macy's."

"Of course it's you. You're the only one I know who

would make a panic call from a men's room," he said sardonically.

"Not a men's room," I hissed. "A men's *dressing* room."

"The point's the same," he said stubbornly. "Is this a medical or a nonmedical emergency?"

"Quit joking around. I've got a pack of reporters looking for me, and I'm trapped. I need you to come and get me out of here."

"Which Macy's?"

"Biltmore Fashion Square."

"Tony Bahamas, Ralph Lauren, or Nathan Nash?"

"Ralph Lauren."

"Any sales?"

"I think there may be a ... wait a minute. That's irrelevant. You're not going shopping; you're going rescuing."

"Who's to say I can't do both?"

"Get me out of here, Sam. Now!" I growled before cutting the connection.

I divided my time during the next twenty minutes between attempts to correct my makeup and starting at every sound. Department stores are noisy places, even when relatively empty; the air-conditioning turning off and on, creaks and groans, and scurrying vermin (at least I assumed it was vermin, although in Arizona lizards and termites are also possibilities).

I was removing blue-green eye shadow from my

forehead (a result of the pink bib relocation process) when I heard approaching footsteps. I didn't call out in case it wasn't Sam. The footsteps hesitated, and then I heard the door of the adjoining stall open and close. I tensed and readied myself for a mad dash.

A pair of man's pants flew over the divider between the two stalls, barely missing my head.

"Duck," whispered Sam.

"You say that *before* you throw," I hissed.

A man's suit coat and shirt flew over and made four-point landings on my head.

"Shoes and hat next," warned Sam.

I flattened against the far wall, and the projectiles missed me by inches. It seemed to me that they weren't tossed so much as thrown with unnecessary force.

"What, no tie and socks?" I snapped.

They hit me on the face and shoulder, respectively.

I changed into the clothes Sam had brought, after which, per his instruction, I hurled my skirt, blouse, and shoes into his stall. Unfortunately, I put a little too much heft into the shoe toss.

"You missed," he hissed. "They went into the next stall."

I heard him go out to retrieve the shoes as I tried to figure out how to tie the tie.

"I can't do the tie," I finally whispered.

I heard an exasperated sigh. "If you're decent, I'll come in and take care of it for you."

"I'm never jus' decent; I'm always gooooood," I countered, quoting one of Tuwanda's oft-used lines.

A few seconds later there was a soft knock. I opened the door, and Sam quickly side-stepped into the small room and locked the door behind him. He was holding a large shopping bag.

In three swift movements he had the tie issue resolved. Pointing at the shopping bag, he ordered, "Put your purse in there!"

Separating a woman from her purse is no easy task; it's like asking her to chop off an arm.

"Must I?"

"You must. If I can change out of a pair of Chanel pumps for this little escapade, you can sack a purse."

I reluctantly placed my purse—the equivalent of my home away from home—into the bag.

Sam pulled a package of sanitary wipes out of his pocket and handed me one. "Lose the Dolly Parton eye shadow and the Emmett Kelly lips."

I scrubbed my face.

He handed me another wipe.

I scrubbed some more.

"Listen, Sam. I think I may become a suspect in Queen Ta Ta's murder," I said midscrub.

"You already are. Every expert in the country is on television saying that there's no way any normal person would jog in Phoenix in August. They're painting you as some kind of psycho fan, like Mark David Chapman."

"Mark whozits?"

"The guy who killed John Lennon. Have you lived in a cave all your life?"

He was the second person to ask me that today. Maybe I *should* get out more.

"I didn't even know who Queen Ta Ta was until this morning!" I protested for the umpteenth time.

Sam resignedly shook his head. "I believe you because I know how clueless you are when it comes to nonwork matters."

"But wait, I heard she came into Saks yesterday and ..."

"We'll talk about it later," said Sam. "Get your 'guy' on. We're getting out of here."

We slipped out of the dressing room and hit our man strides as we crossed the department toward the exit. Since the shoes Sam had given me were a little large, my gait was more of a shuffle than a stride, but I did my best to make it a manly shuffle. I was impressed by how well the rest of the clothes fit, though. Sam must have borrowed them from a much shorter friend, because Sam is about six-two to my five-seven. On the down side, the coat was thick wool tweed and the hat was wool felt. While I was dressed appropriately for the ice-cold temperature in the store, I was going to fry in the 110-degree heat outside.

Halfway to the exit Sam gasped and stopped so short that I ran into him.

"What's wrong?" I whispered nervously, afraid to raise my head to look.

"Canali shirts on sale for half price," breathed Sam.

"No! Keep moving," I ordered sotto voce.

Sam ignored me and pawed through a pile of shirts.

I dug a finger into his ribs, and he slapped my hand away.

"This will go a lot faster if you help. Look for sixteen and a half neck and thirty-four sleeve," he hissed.

I did, trying to keep my pink polished nails hidden as I searched. "Any particular color?" I asked, dropping my voice a few octaves.

"Blue striped with a white Eton."

Miracles of all miracles, I found one. "Here," I said, shoving it into his hands. "Buy it and then let's get out of here."

"I could use a yellow one too," he said, clamping the shirt I'd given him under his arm and continuing to dig.

"May I help you?" A young man with perfect skin and dark hair gelled into spikes had quietly slipped up behind us. The name badge on the lapel of his Italian suit identified him as *Randy, Customer Service Representative*.

I shoved my hands in my pockets and stared at the floor as Sam turned to address the young man. "Do you have a yellow ... Randy! Hi."

"Omigod! Sam! I didn't recognize you from the back, which is odd because that's the side I usually recognize,"

Randy gushed. "How *are* you? Gawd, with this sale going on I should have known you'd show up. In fact, I was thinking of calling you. So Sam, who's your shy friend?"

"It's my boss, Kate," said Sam, lowering his voice.

"That is so cool," enthused Randy. "I had no idea you worked for a tranny!"

"Listen, Randy, we could use some help getting out of here incognito. Kate's the one who found Queen Ta Ta this morning, and the press is hounding her."

I noticed that Sam didn't correct Randy's assumption that I was a transvestite.

Randy's fingers flew to his lips, and he gasped dramatically. "*That's* why there are news vans parked all over. And I saw that luscious reporter from Channel 15 wandering around. You know, the one with the blond hair and the deep blue eyes."

"Greg Borden?" asked Sam excitedly. This time *his* fingers flew to his mouth. "He is so *hot*."

"Hey, Paris and Nicole: focus. I need to get out of here," I hissed.

"She's kind of testy, isn't she," said Randy. "Is she always like this?"

"This is nothing. Once she accidently took some LSD, and—"

"I'm standing right here," I said in a clipped voice.

"Oh, right," said Sam. "Sorry. So Randy, can you hold this shirt for me, and a yellow one in the same size if you find one—"

"Sam!"

"Fine. All right. I get it. Randy, can you can sneak us out of the mall?"

"We'll take the elevator to the employees' underground lot. You can take my ride, and if you tell me where you're parked I'll take yours. We can meet for drinks later and do an exchange."

"Of vehicles?" asked Sam wiggling his eyebrows.

Randy smiled and blushed.

"Oh, for God's sake," I hissed. "Get a room."

Sam blushed this time. "All right, let's get going," he said, suddenly businesslike.

It was about time.

Randy clapped his hands. "This is so great. So much *drama*. I *love* it."

I did not share Randy's enthusiasm.

"First that hunky guy comes in yesterday and buys half the new Abboud and Paul Smith collections, and now a chance meeting with you. This is going to be a good week," Randy said, oblivious to my lack of enthusiasm.

"Joseph Abboud? No way," gasped Sam. "Even the stuff off the rack costs thousands. Who was this guy?"

Randy asked another clerk to cover for him before answering. "His name's Joey Perroni. He's Queen Ta Ta's manager. Poor schmuck is probably out of a job now. I hope that doesn't mean he's going to return the Abbouds. My commissions will take a nasty hit if he does."

"Did he say anything of interest? I mean, his client

was found dead the next morning. He might have known something," said Sam.

"You mean did he tell me he was going to kill her? I *wish*. I could've sold that kind of information to the *Enquirer* for millions."

So far no one had mentioned performing their civic duty to tell the police; these days everyone went to the highest bidder.

"When I asked him if he was shopping for a special occasion, he said it was 'retail therapy' and then muttered something about how stressful it was to have to hold someone's hand twenty-four-seven. Before I knew he was Queen Ta Ta's manager, I thought maybe he was hooked up with a difficult sugar daddy. He was too well groomed and tanned to actually work for a living; not that handling a sugar daddy is a piece of cake."

Randy led us to a door at the back of a storage room. I assumed it led to an outside parking lot, but instead it opened onto a stairwell.

"Why did you think it was a sugar daddy and not a sugar momma?" I asked.

"Because he had me measure his inseam *three times*, and I'm not a tailor. I don't even have a tape measure. I had to make do with gift-wrap ribbon and a ruler."

We followed Randy down two flights of stairs to an employee-only parking lot that until then I didn't know existed. As we crossed the lot, Randy crouched down and tiptoed spy-style from car to car. Sam and I followed with normal postures and paces, pausing every so often while Randy took temporary cover behind yet another vehicle.

Midway through the garage he stopped. "Your valiant steed awaits," he said with a sweep of his arm.

I headed for a Toyota wagon parked in the direction he was pointing.

"No, madam. 'Tis this," he said, stroking the seat of a small motor scooter affectionately.

Sam looked frightened. "The valiant steed is a miniature horse," he side-whispered to me.

"Randy, I've never driven a motor scooter before," I began hesitantly. "Heck, I haven't even ridden on one before. I'm not sure Sam has either."

"It's easy. It's like riding a bike except you don't have to pedal."

"But it's rather small …"

"Don't worry; you'll both fit. I'm in a car pool, and I drove another guy to work today. Of course, we had to sit real close." Randy got a dreamy look.

I cleared my throat to snap him out of it.

"Just take it for a spin around the garage for practice. Come on, Kate. Don't be a chicken," he said challengingly, holding out the keys.

I weighed the alternatives of another confrontation with the press or dying in a fiery motor-scooter crash and took the keys.

Chapter Eight

I sat astride the little scooter, found the ignition, and turned it on. The engine didn't roar like a Harley, but made a soft moan, caught, and then puttered like a lawn mower. Randy showed me how to shift the gears and work the brakes, and I took a turn around the garage in first gear.

He was right. It wasn't that hard. It was actually kind of fun.

Sam crossed himself even though he's not Catholic or part of any other organized religion that I know of. He handed the Honda's keys to Randy (Sam had driven my car and apparently preferred to leave Julia in the mall lot rather than let Randy drive her) and then got on behind me.

Randy giggled. "Hey, Sam, some people call that the bitch seat, you know."

"So this is where you usually sit?" Sam shot back testily.

I started out slowly, swerving back and forth a little until I figured out how to rebalance with Sam's added weight. Then we headed up the curved ramp into the sunlight with Sam sticking to me like a limpet.

"Stop pleading with God to give you mercy. It's distracting," I said through gritted teeth.

We emerged from the ramp into a narrow alley. At the junction of the alley and the main road, I slowed and stopped to check for traffic. I placed my foot on the ground to steady the scooter, but Sam leaned with the scooter and it started to slide out from under me.

"A little help," I hissed.

Sam obliged by throwing his foot to the ground as additional support but then kept going in an attempt to dismount.

"Sit," I ordered a little too loudly.

A couple of young men taking a cigarette break started at the sound of my voice and turned to look in our direction.

"It's her!" one of them yelled. He bolted down the sidewalk in the direction of Camelback Road. "Quick! Over here!" he screamed, gesturing wildly.

A squad of cameramen jogged into sight.

"Hold on," I warned Sam. I revved the little engine and threw it into first. The bike reared up, and Sam expanded the deities to whom he was appealing to include the Buddha, Vishnu, and someone named Jack.

My hat flew off during our rapid acceleration, and when I glanced over my shoulder, I saw one of the cameramen waving it over his head like a trophy.

Fine. They can take as many photos of the hat as they want, I thought.

Instead of turning left toward my condo building, I continued south on Twenty-Fourth Street.

Sam interrupted an especially elaborate (and detailed, I might add) confession to yell, "Where are you going?" into my ear.

"You'll see," I answered. Since I had no idea where I was heading, it would be as much a surprise for me as it was for him.

Two intersections down I had an inspired thought and made a hard left; I would take us to Tuwanda's apartment. Tuwanda, who would be asleep, hated having her beauty rest interrupted, but this was an emergency.

I drove around the back streets for a while to make sure no one was following us and then pulled in behind Tuwanda's apartment building.

I dismounted, but Sam stayed seated. "I think I wet my pants," he said.

"I don't think you did, because that's something you'd *know*. Plus I would have felt it." I surreptitiously checked the back of my suit just in case. Except for what looked like sweat marks where Sam was holding on to me during our wild ride, I was dry.

"Come on. Let's go," I said, suddenly feeling the heat and the weight of the wool suit.

I looked the other way while Sam dismounted and did a crotch check (he was fine), and then we went into the building's foyer and buzzed Tuwanda. I waited a polite sixty seconds before buzzing again. The third time, I leaned on it.

An angry disembodied voice sounded over the speaker: "Dammit. Who the hell is this? You better not be sellin' anythin' 'cuz I'll shove your inventory up your ass if you are."

"Tuwanda, it's Kate," I said, raising my voice to be heard over her rant.

A few beats of silence ensued. I thought maybe she'd fallen asleep. "Tuwanda?"

"I'm gonna buzz you up, but you better have some doughnuts. You wake me up, you gotta feed me."

"No doughnuts; just Sam," I answered. "But it's an emergency."

A sigh floated out of the speaker, but the buzzer went off and the elevator door opened for us.

Tuwanda was waiting for us outside the elevator when we got to the fourth floor. She wore a red satin robe with a matching nightgown and high-heeled white sandals.

"Wow," said Sam appreciatively. "You look hot."

"I ain't sure whether to take that as a compliment,

you bein' gay an' all. You might be sayin' I look like a hot man."

She looked pleased, though.

We followed Tuwanda into her apartment, where I could smell coffee brewing. Tuwanda motioned for us to sit at the kitchen table (a mahogany Chippendale-style affair that probably cost more than my condo) and handed us cold bottles of water.

Tuwanda's dog, Walter, strolled in looking a little mussed, like he'd just gotten out of bed. He was wearing a velvet doggy robe and black silk doggy jammies.

"I'm assumin' that in light of the weather you two ain't in the mood for a hot bev'rage," she commented.

"Actually, I wouldn't mind a cup of coffee," said Sam, staring at his still shaking hands. "Or anything stronger if you have it."

"What did you do to that boy?" Tuwanda asked me, chin jerking toward Sam. "And while we at it, why you wearin' a man's wool suit an' a tie in this godawful heat?"

I gave her a quick rundown on what happened at the mall with Sam providing sound effects (mostly groans) to emphasize certain parts of the story.

She took a bottle of twenty-year-old Scotch and a couple of glasses out of an elaborate minibar and set them down on the table between Sam and me. Sam filled his glass to the brim and took a swig before pushing the bottle toward me.

"No thanks," I said. "I'm the designated driver."

"I'm not riding on that scooter again. I'll walk from here, thank you very much," he said after another swig of Scotch.

Sam had a notoriously low tolerance for alcohol and was already slurring his words.

"Have you tol' Demple 'bout this?" Tuwanda asked.

"Not yet," I said, shaking my head.

"You better call him and let him know wha's goin' on so he can do damage control."

I nodded miserably after correcting the gender she'd assigned to Demple. I reached for my purse and then remembered that I had stashed it in a shopping bag per Sam's instruction.

"Sam, what did you do with the bag I put my clothes and purse in?" I asked nervously.

Sam appeared to give the issue serious thought. "I think I left it in the garage at Macy's. Don't worry; Randy will take care of it."

I doubted it. Randy would probably max out my credit cards and sell my Louis Vuitton handbag on eBay.

"You have to get it back," I said, trying to keep the hysteria out of my voice. "Now!"

"May I borrow your car, Tuwanda?" asked Sam as he half rose from the table and then swayed and fell back into the chair.

"Uh-uh. I wouldn't even let you walk. You ain't capable of stayin' on the sidewalk." Turning to me, she said, "Don' worry, Katie; I'll ask Marge to swing by and get it on her way to work. Call Demple and Randy on my phone and I'll call Marge on my cell an' get things set up."

"Could she bring a friend and pick up Sam's car, too?" I knew a sober Sam would be worried about his precious Julia.

"I'll ask."

But before either of us could make any calls, Sam's cell phone rang. And rang.

Tuwanda finally frisked him and dug it out of his back pocket.

Punching the "accept call" button, she prissily announced, "I'm sorry, but Samuel is indisposed at the moment. May I take a message?"

The caller was silent at first and then asked, "Tuwanda?" in a voice loud enough for me to hear.

Tuwanda looked at me nervously and cupped her hand around the receiver, but it was too late; I had already identified Bryan as the caller. I motioned with my hand for her to continue talking. She pressed the speaker button and placed the phone on the table between us.

"Hey, Bryan. I was doin' my tight-ass-white receptionist impression. How'd you know it was me?"

"You can't hide that low, sexy voice," he said. "Why are you answering Sam's phone?"

"It was ringin', an' Sam ain't in no condition to answer."

Bryan chuckled. "Somebody slip him a glass of chardonnay?"

"Try ten fingers of Scotch."

"God, he must be comatose."

"Close to it. What you need him for?"

We waited through another pause. "Is Kate with you?" he asked with forced casualness.

I ferociously shook my head "No."

"No, jus' me an' Sam."

Bryan made an exasperated noise. "I've been calling her since noon. She's not answering her mobile, and Beth won't tell me where she is."

Tuwanda raised an eyebrow and mouthed, *What the hell?* "Why you need to find her so bad?" she asked.

"I don't want to find her. I want to warn her." His voice now sounded strained. "There's an APB out on her. The police have a warrant for her arrest."

I went cold and still. I'd represented thousands of people accused of crimes, but this was the first time I'd stood in their shoes. I was scared; probably more so than any of my clients, because the majority of them, while overwhelmed by the legal system, were ignorant about its inner workings. I, on the other hand, knew how the process worked; innocence didn't guaranty acquittal.

"Uh oh. That ain't at all good. Why they wanna arrest Katie?" continued Tuwanda, keeping an anxious eye on me.

"Queen Ta Ta's murder. Kate was their chief suspect

from the start, and now they've got an eyewitness. He spoke to a young officer at the crime scene, but by the time the information made it up the food chain, Kate had already left."

It's a good thing I was sitting down. *How could there be a witness to something that never happened?* The practical side of me immediately came up with an answer. *Because he's lying to cover for himself or someone else. He probably waited to contact the police to see if any other eyewitnesses would come forward.*

"Who they say that witness is?" asked Tuwanda.

"Queen Ta Ta's manager. Some Guido by the name of Joey Perroni," he said, spitting out the name.

Why does everyone know about Queen Ta Ta and Guidos except me? I have *been living in a cave.* A section of my brain cells took the metaphor further: *And a cave is exactly where you should be; a hole in a rock where you can hide until this thing blows over.*

Another loosely bound coalition of brain cells thought this was hysterical and threw the switch on the giggle reflex.

Tuwanda held down the mute button and whispered, "Shut up."

"Who's that laughing?" asked Bryan suspiciously.

"Tha's the television. I'm watchin' one of them reality shows about a bunch a' rich white girls livin' in Cal'fornia. They always either gigglin' or whinin'. That ain't a lot of emotional range in my opinion."

There was silence on Bryan's end of the line.

"Bryan, you still there?" asked Tuwanda.

"Yes. I just had to, um, get a drink of water."

I could tell he'd been laughing, which I thought was terribly inappropriate in light of the circumstances—*my* circumstances, that is. My recent giggling fit was excusable because I was in shock, darn it.

"So did the police tell you what this Joey guy *says* he saw?"

"Pretty straightforward. He said he watched it all from a hotel window: Kate met Queen Ta Ta on the path; they argued and struggled, and Kate strangled her."

"Jus' like that. She don' even know this woman, but she runs into her out on a joggin' path an' thinks, 'Damn. She gotta die.'

"You talkin' 'bout a woman who apologizes to furniture. She bumped into a chair the other day and tol' it she was sorry. Any normal person woulda' kicked the hell outta that chair."

Now this was taking it too far. She was making me sound like a nut. I did *no*t apologize to inanimate objects.

Well, okay; there was that vase at Demple's office. But the poor thing almost fell on the floor.

"Don't forget, Tuwanda. Kate killed a man a couple of months ago," said Bryan levelly.

"Uh-uh. Uh-uh. Don' go there. That man was about to kill Sam an' her, an' then pro'bly woulda' got around to Emily. That ain't got nothin' to do with this. It's apples an' oranges. Hell, it's apples an' bowlin' balls."

"I agree with you, but the police aren't seeing it that way. To them, it means she's got a history of violence."

"So they sayin' self-defense is kinda like a gateway drug; first you kill in self-defense, an' before you know it you mowin' down people at McDonald's?"

"Apparently." I could hear the shrug in his voice.

"Law enforcement people think with they intestines. [Tuwanda had taken several nursing courses at the community college in addition to the chemistry course, so anatomical metaphors were also part of her vernacular.] Diarrhea is their idea of a brainstorm."

Bryan was silent for a few beats, probably waiting for Tuwanda to realize her faux pas: after all, *he* was a member of the law-enforcement community too.

"Present company excluded," Tuwanda corrected. "I get a take-back though if you jus' callin' to tell me all this so's I can turn Kate in … if I see her."

"It's no good if she tries to run, Tuwanda," he said wearily. "You know and I know, and she knows too, that running is an admission of guilt."

"An' you know as well as I do that as soon as them police pick Kate up they gonna stop lookin' for the real murderer. They so lazy, they'd confess to it theyselves if it meant they could go home early."

"I can guarantee that my department will not pull

back on its investigation efforts if Kate is taken into custody," said Bryan in a steely, formal voice.

"Your department better get movin' an' find the real murderer, then," said Tuwanda.

"You promise if you see her, you'll tell her to turn herself in?" asked Bryan.

Tuwanda ostentatiously held up her hand for me to see and crossed her fingers. "Yes, boss. I will."

"And you'll call me and tell me where she is?"

Fingers still crossed, she said, "Yes, boss."

"I don't believe you," said Bryan. "But thank you for the gesture."

"No problem."

Chapter Nine

After they ended their conversation, Tuwanda said, "Ain't no way you turnin' yourself in, Katie. You stayin' here till we figger out who did it."

"We?" I asked.

"Yeah. Me, MJ, Beth, an', as soon as he sobers up, Sam."

I was grateful for the offer but afraid for my friends. They stood a good chance of being charged with interference in an ongoing criminal investigation, not to mention harboring a suspect. We could all end up in jail. The problem was that when Tuwanda decided to do something there was no stopping her. Considerations of impossibility, risk of injury, or other danger to self and others—the negatives weighed by reasonable people against outcome—were irrelevant. That MJ, Sam, and Beth had not yet agreed to the plan was also neither here nor there. I knew that they would be on board as soon as Tuwanda asked them to jump off the nice, safe dock into the boat, even if the boat was a leaky kayak with no paddles.

I moved from resigned acceptance into the next stage: annoyance.

"So you're going to find the bad guy, or woman, while I sit here and twiddle my thumbs?"

"You do whatever you want to do with your thumbs. You just gotta stay outta sight. You know they gonna be watchin' your buildin' and pro'bly mine too. So you gotta keep quiet and keep down. Kinda like that Anne Frank child."

"Anne Frank died in a concentration camp," I pointed out sullenly.

"Anne Frank din't have no Tuwanda aroun' to protect her."

True enough. How differently that sad story would have ended had enough people like Tuwanda been around.

"I have to do something or I'll go crazy," I said.

"You can maybe do stuff on the Internet—you know, like that pigtailed girl on *NCIS* or that weird blonde chick on *Criminal Minds*."

I drew a blank on the television characters, but the concept intrigued me. I could do background research on Queen Ta Ta and her manager, for starters. Obviously, her manager was at the top of my list of suspects because he'd outright lied about seeing me strangle his client.

"What are you planning to do?" I asked curiously.

"First thing we gotta do is have a strategy meetin'. I'll get holda' MJ an' Beth an' tell 'em to come over here pronto. After Sam comes to, we can get started. You got any idea how long he usually stays down?"

I shook my head no. "At my Christmas party he was out for two hours after half a glass of eggnog."

"We may hafta strategize without him and let him know what's goin' on later."

"I guess we should forget about calling Randy or Demple."

"Police no doubt heard 'bout your great escape from Macy's an' already talked to Randy. That bein' the case, they likely got your handbag and car now. I'll ask Marge to stop off at Macy's on the off chance that ain't what happened, but at this point gettin' your stuff back don't look hopeful.

"As for Demple, I'll call him ... her ... an' tell her what's goin' on—all except the part where you're hidin' out from the law in my condo. Then I'll tell her that, 'cuz you got a tendency to get hit on the head a lot, you gave me instructions to act on your behalf should you become incapacitated or unavailable."

This last bit did not involve a stretch in logic; I've had more concussions in the last year than a professional boxer after a lifetime in the ring.

I nodded. "Sounds good to me."

I resigned myself to the probable loss of my car, mobile

phone, and my favorite purse, not to mention my credit cards, driver's license, three bottles of aspirin, a can of Sterno, an unopened pack of gum, a half roll of Rolaids, a jar of honey, a new pair of panty hose, my office, car, and house keys, and a tube of lipstick in my favorite color (which, of course, had been discontinued). The latter item was not the lipstick I smeared all over my face while on camera. I had disposed of that in Beth's wastebasket.

Tuwanda, now on a mission, trotted into her bedroom and returned a few minutes later dressed in a velveteen jogging suit. Walter had likewise changed into a matching jogging suit. Walter was an extremely intelligent and talented animal, so it was anyone's guess as to whether Tuwanda dressed him or he handled matters himself.

After pointing me toward her laptop, she got busy making phone calls.

Despite the heat outside, I poured myself a cup of coffee and sat in front of the computer.

I had reviewed everything on Wikipedia and Queen Ta Ta's official site and was starting on fan sites when MJ and Beth arrived.

MJ had changed into what she called her "detective clothes," which consisted of a tight leatherette miniskirt, black Doc Martens, and a low-cut black T-shirt with *Shhhhhh* printed on it.

"Where's your black stocking cap?" I asked.

"Too hot," she said.

Beth, too, had changed and wore neatly pressed jeans,

a collared shirt, and tennis shoes. The two of them were obviously expecting some heavy action.

Tuwanda showed them into the dining room, and they sat on either side of Sam. MJ poked him a couple of times in the arm. When he didn't respond, she started rummaging through her purse.

"No, MJ," I said sternly as I took a seat across from her.

MJ had taken advantage of the few times Sam had passed out at holiday parties to express her creative side by covering him with graffiti. At my Christmas party last year, she used him as a guest book and invited everyone to sign him.

MJ muttered something about First Amendment rights but obediently put the Magic Marker back into her purse.

"Are we going to start without Sam?" asked Beth.

"Sam's right here," said MJ, giving him another poke with her finger.

"I meant are we going to wait for Sam to be conscious?" Beth corrected.

"I don' think so," said Tuwanda as she took a chair at the head of the table. "He had a glass of Scotch—an' I ain't talkin' 'bout one of them tiny shot glasses neither. I'm talkin' 'bout a reg'lar water glass."

Beth covered her mouth in horror, and MJ guffawed.

"Should we take him to the hospital?" asked Beth worriedly.

"He still breathin', so he should be fine," said Tuwanda. "He maybe got a little brain damage, but I doubt anyone'll notice."

"What?" yelped Beth, half rising.

"Take it easy, Beth. She's kidding about the brain damage," said MJ. Turning to Tuwanda, she asked, "Aren't you?"

"Yeah, I'm kiddin. He gonna be fine. But we can't wait for him to wake up. We got important things to figger out, an' we don' got much time, Kate bein' on the lam an' all."

I grimaced upon hearing my status restated and shrugged apologetically as the three of them shifted their gazes to me.

"It ain't her fault," continued Tuwanda. "She jus' at the wrong place at the wrong time, an' some guy's lyin' about what he saw." Tuwanda proceeded to summarize her conversation with Bryan.

Beth looked at me thoughtfully when Tuwanda finished. "That was nice of Bryan to call and give Kate a heads-up," she commented.

"I don't think he was trying to help," I scoffed. "It's more like he was trying to track me down and arrest me."

Beth smiled softly. "By talking to your best friend, giving her detailed information about an investigation, and asking her to turn you in when he knew she never would?"

"If he wants to help me, then why isn't he pleading my case to the police? He knows I could never kill anyone," I said heatedly.

MJ raised an eyebrow.

"Unless they're pointing a gun at me," I amended.

"Maybe he's trying to reason with the police and you just don't know it," said Beth softly.

I crossed my arms and shook my head stubbornly. "He only cares about his political future. He's not going to risk losing the election by sticking his neck out for me."

"We c'n all see that the sheriff's a real touchy subject for Kate," broke in Tuwanda. "So I suggest we move on an' decide how we gonna handle our investigation.

"We gonna do this the same way we do at Pole Polishers durin' our bid'ness development meetin's." She disappeared into the hallway, returning a few seconds later with a whiteboard, a felt pen, and an easel. Once she finished setting up, she wrote *Goal: Find Killer* at the top and the numbers one through five underneath. Turning to us, she pointed to the heading and said, "This here's our bid'ness goal. These numbered lines underneath's gonna be our action plan for accomplishin' the goal. Now we gonna brainstorm to get some ideas for our action plan. I want each of you to call out whatever idea pops into your head, an' I'll write it down. When we got ten ideas, we gonna discuss 'em an' finalize our plan."

"You do this at Pole Polishers?" asked MJ.

I think MJ, Beth, and I were all wondering how this worked in Tuwanda's line of business.

Tuwanda nodded her head proudly. "Yes, ma'am. Ev'ry month we rent a conference room at the Hyatt and me an' my Care Bares meet to set bid'ness devel'pment an' customer-care goals. We break into discussion groups cuz we got so many people an' come together again later to develop our action plan. People buy into a plan easier if they part of the plannin'."

I briefly considered doing the same thing at my firm but then dismissed the idea in view of the low probability of MJ and Sam agreeing on anything.

"Now don' be shy. Shout out whatever comes to mind," directed Tuwanda. "We ain't here to judge."

Beth raised her hand.

"You don't gotta raise your hand, Beth. Jus' go ahead an' say what you're thinkin'," Tuwanda said kindly.

Beth retracted her hand. "I think one of us needs to talk to that Joey Perroni guy," she said.

"Excellent!" said Tuwanda as she wrote, "Interview AH," on line 1.

"Who's AH?" asked MJ.

"That's short for asshole. If we gonna figger this out we gotta think like cops, which means we gotta talk like cops. We all seen *Law & Order*. Tha' show's on ev'ry hour in reruns. No way you ain't seen that show. Anyway, we gotta act like them. They's always assignin' suspects acronyms and nicknames and the like."

"Are we supposed to act like the cops on *Law & Order: SVU, Law & Order New York, Law & Order Los Angeles, Law & Order Miami, Law & Order: Criminal Intent*, or the original *Law & Order*?" asked MJ interestedly.

"Take your pick," Tuwanda responded.

"Okay. Then I want to be Agent Benson on *Law & Order: SVU*," said MJ.

"Hey, that's who I want to be," objected Beth.

A discussion ensued over who got to be whom until it was resolved that all three of them could be Detective Benson since there can never be too many Detective Bensons.

The matter settled, the group went back to brainstorming. Eventually we came up with a plan: Tuwanda would assume a disguise provided by Sam, who was a whiz at that sort of thing, and would register under an alias at the Biltmore Hotel. MJ would find out who among Queen Ta Ta's staff and associates were still at the hotel and provide background information on each.

MJ volunteered on Sam's behalf for him to use his connections at the police department and sheriff's office to get information on the status of their murder investigations. (Sam worked as a detective for the county prosecutor's office for years before he came to work for me, so he had good contacts on the "other side.")

"I'll try to get hold of the autopsy report too," mumbled Sam.

"Sam?" asked MJ, scrutinizing what, until then, we'd thought was an unconscious man.

"Yes," he answered, lifting his head slightly and wincing at the pain caused by even this minimal effort. "And if you poke me again, I'll tie you to that chair and leave you there to die."

He let his head fall back on the table and added, "By the way, I want to be Detective Benson too."

Tuwanda briefly outlined the other matters for which he had volunteered while unconscious before we moved on.

I gave them a rundown on the Macy's incident and then passed on what I'd learned thus far about Queen Ta Ta through my Internet research. They already knew much of what I had to say about Queen Ta Ta, but I did come up with some facts that were new to them. First, Queen Ta Ta's mother, Beatrice Butoff, lived in an adult living community west of Phoenix. She and Queen Ta Ta's father were divorced, and the latter lived in a correctional facility in southern California not far from Yuma. Next, Queen Ta Ta recently fired her longtime assistant, Che Che Herrera (longtime in the music industry, that is—she'd been her assistant six months). Che Che was originally from Tucson, Arizona, and Queen Ta Ta had attended high school in Tucson. All in all, Queen Ta Ta had quite a few connections to Arizona.

Interviews with Herrera and Butoff became items three and four of the action plan.

We then turned to assignments and housekeeping matters. My condo was likely being watched by the police twenty-four-seven and was therefore off limits. Sam and Beth volunteered to go shopping for clothes and other personal supplies to tide me over for a couple of days.

Tuwanda would contact my neighbor Macy to ask her to watch Ralph. I gave her strict instructions not to let on to Macy that she knew of my whereabouts. (I didn't want to expose any more friends to charges of criminal conspiracy.)

Sam volunteered for the Herrera interview. Since, among the four of us, Beth was the most qualified to talk to a grieving mother, we assigned her the task of interviewing Mrs. Butoff. (It's not that the rest of us aren't compassionate, it's just that we don't have a lot of practice with mothering or grandmothering, so our range was limited.)

As the last item on our agenda, we agreed to meet at ten o'clock the next morning at Tuwanda's condo to bring each other up to date. In the meantime, we would stay in contact by coded e-mails and texts (I would be referred to by the name of a previous client).

When we were through, MJ gave Sam a ride back to the office, which unfortunately for him meant sitting on the back of a Harley Hog. (Sam accepted MJ's offer of a ride when he was presented with the alternative of taking the far less substantial scooter.)

Beth headed in the direction of the nearest Target to pick up some provisions for me (underwear, toothbrush, pajamas). Sam would handle the outerwear purchases at Macy's or Nordstrom, although it was clear that his beloved car, Julia, and her welfare were his primary concerns, and her rescue would be first on his list of to-dos.

Tuwanda changed into work clothes (a Michael Kors pantsuit and Chanel spectators) and left for her office. According to Tuwanda, it was important that they all appear to continue their normal routines so no one would get suspicious. She didn't see the irony of including management of a prostitution ring as part of a "normal routine."

Chapter Ten

Left to myself, I became depressed and anxious in under a minute. It was apparent to me, at least, that I could not play a passive role in the investigation.

Sam had once provided a disguise for me that was so effective that even Bryan didn't recognize me. He could do it again, only this time I would give firmer direction regarding my assumed persona. (Last time, he had made me into an older, uglier version of the Wicked Witch of the West.) I would raise the matter at tomorrow's meeting but would tip off Beth and Sam via e-mail now. I wanted my transformation and back-up documentation completed in enough time for me to accompany Beth on her interview with Mrs. Butoff.

I returned to my Internet research task with renewed energy, only breaking for a quick dinner consisting of a peanut butter and banana sandwich (Tuwanda's cooking skills were almost as limited as mine, so provisions were sparse) and to let Walter out at six for his nightly dump. (The latter was accomplished by sending Walter to the ground floor in the elevator and then, upon hearing his signal [a bark], sending the elevator back down for him. I tried to train Ralph to do this, but all I got was a dog that adores elevator rides and would rather go up and down all day than disembark for pooping or any other purpose.)

I read every site identified in AOL, Google, and Yahoo searches of Queen Ta Ta. I also listened to several Queen Ta Ta songs on iTunes, and while some of them were quite catchy, her musical talent did not justify the mass hysteria surrounding her personal life and public performances, the line between the foregoing being indistinguishable. As best as I could tell, her primary talent was outweirding the competition. During a concert in Los Angeles, she stripped down to her underwear, a thong and a French demi-bra. The next day every middle school girl in LA was stripping down by lunch and grade schools scrambled to expand dress codes to address inappropriate underwear exposure. When Queen Elizabeth invited Queen Ta Ta to tea (a decision which, in my opinion, provides further evidence of the negative effects of both inbreeding and senility), Queen Ta Ta showed up in a boat-shaped hat (a replica of Lord Nelson's ship, to be exact) and a tight-fitting dress made out of what appeared to be Saran Wrap. Schools rushed to ban apparel made out of food wraps from classrooms. From what I could tell, the outfit she was wearing when I found her was a relatively conservative choice for her.

Queen Ta Ta's personal life was equally bizarre. She was, according to one magazine, "sexually ambiguous," which appeared to mean that she had no preference in lovers with respect to sexual orientation or species. That might explain her poodle's desperate expression in one of the photos.

Among the humans connected romantically with Queen Ta Ta were DeDe Machotti (a back-up singer), Joey Perroni, and her former assistant, Che Che Herrera, indicating that Queen Ta Ta either preferred to hit on her employees or employed people she hit on.

She was also the owner of a menagerie that included a chimpanzee, a ferret, a parrot, and an emu, all of which probably needed long-term therapy.

In light of Queen Ta Ta's notoriety, her entourage likely included more than just Perroni. Those with the most access to Queen Ta Ta would include her personal assistant, manager, agent, bodyguards, drivers, and lovers, including the "significant other" mentioned by the cosmetician at Saks. I eliminated consideration of the nonhuman species, which shortened the list considerably.

I had just started a background search on Perroni when Tuwanda returned.

"Whoa, you been workin' since I left?"

I was so engrossed in my research project that I didn't

notice how long I'd been at it. I checked the clock and saw that it was two a.m.

"Time flies when you're evading the law," I said ruefully.

"Tha's good. I was afraid you'd get bored and climb out the window."

"As a matter of fact—Wait, why would I climb out of the window instead of walking through the door?"

"Habit."

I did have a history of climbing out of windows during stressful situations.

"As I started to say before I interrupted myself, I'm going to ask Sam to create a disguise for me too. I want to interview Mrs. Butoff with Beth. I'll go stir crazy if I stay here."

"You gonna go *stir* crazy for real if you get caught."

"I'll take that chance."

Tuwanda shook her head resignedly. "I guess you gonna do what you gonna do."

Look who was talking.

"By the way," she continued, "Sam called me. The police got your car, and the tech guys are pullin' it apart for clues."

I moaned and apologized softly to my little Honda. It was, like me, an innocent bystander.

"What about Sam's car?"

"Safe and sound. It din't belong to you, so they weren't lookin' for it."

This, at least, was good news.

"Did you get a room at the Biltmore?" I asked.

"Let me pour myself a glass of wine, an' then I'll tell you what's goin' on in Tuwanda-world. You want some?"

"Yes, but you've been working all night. Let me get it. You sit and relax."

"You actin' like one of them fifties wives on TV. You gonna make pancakes for breakfast an' all that shit too?"

"I don't know how to make pancakes," I said as I poured a glass of chardonnay for me and a cabernet for Tuwanda. "So unless you have Eggos in the freezer, you're out of luck."

She chuckled as she took off her shoes and snuggled into a comfy armchair.

I handed her the cabernet and took a seat on the sofa. Between swigs of wine she told me what had happened since she left.

Marge had managed (the way only Marge can) to reserve Tuwanda a room at the hotel for a three-day stay. The only room available was a cottage suite next to the pool: a premium location at a premium cost. I whistled when I heard the nightly charge.

"We'd better solve this murder quickly. I can't afford a long investigation," I said.

"Don' worry 'bout cost. Takin' on debt ain't nothin' compared to bein' in jail."

"You mean taking on *more* debt. It's been a tough couple of months, and it's going to get worse; it's hard to conduct business when you're on the lam, especially when that business requires that you show up in court every so often."

"I don' think you'll be missin' out on much bid'ness. Things is always slow in the summer, even in my line of bid'ness. People's too hot to do anythin'. Ain't no one wanna leave the air-conditionin', so we gotta depend on yellow page an' newspaper ads an' goin' door to door to drum up bid'ness."

I desperately wanted to know more about her door-to-door marketing program. Did they leave pamphlets? Give out samples? Provide demonstrations? I barely managed to keep my curiosity in check and my focus on task.

"When are you going to the hotel?" I asked.

"Sam's gonna bring his makeup an' shit over tomorrow mornin', an once I get my new look, I'm off to the hotel. I'm hopin' by that time MJ'll find out who's stayin' there an' which rooms they in. Tha's a big hotel, an' I don' wanna hafta make no room-to-room search like las' time."

Tuwanda was referring to an unpleasant incident where we went undercover as maids to search for a kidnapped Pole Polisher employee. You'd be surprised by what you see when you walk in on people in hotel rooms and how poorly some of them take the interruption. But then the ones who liked the audience were downright scary.

"Assuming you have their room numbers, how are you going to arrange to meet them?"

"Easy. I wait in the hallway, an' when they come out I pretend I'm a guest doin' the same thing they doin'. If they goin' to get ice, so'm I; if they goin' to the bar, damned if I ain't thirsty too."

"What if they're going to work out in the exercise room," I smirked. Tuwanda is notoriously hostile toward exercise. She once threw a half-eaten cake at the television screen when Jillian Michaels came on. "Tha' woman's the devil!" she'd screamed, after which she scraped the cake off the TV and ate it.

"Then I'm jus' goin' in to check out the equipment. I don't gotta use the shit, I just gotta look at it an' maybe ask a few questions."

"Sounds like a good plan. By the way, did Marge check on my purse?" I asked.

"I called Randy, but he wouldn't say too much over the phone. I found that suspicious. So I sent JJ over to follow up. [JJ handled Pole Polishers' collections. He was 250 pounds of solid muscle and rarely had to do more than show up to convince people that they should pay what they owe ASAP.] JJ had a discussion with Randy an' found out that Randy sold your purse an' everythin' in it to *Innuendo* magazine for nine thousan' dollars."

"So, in other words, I'm not going to get my purse back."

"I'd say the purse is a goner. But at leas' you got nine thousan' dollars."

"What?! How did that happen?"

"You know how persuasive JJ can be."

"Geez, I'm surprised JJ didn't end up with the deed to Randy's house."

"He rents," Tuwanda explained apologetically.

I had to get a JJ.

Even though I was still wired, Tuwanda convinced me that I should get some sleep before our ten o'clock meeting. She handed me a sack of clothes from Target that Beth had dropped off at Pole Polishers and steered me toward her guest room.

The master bedroom where Tuwanda slept had a red-velvet, canopied, gilt bed on a raised platform at one end and was separated from the humongous dressing room and three-way mirror at the other end by an elegant sitting area. The guest room was only slightly less ostentatious. The gilt, white-canopied bed was covered with a light-blue, raw-silk comforter. Oriental rugs in blues and browns covered the hardwood floor. The dresser looked like something Marie Antoinette might have used. I would have felt like a queen, too, but for the fact that the pajamas Beth bought me were pink with a picture of Justin Bieber on the back and "I'd Bang Bieber in a Heartbeat" written on the front. Beth said they were on sale and she couldn't resist a bargain. From my perspective,

Beth would have had the raw end of the deal even if she'd gotten the pajamas for free.

On the plus side, though, it felt good to get out of Sam's itchy wool suit.

I showered and dressed in the surprisingly comfy Bieber jammies. I could hear the sound of Tuwanda's television and thought maybe a little TV would help me get to sleep too. The guest room was equipped with a forty-eight-inch TV loaded with premium cable channels. I lightly punched the remote, and the screen sprang to life.

The door to my bedroom burst open. Tuwanda marched in and pulled out the TV's plug.

"Hey! Why'd you do that?"

"You don' need to see the shit they puttin' on the television these days. It'll rot your mind."

"Who are you, my mother?" Actually, this was not an apt comparison at all: my mother never swore, had impeccable grammar, and spoke in a modulated voice reminiscent of Queen Elizabeth, which was odd because she'd never been outside of Minnesota.

"I'm jus' tryin' to protect your tender sensibilities."

That was a new one. No one ever accused me of having tender sensibilities before. Quite the opposite. Bryan once accused me of emotional insensitivity when I didn't cry during *Marley and Me,* which I thought was unfair. I'd gotten misty-eyed during *Mamma Mia* just the week before.

"What the hell you lookin' like that for? You thinkin' about that *Mamma Mia* movie again?"

I paused the tape of *The Winner Takes It All* playing in my head. "No. Of course not."

"Good. Jus' get to sleep. No more television, got it?"

Then it dawned on me. "I'm on the news, aren't I?"

Tuwanda nodded and sat heavily on the side of the bed. "All I gotta say is that if you gonna be runnin' aroun' Phoenix, Sam had better do a damn good job of makin' you look like someone else. By now everyone in the country has seen you—all of you, except for maybe that bitty part covered by Precious."

Precious was the Chihuahua I was holding in front of me in the naked-woman-running-from-the-fire photo.

"Why do they keep showing that picture? It's over a year old."

"'Cuz the photographer got a big award for it; a Pulitzer or some shit like that. In a way, though, you should count your blessin's. That picture's better than the shot of you smearin' lipstick all over your face. You look like a crazy woman. What the hell was you thinkin'?"

"I was thinking it was ChapStick," I snapped.

Tuwanda appeared to consider this. "That kinda makes sense. 'Specially when you include the Kate factor."

"What do you mean by the 'Kate factor'?"

"It's like you got all the same facts as everyone else, but when you or your fate angel add 'em together, the results is different from everyone else's. Then you usually get hit in the head or shot at."

I had a fate angel?

"That is a disturbing insight into my psyche," I said.

She patted my leg and rose to her feet. "See you in six hours," she said as she shuffled wearily out of the room.

Chapter Eleven

I fell asleep soon after Tuwanda left, but it was not a refreshing, deep sleep. Rather, it was a dream marathon. I was chased by a variety of pursuers that included Queen Ta Ta, Bryan, Detective Webber, and, at one point, my paperboy. (I'd refused to tip him at Christmas because I had canceled the paper and didn't think he should be rewarded for continuing to deliver something I didn't want, even if it was free. He still drops it at my door every morning out of spite.)

I woke to the sound of the doorbell ringing. After the fifth ring, Tuwanda sleepily called out, "Is that you, Walter?"

The dog can ring the doorbell? Ralph had another training session coming.

A sarcastic "Arf-arf" came from the other side of the door.

I heard Tuwanda's footsteps accompanied by

mumbled obscenities and then the sound of the front door opening.

"You're just getting up?" accused Sam.

"Tha' sounds like sumpthin' you said to your boyfriend las' night," countered Tuwanda.

A few seconds later Tuwanda appeared in my doorway. "Get your ass outa' bed," she ordered.

"Okay, okay. You don't have to be so rude," I said.

"That ain't rude. Tha's how my momma woke me up every day for school. Rude is when you get hit in the face with cold water, which is what happened if I din't hop outa' bed when she asked the first time."

"My mother said, 'rise and shine,'" I said, hopping out of bed in case the cold water treatment was part of Tuwanda's repertoire as well.

"See now, I like my momma's way of doin' it better," commented Tuwanda as I followed her to the kitchen. "Tellin' someone they gotta shine in the mornin' is puttin' 'em under too much pressure. It' hard enough jus' gettin' outa bed. Why you gotta smile about it too?"

Sam had already started the coffeemaker, and the wonderful smell of impending caffeine permeated the air.

"What the hell are you wearing?" Sam asked me.

"Good morning to you too," I responded sardonically as I took the chair closest to the coffee pot.

"Them's the PJs Beth got Katie," provided Tuwanda.

"Justin Bieber? Are you serious?" he asked teasingly.

A few beats later he asked, "Can I have them when you're through with them?"

I looked at him to see if he was kidding. He was smiling softly, and his eyes had a faraway look.

"He gave a concert at the fairgrounds a week ago. I was there," he went on dreamily.

"You an' a couple hunnert thirteen-year-old white girls," said Tuwanda.

"Is the coffee ready?" I asked, sensing that the discussion needed to be interrupted.

"Where are your cups, Tuwanda?" asked Sam.

"Make mine a large mug," I said. "If you can't find one, a soup bowl will work fine."

Tuwanda showed him where the cups were and then sat down next to me.

"Where is everyone else?" I asked.

"They should be along any minute," said Sam as he efficiently poured out two cups and one large mug of coffee. "I left the office just before MJ and Beth. They probably got held up in traffic."

As if on cue, we heard a knock at the front door, and Sam hurried to let in MJ and Beth.

"Sorry we're late," apologized MJ as she walked into the kitchen. "But Beth drives like an old lady."

"I *am* an old lady," countered Beth from behind her.

"Hi, Beth," I greeted. "Did you manage to get hold of Mrs. Butoff?"

Beth nodded. "I set up a meeting with her today at noon."

She placed a bakery box on the table, and I snagged a cherry Danish between exclamations of delight and thanks. Sam pulled off a bunch of paper towels and handed them around, muttering something under his breath that included the phrase "pigs at the trough." I didn't care. The Danish looked delicious, and I was starved.

MJ was oddly restrained, however, and daintily picked at a sprinkled doughnut between slurps of Coke from a Big Gulp. Today she wore her black hair in high pigtails, her too-small plaid schoolgirl skirt, black army boots, and a low-cut black T-shirt with a picture of two owls with "Hooters" written underneath.

"You okay, MJ?" I asked. "You don't seem very hungry."

"She's fine," Beth answered for her. "There're a dozen pastries in that box. When we left the office there were two dozen."

"Since MJ already had breakfast, maybe she oughta' go first with her update," said Tuwanda through a mouthful of chocolate croissant.

MJ licked her fingers carefully and then looked around the table to make sure we were all paying attention. "I have, through a series of brilliant decoding combinations, managed to gain access to the registration records of the hotel."

"Wait a minute," said Tuwanda, waving a chocolate-covered finger toward MJ. "I got it. You tryin' to be like that pigtailed girl on *NCIS.*"

"I thought we were doing *Law & Order*?" piped in Sam. "If we're doing the *CSI* shows too then I want to be Catherine Willows."

"Who's that?" I asked.

Tuwanda sighed in disgust. "Don't the dark an' damp of that cave you live in ever get to you? Catherine Willows is the red-haired lady in the Las Vegas *CSI*. She gets to wear tank tops that are real clingy and low cut, an' everyone else on the show has to wear turtlenecks 'n' shit."

MJ cleared her throat loudly. "If it is settled then that I am Abby, may I proceed?"

"Abby?" I asked weakly.

"The pigtailed girl on *NCIS*. Maybe we should force you to watch television for a week to get you up to speed on popular culture," said Sam.

"Tuwanda won't let me watch television," I pouted.

"Everyone, please focus on *me*!" interrupted MJ.

We all dutifully gave her our attention.

MJ took another slurp of Coke and took up where she left off. "I got into the registration records of the hotel and have a list of all guests staying at the hotel when Queen Ta Ta was murdered. I also have room numbers for the ones still registered."

"Tha' better be Diet Coke, you know," said Tuwanda. "Abby drinks Diet Coke."

I shot her a narrow-eyed look and turned back to MJ. "That was wonderful work, MJ. Now all we need to do is find out which of the guests had a connection with Queen Ta Ta."

"Done," she said. "I conducted a search for names of people who worked on her last three concerts, including musicians, dancers, lighting and sound technicians, makeup artists, hair dressers, wardrobe workers—everyone I could think of. Nine of the same people who worked on one or more of her previous concerts were staying at the hotel during the time of the murder."

"Great! That's wonderful!" I enthused. "Did you bring copies of the list?"

"No. Abby never writes stuff down. She just calls everyone down to her lab and points to it on a computer screen."

"I see," I said, even though I didn't.

"Fortunately, unlike the *NCIS* agents, you have a secretary," said Beth as she pulled a stack of sheets out of her purse and handed them around. "*NCIS* is all well and good for a television show, but it's too top-heavy to be a real, functioning office."

I gave her a grateful look that I hoped canceled the nasty one she got from MJ for stealing her thunder.

After a short period of silence during which we all perused the list, Sam remarked, "These can't be their real names: Sunshine Peacemaker? Violet Flowers? Hi Flyer? Moonlight Gould?"

MJ shook her head. "I checked on that too. Those are their birth names."

"Tha's what happened to children in the seventies. They parents come outta the marijuana haze ten years later an' say, 'Why's my chile named Moonlight?'"

I gave silent thanks that I wasn't born in the Age of Aquarius.

"Are all the people on the list still staying at the hotel?

"Just Perroni, Peacemaker, Flyer, and Stanley Dorfman, and to answer what I'm sure will be your next question, Stanley is only twenty-seven, so he missed the generation of love," contributed MJ. "The numbers next to their names are their room numbers as of last night."

"Tuwanda, it looks like you've got your work cut out for you," I commented. "That's still a lot of people to accidently bump into," I commented. "Don't you think the hotel employees will get suspicious with you lurking around and stalking so many guests?"

Tuwanda looked thoughtful. "Hmmm. Is all these people white, MJ?"

"I couldn't find pictures of all of 'em, but the ones I found are Caucasians. I'll e-mail the pictures as soon as I get back to the office," she added sheepishly, recognizing another oversight.

"If they all white, that's gonna make it 'specially hard. Plus I'm guessin' overall there ain't a lot of black guests at the hotel, so I'm gonna stick out even more. Add to that my strikin' good looks that no amount a' makeup's gonna hide, an' I'm pretty damned identifiable."

"Are you getting cold feet?" asked Sam.

"Uh-uh. I never get cold feet. I'm as hot-blooded as they get. But I'm thinkin' it would be better if I had a partner to share the duties." Her eyes shifted to me.

"Wait a minute," I demurred. "You said I should keep low and stay out of the way."

"Yeah, but then *you* said you couldn't take doin' that no more, an' Sam's gonna disguise you."

"For purposes of going with Beth to interview Mrs. Butoff. That's different from staying at a hotel and mingling with lots of people," I protested. "Plus, it was a miracle Marge found Tuwanda a room. It's going to be impossible to get another one."

"If Marge can do it, so can I," Beth said testily.

Great: a secretary showdown.

"I'm sure you can," I said soothingly. "It's just that I …"

"I can disguise you so your own mother wouldn't recognize you," said Sam.

I sighed in surrender. "All right. We'll use the visit to Mrs. Butoff as a test case. She's likely to be more trusting and won't be on the lookout for me," I said, envisioning a sweet, older lady who baked cookies and knitted sweaters. I had no idea why. My mother had never baked a cookie in her life and was confused by clothing without designer labels. But I always considered her the exception. The real moms were the ones in the TV ads who made their families' socks whiter than white.

Tuwanda raised an eyebrow. "You better hope Mrs. Butoff ain't nothin' like her daughter. I read an article about Queen Ta Ta in *People* magazine that said she was real sharp and had a lot a' bid'ness savvy."

"There are no articles in *People*; just pictures," said MJ.

"Okay, then maybe it was a picture caption. But tha's what it said."

I rolled my eyes and asked Sam what he'd found out.

Sam had managed to get his hands on the preliminary autopsy results. Nothing was a great surprise. The cause of death was temporarily established as strangulation pending receipt of toxicology, DNA, and tissue-test results. Interestingly, however, part of the report was sealed, and even Sam's contacts in the police department did not have access to it. Also, it seemed that a cadre of Queen Ta Ta's personal lawyers had arrived in town and was camped out at the prosecutor's office and the police department. They were taking turns threatening the city, county, and state with lawsuits if certain information was leaked to the public, claiming that the estate of Queen Ta Ta had a proprietary interest in such information. In other words, Queen Ta Ta's heirs and assigns wanted to sell the information to the highest bidder and preserve their profit by preventing departmental leaks to the press.

If Mrs. Butoff was one of those heirs, maybe she wasn't the Ivory Snow mom I'd pictured. It was possible, though, that at this stage of the game, she knew nothing about the attorneys' machinations and they were proceeding unilaterally to protect the estate's assets.

Chapter Twelve

As soon as our meeting concluded, Sam dashed to his car to get clothing bags and his makeup kit. MJ, who had offered to help him, followed at a sedate pace.

Now would be a good time to explain that Sam and his friends had started a Friday-night tradition of dressing like their favorite actresses and performing for each other. The idea had caught on, and now hundreds of people attended and/or participated in these shows, necessitating a change of venue from Sam's apartment to the first floor of As You Like It, a former subsidiary of Pole Polishers and now a thriving, independent operation. Sam, whose costumes and makeup were unrivalled, was a frequent winner of the weekly talent contest.

"This is excitin'!" exclaimed Tuwanda. "I can't hardly wait to see how I end up lookin.'"

"Yes, well, you weren't turned into Nanny McPhee the last time around," I grumbled and started another

Danish. If Sam was going to make me look ugly again, who cared if I put on a few extra pounds.

Sam and MJ made four trips in all (MJ made one; Sam three). By the time they finished, the living room was piled high with clothing bags and suitcases. Sam resituated an armchair and motioned for Tuwanda to take a seat.

"Why does she always get to go first?" I whined.

"Because I said so!" snapped Sam, employing the autocratic logic of a parent.

He proceeded to putty and layer foundation, shade, and powder. The final touch was a long black wig.

Tuwanda looked gorgeous. She reminded me of someone, but I couldn't put my finger on whom.

He pulled a plastic card out of his pocket and handed it to Tuwanda.

"Pretty damn good ID," she said. "But how'd you get a picture of me all made up before I was all made up?"

"That's a picture of the person I made you up to look like, with a few modifications courtesy of Photoshop."

"Can I see what I'm going to look like when I'm done?" I asked.

"Be patient. Wait until I'm through with your transformation," Sam said smugly.

I narrowed my eyes. "Why, because I'll run screaming from the room if I see a picture?"

Sam rolled his eyes. "Next!" he commanded, giving

Tuwanda a light shove and motioning for me to take her place.

"Do I got special clothes?" asked Tuwanda.

Sam pointed to one of the clothes bags. "Those will get you started. You can go through your closet and find other stuff once you get the gist of your new persona."

Tuwanda grabbed her clothes bag and trotted happily off to her room to play dress-up.

Sam pulled up my hair and covered it with a skull cap and then went to work on my face. I was glad to see he was going heavy on the lipstick and mascara and laying off the nose putty and fake warts this time.

When he was through, he gave me a hand mirror and stood back.

I recognized the new me immediately. "Liza Minnelli," I said without hesitation.

"A younger version, of course," said Sam. "More *Cabaret* than *Liza Does Vegas*."

"But won't people be suspicious? I mean, I look *just* like her."

"She does," agreed Beth.

Then I thought of something else. "And Tuwanda looks like a black Cher!"

I do *performers,* sweetie," said Sam. "Our little Friday-night bashes are all about dressing up as your favorite performer. So my repertoire is limited to stage folks."

"But last time you made me into an old woman with a really bad complexion," I said.

"You were the Wicked Witch of the West," he said, "minus the green makeup."

I *knew* it.

"Why don't you change something so it won't be so obvious," commented MJ, who had looked up from the computer screen to check the results.

"Well, I could make a bigger nose and add a few blemishes and—"

"No!" I screamed. Getting hold of myself, I added calmly, "It's fine the way it is."

We decided instead that I would dress as I normally do to tone down the likeness to Ms. Minnelli, and Sam handed me a bag of new clothes he'd picked up at Macy's. I selected a lovely Michael Kors linen suit and wondered if I could afford it.

A half hour later, Tuwanda, wearing a clingy silk blouse, high-heeled wedge sandals, and tight satin pants with see-through lace strips down the legs, was Biltmore-bound in a limo, and Beth and I, in more conservative dress, were on our way in Beth's 1999 Buick Regal to meet Mrs. Butoff.

As Beth drove to Sun City, I continued my Internet search on the iPhone Sam had loaned me, pausing only to scratch under my Liza wig and check my makeup in the mirror from time to time.

When we were at the halfway point (Sun City is about a thirty-minute drive from downtown on a good day), I found something of interest in my search of Joey Perroni.

"It says here that Perroni grew up in Arizona. I wonder if he knew Queen Ta Ta before her star ascended."

"That might explain how he came to be her manager," said Beth. "Lots of show people keep managers on that they hired before they were famous because they think maybe they can trust them more; you know, because they were friends before the whole fame thing happened."

"Maybe he's just really good at what he does," I said, trying to be fair.

"He's really good at lying; we know that much," scoffed Beth. "I can't believe he convinced the police that he saw you kill Queen Ta Ta."

"It could have been someone who looked like me," I said, still trying to give him the benefit of the doubt. "But the timing doesn't work.

"Perroni couldn't see anything before five o'clock because it was too dark, so the killer he saw had to have been there between five and when I found her at five thirty. From what I observed, she'd been dead much longer than that."

I shuddered, remembering the red ants.

We rode the remaining distance in silence. Eventually Beth braked and pointed to a gated subdivision coming up on our right. "Mrs. Butoff lives in there."

A stone monument at the entrance proclaimed it to be

Birch Meadows: *A Regular Community for Active Adults.*
The logo underneath was a B intertwined with an M.

"That must be one of those subliminal messages," said Beth. "After sixty, bowel movements get to be real important. Whether you have a successful BM in the morning can make or break your whole day."

I gave her a side glance. "So how are you feeling today?" I asked politely.

"I'm feeling pretty good."

We arrived at the gate, and I was saved from having to decide if congratulations were in order.

"We're here to see Mrs. Butoff," Beth said in response to the guard's inquiry.

The guard, an elderly man who looked as if he was past the "active adult" stage, looked into the car suspiciously.

"You ain't reporters, are you? We've been getting a lot of reporters here. Camera crews too."

"No," I said. "We have an appointment to see Mrs. Butoff about a personal matter. If you give her a call, she'll confirm it."

"Whoa, I didn't spot you right off, Ms. Minnelli. You look real good. Been to one of them Hollywood plastic surgeons, huh? I guess you being who you are I can let you through. I gotta warn ya' though: You're gonna have a lot of company. There's a bunch of people in there already."

I shot Beth a concerned look.

"Probably family members here to support her in her time of grief," said Beth. She turned to the guard for confirmation. "Right, er, Benny?" she asked, reading the name on the guard's badge.

Benny shook his head and then made a choking noise. I was dredging up what I remembered about CPR when the choking noise grew louder and turned into a series of guffaws.

Benny managed to croak, "Go on in, ladies," between mirthful eruptions, and the gate swung open.

"Don't you want to call Mrs. Butoff first to let her know we're here?" asked Beth.

He waved us in, shaking his head and gasping for enough air to fuel more laughter.

"What the heck was *that* all about?" asked Beth, checking the rearview mirror nervously.

"It's possible he's senile. I mean, come on; I don't look *that* much like Liza Minnelli," I said.

Beth glanced at me. "Oh, yes you do."

"By the way, how did you manage to set up a meeting with Mrs. Butoff?" I asked, suddenly, and belatedly, suspicious.

"I told her the truth—that we're from a law office," answered Beth.

"And she didn't ask which law office? Or why we wanted to see her?"

"Yes," said Beth. "I may have implied that I had information concerning her daughter's estate. I also said I would take her to lunch."

I had no prepared script and no idea what I was going to say.

"By the way, your name is Louella Ann Rankle," added Beth, handing me a fake license with a picture of a very young Liza.

"Geez. That makes me sound as if I'm from the Ozarks."

"It's my niece's name," Beth said drily.

We easily found the right street, because the subdivision was laid out in a grid pattern with all east-west roads arranged alphabetically. Mrs. Butoff lived on Eli Lilly Lane. Once we turned on her street, there was no mistaking which house was hers; cars and news vans filled its driveway and then continued down either side of the road, some of them double-parked. We had to drive a few streets over to find a parking spot.

We heard voices inside as we approached the door, and it took two doorbell rings and some heavy knocking before someone heard us. Just as I wound up to pummel the door again, it swung open. The man who greeted us at the door wore a diamond earring in his left ear that had to be three karats, minimum, and a trendy Paul Smith suit with a narrow tie. His balding pate was surrounded by an overlong fringe of fine, curly red hair a la Larry of the Three Stooges. He was about five feet tall and would be slightly taller lying on his side.

"May I help you ladies?" he asked. His eyes reflected no sign of recognition of either Liza or me.

I froze, suddenly nervous. Beth gave me a concerned side-glance and took the lead.

"We have a noon appointment with Mrs. Butoff regarding her daughter's estate," she said, sounding professional and businesslike, with just the right touch of imperiousness. "And you would be?"

"Dick Burton. I'm Ms. Butoff's attorney."

Just the way he said his name set off my good-ol'-boy radar.

"So, um … Richard—do you mind if I call you Richard?" asked Beth.

"I prefer Dick," he responded.

I felt a giggle coming on. *It's just a name,* lectured my left brain. *He said, "Dick,"* guffawed my right brain.

I dug my nails into the palm of my hand.

Beth introduced herself as Martha Gibson (which I thought was a much better name than the one she gave me) and nudged me in the arm.

I cleared my throat and introduced myself in what I hoped was a voice different enough from my own that no one could recognize it as that belonging to the lipstick lady on TV. Unfortunately, what came out sounded like Betty Boop.

Burton shook our hands, holding mine a little longer than was socially appropriate.

Bringing his mouth close to my ear, he whispered, "Has anyone ever told you that you look exactly like a young Liza Minnelli?"

"Practically everyone," I answered in my fake voice.

"I've always had a crush on Ms. Minnelli," he said, still in a whisper, still in my ear.

"So does our office's investigator. He's …"

Beth shot me a warning look.

"He's very nice," I finished lamely.

"Well, come in, come in," he said, slipping back into good ol' boy mode. "I hope you don't mind if I sit in on your meeting with Mrs. Butoff. Since the death of her daughter, she has come to rely on me in all matters."

"What kind of law do you specialize in?" I squeaked Betty Boop–style.

"I've done a little bit of everything, but the last few years I've mostly handled DUI defense work. That's how I came to know Mrs. Butoff."

Chapter Thirteen

We followed him to a small living room packed with turquoise, black, and pink furniture. If you squinted your eyes, it looked like one of those paint 'n' swirl pictures you make at county fairs.

The room's brazen colors did nothing to distract from the woman standing amid a group of reporters, most of whom were thrusting tiny microphones in her face. (The NPR guy was writing on a legal pad.)

Looking to be in her midfifties, she was of medium height excluding her hair and was another couple of feet taller if you included the Dolly Parton–do. Pink lip gloss and dark red lip liner only roughly approximated the location of her actual lips. (My ChapStick faux pas was tame by comparison.) Heavily mascara'd lashes fringed large brown eyes. Flakes of mascara speckled the skin under her eyes like coal dust. She wore a short, low-cut, tight blue dress that bunched and creased around the rolls of flesh at her waist. Her breasts were pushed up, together, and out so far they could have doubled as either extra shelving or a TV tray.

High-heeled blue-and-pink sandals showed off surprisingly thin legs, of which much was required with regard to their weight-bearing abilities. A variety of bangle bracelets assembled without regard to consistency in color or materials covered both arms. A turquoise cross balanced unsteadily over the chasm between her breasts; one quick move would send it plummeting. It would take a rescue team, equipped with flashlights and climbing ropes, to find it.

Dick moved to the woman's side and whispered something to her. She had not noticed us come in, but now she turned and looked at us appraisingly.

With a royal wave of her hand, she dismissed the reporters with enviable ease. She waited until everyone else was gone before approaching us.

Extending her hand to Beth first, she introduced herself in a surprisingly low voice, pronouncing Butoff "boot owf" with the accent on the second syllable. It gave the name a French flair. I guess with a name like Butoff you have to try something.

"I've made reservations for us at Le Petit Cafe," said Beth after introductions were made and Beth and I had extended our condolences.

While she showed little or no reaction at the mention of her daughter's passing, Mrs. Boot-owf grinned broadly and seemed pleased with Beth's choice of restaurants. I suspected that she was a bit of a Francophile.

Since Mrs. Butoff had an appointment at one thirty, we agreed to take separate cars.

The restaurant was not far, and less than ten minutes later we were sitting in a booth in what would have been a romantic setting but for the company.

We chatted lightly about the weather and other neutral topics, and to my relief, Mrs. Butoff insisted that I call her Muffy (a high school nickname that stuck), thereby relieving me of the challenge of pronouncing Butoff correctly. (Of course, the fact that I was sitting at a table with people named Dick and Muffy raised another set of awkward possibilities.)

Muffy and Dick shared a bottle of wine. Beth and I politely declined to partake. By the time the food arrived (steaks for Dick and Muffy, tuna sandwiches for me and Beth), they had mellowed nicely and were ready for a second bottle.

I said very little, leaving most of the polite chatter to Beth, partly because I wanted to have a chance to observe Muffy and partly because I was afraid I would accidentally slip out of my Betty-Boop voice.

With her tongue loosened by burgundy, Muffy held forth about her career as a Vegas showgirl and how, if she'd had the breaks her daughter did, she would have been famous.

Muffy finally paused to saw off a chunk of bloody steak and fixed me with a curious stare.

"You look just like Liza Minnelli," she commented. "You don't look like a lawyer at all."

She shoved the piece of steak in her mouth while she spoke, treating us to a view of open-mouthed mastication.

"I get that a lot," I said.

"When I talked to your associate here I got the impression you had some good news for me."

"I'm afraid Martha may have misled you somewhat," I said, placing my hand on Muffy's arm and giving it a squeeze designed to convey compassion and intimacy.

"What do you mean?" she said, eying me suspiciously while she shoved another piece of steak in her mouth.

I had to hand it to her; I could never accomplish her level of diction with that amount of food in my mouth.

I leaned into her until I could smell the A-1 on her breath. I noticed that she was older than she'd first appeared. The light plastic surgery scars around her ears were a giveaway.

"I am writing a book about celebrity deaths," I said, pulling back a little and wiping secondary sauce off my cheek. "I've experienced the effect of the sudden passing of a well-known family member." I gave it a few seconds for the inference to sink in before continuing. "I think your daughter's tragic death should be part of my book."

Almost simultaneously, Muffy and Dick asked, "How much?"

"As much as you feel comfortable sharing," I said.

"Money. How much *money* are you offering Mrs. Butoff for her story?" clarified Dick, waving his fork full of French fries in the air for emphasis.

"I believe I can answer that," said Beth as she delicately removed a French fry from her hair. "Ms. Rankle cannot make a financial commitment until she knows more about what Muffy has to say."

"You mean you want to try a sample before you buy the product?" said Dick, grinning.

Beth nodded, took a pen out of her purse, and then wrote something on a napkin. She shoved the napkin across the table to Dick.

I thought it was a neat move, except it would have been even cooler if the napkin wasn't covered in ketchup.

Dick picked up the napkin between thumb and forefinger and held it so both he and Muffy could read what Beth had written.

"You realize we could sell Mrs. Butoff's story to *Innuendo* for millions," said Dick.

"Except that Ms. Rankle does not want an exclusive and will agree to only use the information for her book, which will not be published for another six months," responded Beth promptly.

"My client and I need a few moments to discuss your

offer privately," said Dick. "Perhaps you could take your food to another table."

I thought this was rude. If they wanted to be alone, *they* should move.

Before I could protest, Beth picked up her plate and Diet Coke and head-jerked toward the back of the dining room.

We resettled at a table outside of hearing range, and the hostess rushed over to inquire if everything was all right.

"We're fine. We moved because that man over there has a terrible gas problem," I said, pointing to Dick. "He can't help it, poor dear, but there's only so much we could take."

"I understand," she said. "You'd be surprised how often this sort of thing happens. I guess it's because we're in a retirement community. The restaurant has an excellent ventilation system, though. You shouldn't be bothered over here."

I inhaled deeply as if testing her assertion and then politely thanked her.

As soon as the waitress was out of earshot, Beth kicked me lightly under the table and said, "You are a bad person." The grin tugging at the corners of her mouth belied her reprimand.

"How much did you offer Tweedle-Dee and Tweedle-Dum?" I asked.

"Twenty thousand."

"*What*? Where am I going to get that kind of money?" I hissed.

"*You* don't have to. Louella does," Beth answered complacently, taking a bite of her sandwich.

I slumped in my chair and looked at her in disbelief. "Did you snag a glass of wine when I wasn't looking?"

"It's simple: you give them a fake check."

"And where, pray tell, is this fake check?"

Beth reached into her purse and produced a check for my inspection.

"Wow. This is good," I said, scrutinizing it. "How'd you do it?"

"This morning I altered one of the firm checks by changing the name and address and two of the numbers in both the routing code and the account number."

"But what if they want to verify funds or wait for the check to clear?" I said, demurring.

"Then you encourage them to go ahead and verify funds. Here's the contact information for your banker," she said, pulling a business card out of her purse's side pocket.

I glanced at the card. "Isn't that MJ's cell number?"

"Yup. And don't worry; she agreed to play along."

I gave Beth a long look. "You're good at this stuff. I mean, scary good—like you've done this before."

"I've dabbled," said Beth.

I stared at my Bible-thumping secretary in disbelief.

I had second thoughts about Muffy and Dick's offer of wine and raised my hand to get the waiter's attention.

Before the waiter came, however, Muffy and Dick waved us over.

Beth again took the lead.

"Have you considered our offer?" she asked.

"Yes, we have," answered Dick, "and we agree to share a limited amount of information with you."

Beth glanced at her watch. "We still have about fifteen minutes before Mrs. Butoff needs to be at her next appointment. Can you give me a sample of your wares?"

"We should put our agreement in writing first," said Muffy, who appeared to be the more sober of the two.

"Ms. Rankle will draft something, and then we can proceed."

Muffy turned to me in exaggerated surprised. "You're an author *and* a lawyer?"

"You'd be surprised how common that is," I Betty-Booped.

I borrowed a pen from the waiter and drafted an agreement on a napkin. Because I am verbose by nature and training, I was going to attach a cocktail napkin addendum, but Beth motioned to cut it short.

I signed Ms. Rankle's name and handed the napkin *cum* legal document to Dick. After looking it over, he directed Muffy to sign.

Dick pocketed the fully executed napkin. "I'll have

my office send you a copy. Now, may we see the money before my client gives you any information?"

Beth gave him the check. Every body part capable of clenching did so as I anxiously watched him inspect it. The only question he had, though, was whether the address on the check was where he should send a copy of the contract.

After we confirmed the mailing address, Dick ordered another glass of wine and instructed us to "proceed."

"Mrs. Butoff, how did you hear about your daughter's death?" I asked.

"Her manager, Joey Perroni, called. He didn't want me to hear it from the news."

"That's very considerate of him," I commented. "What exactly did he say?"

"That Gladys had been murdered and to expect calls from the press."

"And then?"

She shrugged. "He told me to refer all calls to him because reporters could be difficult to deal with."

I bet he did. Queen Ta Ta's death was big business. He wanted to control as much information as he could.

Based on the number of reporters at her house earlier, I guessed she had ignored Joey's advice.

"Do you remember when Mr. Perroni called?" I pressed.

"About six a.m. on the day she died. The phone woke

me up. I knew it was trouble as soon as it rang. No one calls with good news that early in the morning."

"Did he mention who he thought killed your daughter?"

"He said some crazy lady. Probably a stalker. My daughter was famous, and there are a lot of nuts out there."

And I was the alleged nut.

"Is there anyone else in your daughter's life who had a reason to murder her?"

Muffy shrugged again. "Probably. God knows there's a lot of jealous, spiteful people in the entertainment industry. Why, when I was performing at the Flamingo …"

"Can you tell me more about Gladys?" I interrupted, trying to head off another trip down memory lane. "For instance, who her friends were, what she was like, that kind of thing."

Dick put the check in his pocket. "The sampling is over."

I nodded without taking my eyes off Muffy and instructed her to go ahead and answer.

"Gladys had lots of friends in high school: mostly the boys in her class and older men. They liked to hang out in her room and listen to music real loud. Those kids really loved that music.

"I don't know who she hung out with after she went to Los Angeles except for Che Che and Joey Perroni. They're local kids who went out to LA with her the day after her high school graduation. I didn't see Gladys much after that."

"Was their friendship the reason Joey became her manager?"

"Yeah. Plus Joey was older and more experienced. He graduated a year before Gladys and was working at Best Buy, so he knew the entertainment business."

Selling small electronics qualified you as an expert in show biz?

"How about Che Che?"

"Che Che was and is a hanger-on. She was always jealous of Gladys and figured she deserved the big break, but Che Che has no talent, unless you consider dealing drugs and whoring around talent. Gladys hired her as her assistant out of pity."

"What was the status of their relationship immediately prior to Queen Ta Ta's death?"

I was having a heck of a time staying in character as Liza/Betty but managed somehow to avoid lapsing into my attorney voice.

Muffy dabbed the corner of her eye with a napkin, not to wipe away a tear but to remove an errant lash. "Like I said, I didn't have a lot of contact with Gladys after she moved to LA. I get most of my information from reading *People* and *Us* at my hairdresser's."

By the looks of things, she spent a great deal of time at her hairdresser's, so I suspected she was up to date on the tabloid reports concerning her daughter.

"Did you and Gladys have a falling out?" asked Beth.

Muffy snorted. "If you can call stealing my credit cards and taking off in the middle of the night a 'falling out,' then I'd say yes."

Dick roused himself out of his wine stupor. "I think what Muffy means is that Gladys was an independent child who knew early on what she wanted and focused on that dream."

"Is that what you meant?" I asked Muffy.

Another shrug. (Muffy's body language was limited.) "I guess."

Dick pointedly looked at his watch. "Unfortunately, ladies, Mrs. Butoff needs to leave for her next appointment. Place any additional questions you have in writing and send them to me. I will make sure Mrs. Butoff answers them, provided the check clears."

He smiled and wiggled his eyebrows to indicate that the last part was a joke, but the joke was on him.

Aware that this was our last chance to question Muffy, I blurted out, "One more thing, Muffy."

Muffy and Dick were already on their feet, and Dick, possessively gripping her elbow, guided her toward the exit.

Muffy, perhaps irked at Dick's strong-armed tactics (literally), pulled away and gave me a quick nod.

"When was the last time you talked to your daughter, and what did she say?" I asked hurriedly.

"That's two questions," snapped Dick.

Muffy ignored him. "Last Friday when she arrived in Phoenix, she called me from her limo on the way to her hotel. She told me she loved me and hoped she could drop by this time. Then she asked me to let her know if Che Che or her parents called, which I thought was odd since I wasn't close to any of them."

Dick regained his hold on Muffy's arm and propelled her outside.

Chapter Fourteen

As soon as the door closed behind them, I asked Beth what she thought.

"I think that's one self-involved bitch," Beth responded without hesitation.

I was shocked. I had only heard Beth swear once before and attributed that single episode to the fact that she had just downed five shots of expensive Scotch.

"She didn't look even a little sad," Beth continued. "If something bad happened to one of my children or grandchildren, I'd curl up and cry for the rest of my days. This woman's out having lunch and taking a check for her story."

"I know," I said. "I feel as if I need a loofah and a long, hot shower after being around those two. Based on what Muffy said, though, it seems like Queen Ta Ta was close to Che Che and Joey and they had a long history together. Assuming Muffy was telling the truth, the fact that Queen Ta Ta asked her mother to let her know if Che Che or her family called shows that, even if she fired her as her personal assistant, she still cared enough to keep track of her."

"Or maybe Queen Ta Ta was trying to hunt her down because she stole something that belonged to her or because she forgot to sign a confidentiality agreement or because Ta Ta was trying to kill Che Che or vice versa."

I raised an eyebrow. "Wait; now *I'm* the Pollyanna? What happened to all that Christian compassion for human frailty?"

"You're assuming these people are human," Beth said disgustedly.

Her cell phone rang, cutting our debate (or rather Beth's rant) short.

"Yes?" she answered testily.

I heard Tuwanda's booming response. "What the hell kinda' phone manners is that? You sound like you expectin' a call from a debt collector."

"Sorry," said Beth. "It's just that meeting Mrs. Butoff wasn't a pleasant experience."

"You can tell me about it later. I'm at the hotel, an' Marge just called to say she got Kate a room. She said she tried to call, but Kate musta turned the phone off."

This was true. MJ had warned me that cell phone calls could be traced. Plus, I wasn't clear about who I was supposed to be when I answered.

Beth bristled. "I said *I* would handle Kate's reservation."

Marge had won round one of the most efficient secretary contest.

I held my hand out for the phone, and Beth reluctantly passed it over.

"Hi, Tuwanda. It's Kate. Or Louella. Whatever."

"Louella?"

"Never mind. I'll explain it later. What name did Marge put my reservation under?"

"Lottie Bush."

"Seriously?"

"Yeah."

"That's awful. How did she come up with a name like that?" I asked in bewilderment.

"Hey, tha's not nice. Lottie was our top performer two years in a row. She jus' retired a year ago last March. We still got her picture an' plaque hangin' in the reception area. And we still got her file. Marge made a copy of her driver's license with Liza's picture on it."

"Tell her about the check and business card I made," hissed Beth.

I shook my head no.

"Won't she mind that I'm using her identity?" I asked, hoping she would.

"Lottie lives in Oregon now, raisin' organic shit. She got a new name, so I doubt she'll care if we use her old one. When can you get here?"

"I'll need to pick up some clothes at your apartment, and …"

"Marge already got 'em sent over to the hotel. Your suitcase arrived on an earlier flight, so to speak, and is waitin' for you in your room. Sam said he'd meet you at the Starbucks on Twelfth Street and Camelback to give you your new license and his cosmetics case."

"Cosmetics case?"

"Yeah. I figured we're gonna need to touch up our disguises from time to time, so I asked him to pass it along."

"Good idea. Is he sending instructions too?"

Tuwanda ignored my last question and moved to the next subject on her mind. "I seen that Joey guy. He's sittin' by the pool workin' on his tan, drinkin' a daiquiri, an' talkin' on the phone. He don't seem real down to me. Fact is, he looks kinda happy. I'm gonna go down there so's I can observe him some more. Come an' find me as soon as you get registered. It's too damn hot to lay out, so I'll likely be standin' in the shallow end so as not to get my hair wet."

"Are we supposed to know each other?" I asked.

"Sure. We ol' friends attendin' the same convention."

"Which convention?"

"The only ones goin' on right now at the hotel are Devel'pments in Wastewater Technology an' an AMA gynecologist convention. I figgered we should stick to what we know, so we's signed up for the gynecologist convention."

I was a gynecologist named Lottie Bush. Louella Rankle sounded good by comparison.

Chapter Fifteen

Beth drove me back to Phoenix and waited in the parking lot of Starbucks while I picked up my fake Arizona license, a new mobile phone attached to an account opened in Lottie's name, and the cosmetics case. Sam had thoughtfully prepared paint-by-number guidelines for both Tuwanda and me that showed which pot of gunk should be applied where. "Just remember to blend," he cautioned. "Otherwise you'll look like a Picasso painting."

There were a few television vans outside the entrance to the hotel grounds, but we saw no other signs of the media as we traveled along the graceful drive leading to the beautifully proportioned, art deco main building housing the hotel lobby, two restaurants, and a piano bar. Beth pulled to a stop at the entrance, and a bellman dressed in a collared white sports shirt and khakis opened the car door before I could engage in self-help and asked if I was checking in. After I confirmed that I was but my driver was continuing on, he helped me out of the car, took Sam's case, and escorted me into the main building.

The art deco style continued inside, and, even though I had visited the hotel before, I was so busy admiring the room's understated, elegant appointments that I nearly rear-ended the bellman when he came to a sudden stop in front of the registration desk. A young woman dressed in a khaki suit handled my check-in with the friendly efficiency of someone who majored in hotel management in college and took her job seriously.

I kept a straight face throughout the registration process despite being repeatedly called "Doctor Bush," which, probably because I was tired, I thought was hysterical.

Another khaki-clad young man whose name tag identified him as Dan led me to my room, which was quite a hike from the lobby. I didn't mind, though, because it gave me a chance to check out the grounds and pump Dan for information.

"Have you worked here long?" I started out benignly.

It was like pulling the string on a Chatty Kathy doll.

"I've worked here part time since I started college. I'm a senior now, but it took me a couple of extra years to get that far because of having to earn my own way," he provided.

"What's with the news vans parked outside the front gate?" I asked.

"You don't know? Man, no offense, but you must like, live in a cave."

I was really getting tired of hearing this.

"I've been out of the country doing missionary work in West Africa," I snapped.

"That would explain it," he said. "I'll be honest, though; you don't look like the missionary type. In fact, you look more like Liza Minnelli—when she was younger I mean," he hurried to add.

"Why don't you think Liza is the missionary type?" I shot back.

"I dunno," he said, sounding thoughtful rather than offended. "I guess because she looks high maintenance. It's gotta be tough to be high maintenance in West Africa. Like, where do you get mascara if you run out?"

This was a thinly veiled reference to the spiky fake eyelashes glued to my eyelids and then further exaggerated through liberal application of Maybelline's Ultra Thick Mascara.

"You adapt," I huffed. "I used mud and ground plants, or I went without."

For reference, I had never ground a plant in my life and had no idea how to make mud stick to your lashes.

"The news trucks?" I reminded him.

"We're not supposed to talk about it, but since you've

been in Africa and all, I guess it's okay to tell you. I mean, it's not like you're from the press or the police."

I nodded encouragingly, feeling better about my other deceptions because I was in fact neither from the police nor the press.

Dan looked around nervously before continuing. Although the coast was clear, he still took the precaution of whispering.

"Queen Ta Ta was staying here, and she was found murdered—strangled to death—on a jogging path that runs through the hotel property. The police think a crazy fan killed her."

I widened my eyes, feigning alarm. "Are they sure?"

"Pretty sure. One of our other guests, her manager, says he saw two women fighting—he didn't know Queen Ta Ta was one of them at the time. The other woman was wearing jogging shorts and a tank top, same as the jogger who called the police and claims she 'found' the body."

"Did anyone else at the hotel see anything?"

He looked around again. "Yeah. One of our personal trainers said he saw a man by the casitas next to the spa about the time the police say Queen Ta Ta was murdered. He thought it may have been a guest sneaking back from someone else's room after a wild night. We get a lot of that here, especially during conventions.

"And one of the maids said she saw someone near the spa about the same time, but since I don't speak Spanish, I didn't understand the details."

"They told all this to the police, right?" I said.

"Mark—he's the personal trainer—maybe. I don't know about the maid. Everyone says the detective interviewing her was kind of a jerk and got impatient because of the language barrier."

Interesting. "Do you know her name?" I asked.

Dan hesitated and looked at me suspiciously. "You sure sound like a reporter. Are you?"

"Have the police arrested anyone yet?" I asked, avoiding his question and returning to neutral ground.

"No, but they're pretty sure the killer's left the state."

We rounded the corner of a cute cottage made of the same material as the main building.

"Here you are."

My room was a large suite that occupied half the cottage. Sliding arcadia doors led to a private patio screened from public view by a dense jungle of bougainvillea. The unit included two bedrooms, two baths, and even a little kitchenette. My suitcase had been placed on a luggage rack, and a bottle of champagne was cooling in an ice bucket. A card indicated it was a gift from the management to Dr. Lottie Bush, "valued customer."

I was getting the high-roller treatment. I had no idea how I was going to pay for all of it and resigned myself to the possibility of bankruptcy.

I tipped Dan handsomely, figuring I might as well go for broke, literally.

"By the way, is there more than one pool at the hotel?" I asked.

We'd passed a large pool on the way to my room, but I didn't spot Tuwanda anywhere near it.

"Yes," Dan responded promptly. "There's an adults-only pool behind the spa. It's smaller but quieter than the main pool."

I thanked him, and as soon as he left I opened the suitcase and dug out a bathing suit. I eyed it ruefully, wondering what Sam was thinking when he picked out this little number—and I do mean little. Fortunately, the hotel provided robes for its guests, so I wouldn't be exposed to public ridicule. The private humiliation would be bad enough.

Sam had not included a pair of sandals, so I made do with brown loafers.

I grabbed a towel from the bathroom and headed to the pool.

The hotel robe was luxurious, which meant it was thick and heavy. By the time I reached the pool's gated entry (identified by a discreet sign reading *Pool, Adults Only*), I was ready to shed the robe and jump in the water regardless of the harm to onlookers' sensibilities.

The pool itself, like everything else on the property, was screened from view by vegetation. It occurred to me that the abundance of plant material at the hotel was good for privacy but limited the potential pool of witnesses.

I entered through the gate and, following the scent

of chlorine, walked down a path lined with placards reminiscent of the old Burma Shave signs that used to be strung along the highways. The placards warned that the area was for adults only and defined an adult as a person twenty-one or over (with no mention of emotional maturity, which I thought was the more pertinent criterion) and advised guests of the pool rules, including no glass in the pool area, no eating in the pool, and no more than 165 people in the pool at any one time. These restrictions likely came about after one too many wild parties. Once I reached the pool, I wondered about the fete that gave rise to the capacity limit. It was fairly inauspicious as bodies of water go and looked as if it could barely hold 25, much less 165, people.

I spotted Tuwanda immediately. She was lounging in an open-fronted cabana looking like an African queen. I didn't see anyone else around.

I called out to her, waved, and headed in her direction.

"Damn time you got here. It's hotter'n hell out here. I was jus' about to call an' tell you there was a change in plans."

"What happened to Joey?" I asked.

"He moved his drinkin' inside like any sane person would."

I forbore from pointing out what this implied about her sanity.

"Let's join him then," I said. "Lead the way."

Tuwanda eyed me critically as she gracefully rose and donned an elegant Tory Burch cover-up. "Le's jus' hope they let you in the bar in that getup. That robe with them shoes makes you look like a flasher."

"The robe is better than what's underneath," I assured her.

I followed her into a small but nicely appointed bar overlooking the pool and spotted Joey immediately. He was the only person in the bar other than the bartender, but even were that not the case I would have known him from the Guido description.

He was perfectly tanned with a set of killer abs framed nicely by his unbuttoned linen shirt. His black, faux mohawk was gelled into vertical spikes, and a diamond earring the size of a gumball—even larger than Dick's—weighed down his earlobe. He had Rock Hudson good looks marred somewhat by a weak chin and thin lips. Because he was sitting down I couldn't tell how tall he was, but judging by the bend in his knees I guessed he was between five-ten and six feet.

He looked up from his drink when we entered and flashed Tuwanda a wide grin, exposing unnaturally white teeth.

"Too hot out there for you?" he asked her, ignoring me.

Tuwanda did a Groucho Marx–thing with her eyebrows and said, "I like bein' hot."

She sat next to him, and I took a stool on her other side.

Making contact with Joey hadn't been at all difficult. This detective thing was turning out to be surprisingly easy.

Tuwanda held out her hand to Joey. "I'm Marge Porter, an' this here is my colleague Lottie Bush."

Perroni smirked at my name, and I felt like slapping him. Instead, I managed a polite nod.

A man's voice reiterating the phrase "You my bitch" loosely accompanied by drums and guitars blared out of his phone. Perroni mouthed, "Just a sec," and pulled a cell phone out of his shirt pocket.

His side of the conversation consisted of him saying and then repeating, "That's the deal; take it or leave it." I couldn't make out the other side of the conversation, but the speaker sounded male, and his tone alternated between threatening and wheedling.

After the call ended with what sounded like a hang-up, Joey introduced himself and asked, "What brings you ladies to Phoenix?"

"We at the gynecologist convention," said Tuwanda.

He pulled back slightly in surprise. "You're doctors?"

"She is," said Tuwanda, chin-jerking toward me. "I'm in equipment sales—you know, them tables with the stirrups an' those long-handled spoons? My comp'ny makes that shit. Lottie 'n' me have been gettin' together at these conventions for years."

Joey looked confused. He was probably stuck on the long-handled spoon part.

"How about you?" I asked. "What brings you to this fair city at this ungodly time of year?"

"Business," he said after taking a swig of the amber liquid in his glass.

Not a lot of information there. Maybe this wasn't going to be so easy.

"You my bitch" played again. This time his side of the conversation expanded to include the phrases "cash; no checks" and "full release."

When he got off the phone, Tuwanda asked, "What you drinkin' there?"

"Scotch," he responded distractedly.

"You in the mood for some really *fine* Scotch? Lottie's medical group covers all her expenses, so it's her treat."

I dug my elbow into Tuwanda's side in protest.

"Well, if you're offering," said Joey, "I guess it would be impolite not to accept."

I didn't think so at all.

We got another dose of "You my bitch." Joey answered and had a lively debate with someone about the relative advantages of a sailing yacht versus a motor yacht. Joey took the motor yacht side, and I had to agree with him there. I saw nothing enjoyable about spending a day with people screaming at each other about "coming about" (which as best as I can tell means "duck" in layman's terms), port and starboard (why can't these people just say right and left?), and hiking (which has nothing to do with a pleasant walk in the woods).

Despite my favorable view of Joey's position on the boat debate, I considered the phone interruptions annoying and rude. If you want to hold a conversation with people in the room with you, turn off your phone. If you want to text or talk on the phone, excuse yourself and leave the rest of us alone.

"That's a great phone you got there. Is it one of them smart phones?" asked Tuwanda, leaning closer to Joey to take a look.

Joey's expression softened, and he stroked the phone's cover affectionately as he explained its amazing technology. It was the first genuine emotion he'd displayed.

My eyes glazed over. I signaled the bartender and ordered a glass of wine. Tuwanda managed to look fascinated with Joey's dissertation and made oohing and aahing sounds.

"Can I see your phone for a second?" she finally interrupted. "I mean jus' to look at the screen an' see all them functions and applications."

Amazingly, after giving it a reassuring squeeze, he released custody of his beloved gadget.

Tuwanda bent over it and called out each icon on the screen with a mixture of awe and joy. This took some time, mind you, because Joey was big on applications. (The only one I was remotely interested was a high-pitched whistle only dogs could hear. I imagined hours of fun annoying

Ralph as revenge for all the nights his barking kept me awake.) She stretched out the torture by playing Angry Birds for a full five minutes, during which time Joey wandered away and snagged some peanuts from a bowl on the bar. By the time Tuwanda wrapped it up, I was in need of a second chardonnay.

Joey returned munching on peanuts and smelling like a jar of Jiffy. He took the phone from Tuwanda and placed it back in his pocket, giving it a reassuring little pat once it was home in bed.

Tuwanda ordered two glasses of twenty-year-old Scotch with a brand name I'd never heard of but that evoked images of peat and plaid. I declined the offer of Scotch (technically my offer, since I was paying) and ordered a second glass of chardonnay.

Three rounds of Scotch later Joey showed no sign of loosening up. His pocket hadn't played so much as a note of "You my bitch," though, and for that I was grateful.

When I said he hadn't loosened up, I meant he wasn't spilling any personal information. He had certainly relaxed, though, and had gotten touchy-feely with Tuwanda.

I was on my fourth chardonnay, so I, too, felt the effects of alcohol. I was light-headed and increasingly garrulous, despite clear signals from Joey that he did not appreciate my interruptions.

At one point I even waxed on about the joys of gynecology. Since my experience was limited, a lot of it had to do with Pap smears.

"You look like that old actress … What's her name?" Joey interrupted during an impassioned speech about the discomfort of yeast infections.

"Liza Minnelli," Tuwanda promptly provided.

"Yeah, that's it. Her mom was Judy Garland," said Joey.

Tuwanda leaned into him. "You sure know a lot about show bid'ness," she said.

That's laying it on a bit thick. Even I, the cave dweller, knew that.

But Joey seemed amenable to false flattery, for he looked pleased.

"So, you do somethin' in show bid'ness or you just a fan of ol' movies?" she asked.

He looked at her slyly and gave a noncommittal shrug.

I'd had it. This conversation was going nowhere, and I was having trouble balancing on the stool.

"For God's sake," I muttered. "Queen Ta Ta's murder has been on the news twenty-four-seven, and your name is constantly mentioned." With a silent apology to the Phoenix Chamber of Commerce, I added, "We're two drunk women bored to heck in the middle of a desert oven and thought you might be an interesting companion under the circumstances." Looking toward the far side of the bar, I said, "As it stands, I'd have a better time talking to that cat."

Tuwanda and Joey turned their heads to see where I

was looking. A gray tabby whose coat bore evidence of frequent warfare stared at us unblinkingly through one of the windows.

I stared back at it. No human is foolish enough to believe they can win a staring contest with a cat, but like I said, I'd had a few drinks.

Joey signaled the bartender and ordered another Scotch. A couple of more people had come into the bar by this time and were staring curiously at him. They probably recognized him from the news.

Once Joey had a fresh drink in hand, he dismounted from his stool and gave us a quick salute.

"Thank you ladies for the very excellent Scotch." Then, looking almost (but not quite) apologetically at Tuwanda, he said, "You understand, don't you, that I am subject to confidentiality restrictions."

Tuwanda nodded understandingly. "Police," she said.

Joey looked surprised. "I never thought of that," he said. "That's a good line. I can use it to up the bidding."

He left, heading toward the pool area and looking pleased.

"That was a waste of time," I grumbled. "You realize none of these people will give us information unless we pay through the nose for it, and I don't have that kind of money."

"No, but it looks like Max Goldstein does," Tuwanda commented before taking another sip of her Scotch.

"Who?"

"Mass Media Communications. Los Angeles area code."

It took me a while, my synapses having been slowed by alcohol to the point where they were not so much firing as doing a slow pitch. But then I got it. "You looked at his call history."

"Uh-huh. An' a day's worth of text messages. An' I turned off that damn ringer. That man texts a lot. I got a quick look at his Twitter messages too, but they were dumb-ass boring; like anyone cares how long he leaves on them Crest whitenin' strips. Anyways, from what I can tell, he got himself a biddin' war over an interview about Queen Ta Ta's murder."

"Someone besides Mr. Goldstein is interested?"

"Hell, yeah: Morris Dayside with a San Francisco area code, Greg Peterson with a New York area code, and Ray Ramirez with a Tucson area code. Accordin' to his directory, they all from big multimedia companies except Ramirez. He don't show up in Joey's list of contacts, but he sent a few texts hintin' about tradin' information for cash. Also, your friend Dick Burton made a few calls an' left a text message threatenin' to sue Joey. You know anythin' about that?"

"First of all, he's not my friend. And, yes, he represents Muffy, Queen Ta Ta's mother. I'm guessing he's trying to rope in Joey so Queen Ta Ta's estate doesn't miss out on any of the proceeds from the sale of information about Queen Ta Ta's last minutes."

"Ain't no one around this lady interested in anything besides money? Them television detectives is always sayin', 'If you want to solve a crime, just follow the money.' That don't narrow the field here at all."

We both stared at our drinks and contemplated this sad, but true, assessment.

"You'd think, though, that strangling is more a crime of opportunity and passion, and Joey and Muffy don't seem capable of much passion. They're more the types to hire a lawyer and file a lawsuit."

Tuwanda slapped the bar lightly. "Thas' it. Maybe in this case we don't follow the money; we follow the passion. Who else we got?"

We moved Che Che Herrera up on the list of suspects due to her long-standing connection with the victim and added Ramirez to the list because, although he was admittedly a wild card, he lived in Che Che and Ta Ta's hometown and may have more extensive connections with her than were apparent on the surface. Mark, the personal trainer, and the maid went on the list as well because both had the opportunity.

We agreed that Tuwanda would come to my room at six so we could figure out the makeup thing and then strategize and coordinate tomorrow's efforts over dinner.

Outside, I tossed a couple of pretzels to the cat before heading to my room.

We didn't see Joey later that evening in either the hotel's elegant main restaurant or the adjacent piano bar. Tuwanda surmised that he had finally passed out after a full day of drinking. We did see Stanley Dorfman, however, whom we recognized from one of the photos Beth had e-mailed. Stanley, Queen Ta Ta's audio engineer, was ensconced in a corner booth at the restaurant and looked to weigh in excess of three hundred pounds. He reminded me of Jabba the Hut with glasses. He seemed an unlikely murder suspect unless the victim was a chocolate cake.

He looked around disinterestedly throughout his meal, only showing flickers of emotion when a waiter walked by with a plate of food. Since Queen Ta Ta had not died from a crushing injury, we decided to move him to the bottom of the list.

On our way back to our rooms, we stopped at the front desk and I, having lost the coin toss, signed up for a personal training session with Mark for nine the next morning.

Chapter Sixteen

The next morning I was awakened at seven by loud yowling. The gray cat I'd given the pretzels to was sitting on the veranda, making an unholy racket. I let her in—I assumed it was a her because I didn't see any him parts—and, with apologies to Ralph, who would have loved to be there, poured four little prepackaged cups of cream into a bowl for her. After a quick shower, I made a pot of coffee from the packet of Kauai's Finest provided by the hotel and turned on the television to watch the news while I tried to follow Sam's paint-by-number diagram.

Queen Ta Ta's murder was not only the lead item but appeared to be the only item except for the brief mention of a local man winning a gold medal at the Olympics.

The police still refused to publicly name a suspect, but Kate Williams Esq. remained a person of interest (everyone knows that's another way of saying, "She did it") and was presumed to have left the state. Members of the public were asked to contact the FBI or Phoenix police if they spotted the woman shown. Since the picture that filled the screen was the naked-woman-running-from-fire photo, I didn't think I ran much of a risk of being identified even without the Liza Minnelli makeup. ("Hey, that woman over there looks like—no wait; it couldn't be. Where's the dog?")

Interestingly, Che Che was another missing person of interest. One pundit on the Entertainment Channel went so far as to surmise that Che Che, Queen Ta Ta, and I were part of a love triangle gone wrong.

Interviews of everyone even remotely connected to the event filled the airtime. ("Yes, I was driving to work on the other side of town when the helicopters flew over. I think the jogger did it.") Channel Twelve even interviewed Bryan, who expressed that murder was wrong and that, as a candidate for sheriff, he was against it.

"Wow, he really stuck his neck out on that one," I muttered as I tried to reglue my Liza eyelashes to my lids.

The gray cat, which I had by now nicknamed Her, had found its way to my lap and seemed oblivious to my commentary.

When I heard the next bit on TV I forgot about the eyelashes. The news anchor introduced Max Demple, and her face filled the screen.

"My firm and I represent Ms. Williams, and while I have not heard from her in over twenty-four hours and have no idea where she is, I am convinced that Ms. Williams is innocent and that the fact that she has not come forward does not bode well. We are concerned that she is in danger from the real killer. While the police wear blinders and waste time pursuing my client, my firm and I are actively searching for a murderer on the loose." She then gave a phone number viewers could call if they had any information about Queen Ta Ta's death or my disappearance.

Wow. Good job, Max! I silently cheered. At least one person in the media was on my side—bought and paid for, of course, but, still, I was heartened.

I dressed in Nike gym shorts and a matching top Sam had purchased but had to settle for a pair of MBTs I'd borrowed from Tuwanda because brown loafers would not do for a workout. (MBTs are clunky sneakers the manufacturer swears creates buns of steel after frequent wearing.) The MBTs were a size too small, and I had to practice balancing on the thick, curved soles before taking a test walk, but once I figured it out I began to enjoy the rolling gait forced by the shoes' shape.

After checking the mirror one last time and redrawing one of my eyebrows, which had been about a half-inch higher than the other, I said good-bye to Her and set out for the spa.

I had never used the services of a personal trainer before and was mildly apprehensive. I envisioned a boot camp experience a la *The Biggest Loser.* By the time I reached the spa I had come up with a story about recently healed multiple fractures in a bid for sympathy and lighter training.

An impossibly muscular man, who I assumed was Mark, leaned against the spa's reception desk talking to a tanned, disgustingly healthy-looking blonde whose short shorts disappeared into her butt crack like a thong. Her pink spandex-clad breasts were what my mother would call "perky," this and similar adjectives being one of the reasons my mother and I rarely spoke.

Mark and Miss Perky turned toward me as I entered.

"You must be Ms. Bush," said Perky as if she couldn't be more delighted.

I nodded yes and looked at Mister Universe. "Are you Mark?" I asked.

"Yes. You're my nine o'clock appointment, right?" Mark's powers of deduction were almost as spectacular as Perky's.

I nodded again, doing a fine impression of a bobble-head doll.

"I ask all my clients to fill out a history before we get started so I know what their baseline is," he continued, handing me a sheet from a stack of forms lying on the reception desk.

I raised an eyebrow. (At least I think I did; it's hard to know when it's not your eyebrow.)

"The baseline is the starting point for our exercise

plan," he explained. "I don't want to give you anything too difficult or too easy in light of your present level of fitness. When you're through, give the form to Jan. Then we can get started." Mark left me with Jan, disappearing through a door behind the desk.

Jan smiled happily, as if she lived for this sort of thing.

She handed me a pen and a clipboard, and I sat on an uber-modern couch that looked like a floating inner tube to fill out the form. It took me about fifteen minutes to complete it. Five of those minutes were dedicated to achieving the balance necessary to sit upright on the inner tube.

I included incredible detail as to my accident history on the form, including dates, cross-references, and assignments of blame.

I handed the form to Jan, who, after skimming it, seemed confused, probably due to the length of the narrative and the big words. She disappeared through the door behind the desk and emerged seconds later to announce that Mark was ready for me.

Mark was either a speed-reader or hadn't looked at my form.

Jan showed me into a large room containing all manner of exercise equipment: treadmills, weight machines and free weights, stationary bicycles, a Stairmaster, and sundry machines whose purpose and operation were a mystery to me. It looked like a medieval torture chamber.

Mark was effortlessly doing curls with hundred-pound weights. His grapefruit-sized biceps popped and rolled rhythmically. An anemic-looking man jogged on a treadmill, his eyes fixed on a small television turned to the *Today* show. A middle-aged woman on a stationary bike also watched a television screen but with frequent side glances at Mark.

Catching sight of me, Mark placed his barbells on wall brackets with the same amount of effort I used in reshelving a paperback.

"Hi, Lottie. Why don't you come over and start with some mat exercises," he boomed, gesturing to a blue exercise mat lying on the floor near his feet.

I looked around to see who he was talking to and then remembered that I was Lottie, an appellation I had momentarily forgotten or more likely suppressed. I moved to the mat with a pronounced limp, hoping to impress my fragile physical condition upon Mark.

He started me off with some easy stretches (easy, that is, for people with a modicum of flexibility, which I lacked) and then moved to sit-ups. That's when he got nasty. After five sit-ups, I politely informed him that I had worked my stomach muscles to capacity. Fifteen minutes later, prodded by Mark's taunting, I was still going. My stomach muscles were planning a walkout.

After the sit-ups came push-ups, which made me nostalgic for the sit-ups.

I was getting desperate. How could I ask this guy

questions when he was screaming at me like a drill sergeant and, even if the opportunity presented itself, I was too out of breath to talk? Drastic measures were required.

I faked a faint, flattening out on the mat like roadkill.

"Miss Bush!" Mark said sternly. After a few beats, abandoning the imperative, he asked, "Miss Bush?"

Before I could respond with a suitably groggy "yes," he knelt down, flipped me over, and pumped my chest.

"Stop it!" I sputtered, dropping the Camille act.

Mark stopped in midpump and sat back on his heels. "I did it," he said, sounding awestruck. "I saved your life."

My immediate impulse was to strongly disagree, but then I saw my opening. "You did. Thank you so much. Is there a place I can rest for a bit? And could you stay with me in case I have a relapse?"

The middle-aged woman on the stationary bicycle who had quit peddling and was now apparently coasting shot me a narrow-eyed look, no doubt peeved that she hadn't come up with a similar idea.

I allowed Mark to help me up and leaned heavily on his arm as he escorted me to a side room with a sign reading *Yoga Room; Shhhh!* The room had no furniture, and the floor was covered with mats. Mark brought in a padded bench and motioned for me to lie down. Then he left and returned moments later with a chair, which he set next to the bench. After shutting the door, he sat on the chair and stared at me with concern. He was taking this Florence Nightingale thing seriously.

I struggled to think of a way to introduce the subject of Queen Ta Ta's murder. Mark mistook my silence for a relapse, leaned close to my nose and mouth to check my breathing, and positioned his hands on my chest in case he had to start pumping again.

"I bet if you had been around when Queen Ta Ta was killed, you could have stopped it, or at least revived her long enough for the EMTs to get there."

Not brilliant, but anxiety rarely inspires eloquence.

Mark returned his hands to his lap. "I know I could have," he said grimly.

"Did you see anything the morning it happened?"

He shook his head. "I saw someone near the spa casitas, but at the time I didn't know about the murder, so I didn't think to ask him any questions."

"Him?" I asked.

He shrugged. "It was dawn and difficult to see, but the person moved more like a man than a woman."

"How's that?" For all I knew, Mark might think women usually skipped.

"Hands in the pockets, long strides, head down, big shoulders."

"Could you see what he was wearing?"

Mark hesitated before answering, and I saw a flicker of suspicion flash across his face.

"Athletic shorts, tank-top, socks, and a ball-cap. That's

all I could see. I couldn't even tell you what color they were. Because of the socks I thought maybe he got locked out of his room."

"Did you see where he went?"

"I ... hey, I'm not sure talking about this stuff is good for you. Maybe I should leave you alone for a while to rest."

"No, no," I said hurriedly. "Conversation takes my mind off the pain and helps me focus; you know, keeps me from sliding back into unconsciousness." Whatever.

"Uh ... okay. So, what was I saying?"

"You were telling me if you saw where the stocking-wearing-guy went."

"Oh yeah. One of the maintenance carts pulled up and he got in. I figured he hitched a ride to the main building with one of the groundskeepers to get another key. About a half hour later all hell broke loose."

"Did you tell the police what you saw?"

"Yeah, only the detective I spoke to didn't seem too interested. He was more interested in whether I'd seen any early morning joggers on the canal path. I couldn't see the path from where I was, though, and besides, no one jogs this time of year."

"Are there any rooms in the hotel with a view of the canal?" I asked.

The suspicion returned to Mark's eyes.

I fluttered my eyes and moaned.

"Just the casitas in the back," he answered hurriedly.

"The bougainvillea block the view from most of the rooms."

"Is there a shortcut from the spa area to the canal path?" I asked.

If Mark thought this segue was strange, he was either too polite or too afraid I'd relapse to say anything.

"There's a gate at the far end of the adults-only pool. Other than that, there're a couple of breaks in the bougainvillea people who work here go through to get to the employee parking lot."

I filed this information away for future reference since I planned to walk the property later.

Mark cleared his throat. "Do you mind if I ask you a question, Lottie—by the way, do you mind if I call you Lottie?"

"Not at all." *Pick a name. Any name. I don't care.*

"You, um, seem to wear a lot of makeup."

Not to mention a wig and a fake nose.

"I think you'd look better without it. You've got great bone structure."

Suddenly, I liked Mark. I liked him very much.

"Thank you," I said. "I had bad skin when I was younger, and I'm still self-conscious even though the acne's gone away."

I was getting good at being someone else.

Mark looked at his watch. "I have another client coming in five minutes. Do you think you'll be okay if I leave you alone? The yoga room isn't scheduled until four o'clock, so you can stay here as long as you like."

"I feel lots better," I said, sitting up to prove the point. "I think I'll go back to my room."

"Do you need help? I could have Jan go with you."

"No, no. I'm fine."

I called Tuwanda on my mobile as soon as I was outside.

Before I could say anything about my session with Mark, though, Tuwanda announced that the police had found Che Che.

Chapter Seventeen

"Where is she?" I asked.

"Pima County morgue, I'm guessin'. Her parents found her dead in their garage. Police say it looks like suicide; carbon monoxide poisonin'."

"Did she leave a note?"

"If she did, they ain't sayin'. Looks like she couldn't have killed Queen Ta Ta; they died about the same time."

"And they just found her today?"

"Yeah. The folks was in Vegas and din't get home till last night. Accordin' to the paper, the mother said, 'I lost fifty bucks at the casino, and now this.' I guess losin' your kid is on par with a bad day at the nickel slots."

"Lack of parental concern appears to be a constant in this case."

"Ain't that the truth."

"Did the paper say the police were looking into a connection between the two deaths?"

"Uh-uh. Sam called right as I was readin' about Che Che. He said the police ain't givin' out no information about anythin'. Even his contacts on the inside say the only ones that know the whole story of what's happenin' are the detective in charge, the police chief, an' your ol' boyfriend, the sheriff. Everyone else jus' gets enough info so's they can do their jobs. They tryin' to make the police department an' sheriff's office as leak proof as poss'ble."

"Maybe they're afraid one of Phoenix's finest will try to sell information," I commented cynically.

"One of 'em already did. The initial results of Queen Ta Ta's autopsy an' crime scene photos was published in *Innuendo*. People ain't bothered by nothin' no more.

"By the way, I'm havin' drinks with Peacemaker an' Flyer at five. You wanna tag along?"

I drew a temporary blank. "Who?"

"They's part of Queen Ta Ta's light an' sound crew. They still here, but they leavin' tomorrow. I ran into 'em in the hall outside their room an' we got to chattin' on the way to the pool."

"How long did you have to wait in the hallway until you ran into them?" I asked.

"'Bout an hour. Them two are late sleepers. I got so hungry I finally had breakfast delivered up to me."

"In the hallway?" I asked in surprise. "Weren't the staff suspicious?"

"They was at first, but I tol' 'em it's somethin' my people do an' I din't wanna have no one questionin' my religion like that 'cuz it violated my Fifth Amendment rights."

"Fifth Amendment? That's the right not to incriminate yourself."

"So? I'd say that fits jus' 'bout everythin'."

True enough. Some days I didn't know why I'd bothered with law school.

"Count me in for drinks. In the meantime, do you want to meet for lunch in about an hour?"

"You bet. Them pancakes I had this morning ain't gonna hold me long. What you gonna do in the meantime?"

"I thought I'd check out the hotel grounds." I told her about the man Mark saw the morning Queen Ta Ta died.

"I want to find the most direct route from the spa to the canal. Mark said he saw the man just after dawn, which puts him on the hotel grounds about the time of Queen Ta Ta's murder and just before I showed up. If he was the murderer, he didn't have much time to get from the canal to the spa area."

"I'm gonna mill aroun' the convention rooms so's to perp'trate the myth that we attendin' seminars an' shit. Marge made us some name tags, so we can look legit."

"Stay away from medical equipment discussions."

"Why? I'm a woman. I know as much as anyone else 'bout what gets shoved up my ..."

"I'll meet you in front of the restaurant eleven thirty-ish."

A young woman wearing a hotel uniform with the name Coventina embroidered over its pocket was cleaning my room when I walked in. The cat, Her, was gone. She'd probably escaped when the maid opened the door.

Coventina politely asked if I preferred that she return later. Her soft voice was filled with Spanish r's and y's.

Deciding to seize the opportunity to ask about the maid Dan mentioned as a possible witness, I said no. I sat at the desk and pretended to be at work as I wrote nonsensical phrases on a message pad.

Without lifting my head, I said, "I hear you've had lots of excitement around here."

She said nothing at first, and I guessed she was struggling between being polite and keeping her mouth shut. I turned, established eye contact, and gave her an encouraging smile.

"Djes," she said. "Much reporters."

"Cumplir a reina Ta Ta cuando ella tenía aquí?" [Did you meet Queen Ta Ta when she was here?]

"No, señora. Se quedó en una casita en la piscina pequeña." [No, señora. She stayed in a casita by the little pool.]

"Por lo tanto no limpiar su habitación?" [So you didn't clean her room?]

"El primer día, sí. Pero ella no estaba allí cuando lo limpia." [The first day, yes. But she wasn't there when I cleaned it.]

"Estábamos el día que murió?" [Were you here the day she died?]

"No. Una mujer mayor, quien usualmente limpia el spa, iba a limpiar, pero los policías vinieron y ella bajé el resto del día." [No. An older woman, the one who usually cleans the spa, was supposed to clean, but the policemen came and she got the rest of the day off.]

Coventina sounded envious. Apparently guest murders translated into vacation time for the housekeeping staff. I wondered if she was hoping I'd die so she could have some downtime. I forced a cough to at least give her hope.

She moved into the bathroom to clean. I figured it would seem odd if I followed her, so I stayed put and waited until she came out before resuming my questioning.

"¿La policía pedir a la sirvienta muchas preguntas antes de que dejen entrar a su casa vaya?" [Did the police ask the maid questions before they let her go home?] I asked this in part because I wanted to know if this was the witness Dan was referring to and in part because I wanted to point out the downside of the woman's demise.

She shot me a sly smile and told me that "the detective" was frustrated with talking through a translator and gave up quickly.

She said that Luna hadn't volunteered more information because the detective mentioned something about checking her immigration status. She was here legally, but sometimes the authorities made it hard by asking for more evidence than they should have a right to expect. For instance, how many people do you know of who carry around a certified birth certificate and a passport?

I nodded sympathetically, hiding my elation over having the name of the other witness: Luna.

Coventina finished cleaning and, after inquiring politely if I wanted extra towels or shampoo (I did), took her leave.

I grabbed a four-dollar bottle of water out of the minibar, immediately offsetting the benefit of the free shampoo, and headed out to scout the property.

I returned to the path by the spa, since that was where Mark had spotted the stockinged mystery man, and followed it to the adults' pool. The path curved around the pool but then dead-ended in a grassy "Meditation Area" occupied by a single bench. I searched the small area's perimeter carefully, looking for a break in the jumble of semihostile (thorny) and hostile (spiky) plantings. I found a dirt path between two Spanish Daggers. The path led to a narrow gate that, wonder of all wonders, led into a parking lot next to the canal. I could see the yellow police tape on the other side of the canal from where I stood.

Several green maintenance carts were parked in the lot in addition to miscellaneous sedans and pickup trucks, each of which had a Biltmore employee parking permit on its windshield. This was likely the murderer's route.

It hadn't taken me long to find out about stocking-guy and find this path. Certainly the police knew the same things I did. I couldn't be the only murder suspect they were considering.

Heartened by this thought but still aware that I had a stronger motive than the police to find out the truth, I went in search of Luna. I hadn't thought to ask Coventina if Luna was working today; I was pressing my luck getting the information from Coventina that I did. (I had also stretched my Spanish language speaking skills close to capacity.)

I asked the question of the first housekeeping staff member I ran into, a tiny woman with features indicating Guatemalan ancestry. She shook her head and told me that two people in housekeeping were named Luna and that both were out. I next asked her if she was at work on the morning of the murder. Her response was a frown and a shake of her head.

"Policia?" she asked.

She was right to be suspicious. I was acting like Kate Williams, murder suspect on the lam, not Lottie Bush, conventioneer.

"No. Bored tourist," I said, smiling ruefully.

I had ten minutes before the time Tuwanda and I set for lunch, so I strolled toward the main building, dutifully reading the little signs identifying the various floras along the way and reaffirming my status as a visitor.

I was a few minutes early, so I sat on a couch in the piano bar and ordered a Diet Coke. Several other people, mostly men, were sitting at the bar nursing drinks. They each wore a name tag, from which I assumed they were attendees at one of the conventions. If I had to bet which one, I would put my money on the wastewater technology convention, because each stared into his drink as if to discourage conversation, especially questions about what they did for a living.

I felt the cushion next to me sag, and turned to see who had joined me.

It was Bryan. Our eyes locked, and his blue eyes bored into mine, which I'm sure had a deer-in-the-headlights quality. My body went cold.

Stay calm, I ordered myself. *You are Lottie Bush, who bears a striking resemblance to a young Liza Minnelli.*

"Do I know you?" I asked sweetly, forcing a smile. I spoke a couple of octaves higher than usual and hoped that this, along with the sweetness factor, would throw him off.

"Your nose is peeling," Bryan said through his teeth.

"Oh, my goodness! It must be your Arizona sun. I probably sat by the pool a little too long," I said as my hands flew to my nose. "I'll just go into the ladies room and repair the damage with a little makeup and powder."

As I started to rise he grabbed my elbow and pulled me back down. "Makeup won't do it. You need to re-putty. When you do, work on the shape. You look like W. C. Fields."

"Why, sir, I don't know who you are, but you are the rudest …"

"Stop it, Kate," he said, his voice barely audible. "Why don't we go to your room and have sex?" he said, raising his voice.

The nearby drinkers looked at us with varying expressions of surprise and shock.

I glared at Bryan disdainfully but stood and gestured for him to follow.

Every man within earshot was probably thinking, "That's it? That's all you have to do?" It was going to be a rough day for the bar's female patrons.

Bryan and I didn't speak as we walked to my room, but I could feel his eyes burning into my back.

I swiped my keycard and opened the door. Stepping back, I motioned an invitation for him to enter first. He declined.

He thinks I'm going to make a run for it, I thought disgustedly. That had in fact been my plan, but it still hurt that he didn't trust me.

Once inside, Bryan whistled. "Whoa. This is some setup. How the heck can you afford it?"

"I can't," I said.

I inspected my nose in the hallway mirror. "It's not

that bad," I remarked. "I must have bumped it sideways when I was with Mark. I'm not used to that much physical activity."

"Who's Mark?" Bryan asked suspiciously.

"One of the personal trainers at the spa."

Bryan grabbed my shoulders and spun me around.

"Kate, what are you doing?"

I tried to pull away, but not very hard. A part of me liked that he was holding me.

"I want to get in better shape."

"Not that; why are you hiding from the police?"

"I am trying to stay out of jail," I huffed. "Webber's assigned me the number-one spot on his list of murder suspects, and you guys are doing diddley-squat to find the real murderer."

He pulled me closer and squished me in a bear hug. "Poor Katie," he murmured into my—or rather Liza's—hair.

This time I pushed back for real. "What do you mean, 'poor Katie,'" I snarled. "You make it sound like I lost an earring."

"If you were still a suspect, don't you think I'd have you in cuffs by now?" asked Bryan.

"What happened to change Webber's mind?" I asked, suddenly weary. I flopped into a chair, and my wig slipped sideways. I didn't bother to straighten it.

"The final autopsy report. She was dead before she was strangled."

"But her face was …"

"I know. Still, the strangling was postmortem; barely, but still qualifies," he said, sitting across from me on a leather love seat. (Real leather; I'd given it the sniff test earlier.)

"What do you mean by 'barely'?"

"Whoever strangled her was with her either when she died or immediately thereafter. The cause of death was overdose of, well, just about everything. The list of drugs in her system looks like the table of contents for the *PDR Drug Guide.*"

"Accidental?" I asked.

Bryan shrugged. "No idea. Most of the drugs were prescription, but we didn't find any prescription bottles in her room. According to her manager, she has two doctors—a gynecologist and a family doctor. The gynecologist hasn't gotten back to us, but the family doctor said the only drugs he prescribed for her were Ambien, Xanax, and Prozac, with no recent refills on any of them. The coroner also found that, based on the lividity patterns, Queen Ta Ta died somewhere else and was moved to the path by person or persons unknown."

I immediately thought of the man in the golf cart Mark had seen pick up the stockinged man. Then my brain switched gears.

"Do the police think there's a connection between Queen Ta Ta and Che Che's deaths?" I asked.

"You mean the ex-assistant?"

I nodded in the affirmative.

"No one's considering it seriously. It could have been a suicide pact, but neither woman left a note. So there's no proof."

Her, the cat, appeared out of nowhere and climbed into my lap.

"When did you get a cat?" asked Bryan.

I didn't bother to answer but absentmindedly stroked Her's tangled fur.

"So what happens now?" I asked after a minute or two of petting (me) and staring at Her (Bryan). "I've just got your word that I'm no longer one of America's Most Wanted."

Bryan pulled out his cell phone and punched a button.

"Hello, Detective Webber," he greeted.

I mouthed, "You've got Webber on speed dial?"

Bryan shrugged apologetically. "I'm with her right now. She wants to talk to you."

He put the phone on speaker and placed it between us.

"Ms. Williams here," I said. It lacked originality, but it covered the necessary territory.

"So when are we going to be on a first-name basis?" asked Webber teasingly.

When you quit charging me with crimes, I thought.

"Mr. Turner has informed me that you are no longer

viewing me as a murder suspect," I said with crisp formality.

"Sheesh. So now he's Mr. Turner? I take it you're not going to vote for him this fall." When I didn't respond, he continued in a more professional tone. "Sheriff Turner is correct. You remain a material witness, however, and we'd like to interview you again in light of new information. While the murder theory looks less likely, there's still a chance that she either did not take the drugs willingly or that the strangling was contemporaneous with the overdose. Absent that, we've got a good case for interference with a police investigation."

"So now you want me to give you the results of my investigation because you failed so miserably at your own?"

"You have been conducting an independent investigation?" Webber sounded as if he was talking through clenched teeth.

"If you weren't so busy trying to track me down to throw me in jail, I would've shared the information I discovered with you sooner," I said.

"If you've been withholding evidence, I'll hit you with a charge of obstruction of justice so fast ..."

"Give it a rest, Webber," I broke in calmly.

I heard a clank on Webber's end.

"What was that sound? Did you just punch your phone?" I asked.

"I dropped it," said Webber.

"You did not. You were trying to beat it into submission."

Bryan gave me a cautioning look and put his finger to his lips. "I'll interview Ms. Williams," he said, taking over my side of the conversation, "but she won't cooperate until she gets something in writing from your office giving her immunity from prosecution." I could tell by his tone that he wasn't happy with the way Webber had handled the interview.

"That's gonna take time," said Webber.

"I'll wait," I piped in.

Webber responded by breaking the connection.

"Does that mean he'll do it?" I asked, looking at Bryan.

"I believe the hang-up means, 'I don't want to do it, but I will,' in Webber-ese," he answered.

"I think your translation left out a few obscenities," I said, smiling at him. "Thank you for representing my interests," I added as an afterthought. "It wasn't very sheriffy of you to raise the immunity issue. I'm not sure the voting public would appreciate what you did."

Bryan sighed and placed a hand over his eyes. He did this frequently in my presence.

"Who is she?" I don't know what prompted me to ask, but the words were out of my mouth before I could bite my tongue.

Bryan lowered his hand and looked at me in surprise. "She who?"

"You know damn well who I mean. Macy saw you in DeRoy's parking lot with your tongue down a woman's throat." What the heck: in for a penny, in for a pound.

"When was this?" he asked.

"Last spring."

"During your lizard escapade?"

"Just before. And I was a dragon, not a lizard. I was supposed to be a frog, but I took the wrong costume."

Bryan's eyes reflected enlightenment. "Ahhh, so that explains the scales …"

"Don't change the subject," I snapped.

Loud pounding sounded at the door, and three pairs of startled eyes (two human, one feline) jerked toward the noise.

"Katie? You in there?"

Tuwanda! I'd forgotten all about our lunch date.

I dumped Her off my lap and hurried to let in Tuwanda, an apology already forming on my lips. I didn't get a chance to deliver it, though. As soon as I had the door open, she pushed into the room and announced, "I jus' talked to Sam. You free, girl. You no longer a wanted criminal."

Tuwanda drew up short when she caught sight of Bryan. "What he doin' here?" she demanded.

I explained how and why Bryan came to be sitting in my casita.

"So he tell you who *she* is yet?" asked Tuwanda, pulling a chair up next to mine.

The cat jumped on her lap, and she began stroking Her without taking her eyes off me.

"Not yet," I said. "I had just raised the issue when you arrived."

I retook my seat, and Tuwanda and I looked expectantly at Bryan.

He stared at the floor and picked at an invisible thread on the hem of his suit coat.

"That there's a sign of a guilty conscience," Tuwanda hissed out of the side of her mouth.

We waited for the pressure of silence to prompt Bryan to speak.

"She was a police officer," he said finally in a barely audible voice.

Tuwanda tensed, and I could tell she was revving up for a verbal barrage. I placed a restraining hand on her arm. She sucked in her breath, and we waited in continued silence.

"We were assigned to a joint task force on illegal drug use prevention. I asked her to dinner. She was so … normal."

I tensed, ready to spring, and this time Tuwanda had to provide the restraining hand.

"An' what would you be meanin' by 'normal'?" asked Tuwanda in a tone I recognized as her therapist voice. (Tuwanda believed the psychology course she took at the community college last spring qualified her to practice psychiatry.)

Bryan looked up defiantly. "I mean she doesn't defend criminals, wear weird disguises, scale down the sides of buildings, or regularly get kidnapped, chased by clients, and trapped in burning buildings."

Uncomfortably aware of my current weird disguise, I lashed back defensively. "The wall scaling thing happened *after* you and Ms. Normal went tonsil-diving."

"It was only a matter of time," countered Bryan.

"Admit it; you want to be sheriff and you dropped me like a hot bun because I'm bad for your image," I said through my teeth.

"Hot bun? Interestin' simile," commented Tuwanda, the therapist.

"Oh come on, Kate. Be fair," said Bryan heatedly. "You'd be bad for anyone's image. Every time the paper published a story about you they used the naked-woman-running-from-fire photo, and now they can switch between that and a still shot of you looking like a circus clown. Anyone in a long-term relationship with you is looking at a lifetime of explanations and apologies."

"I have no control over what the newspaper publishes, and you know it," I spat, leaning forward in my chair belligerently.

"Those photos are not doctored, Kate. They reflect moments in the life of Kate Williams, and there are many more moments like them." The anger had bled out of his voice, and now he only sounded weary.

"I hired a PR agent. In case you didn't notice, there

was a very positive interview about me on TV recently, and Max …"

A moment of self-awareness interrupted my defensive rant.

"I'm a mess," I said matter-of-factly.

"Why do you think that?" asked Tuwanda, resting her chin on bridged fingers. All she was missing was a couch, a notebook, and a degree.

"There's something in my brain I can't turn off," I said. "I have to know the truth. I can't let go of an issue until I figure it out, and I don't trust anyone else to do it for me. I wish I could let things slide or let someone else take over, but I can't."

Tuwanda and Bryan both leaned forward and looked at me earnestly. I was being psychoanalyzed in stereo.

"Do you think you feel that way because you're an attorney, or were you that way before you became an attorney?" asked Bryan.

"A little of both," I answered honestly. "I've never been big on trust. I *expect* people to lie to me."

"What about your mom and dad?" asked Tuwanda.

"Especially them." Even I was surprised by the level of anger and bitterness in my voice.

"Why?" Tuwanda prodded after a moment of silence.

"Enough of this! I will not sit here and be psychoanalyzed by amateurs. I'm not a bad person, Bryan. If you can't handle the way I am, then screw you."

I stood abruptly, and my wig, which had fought valiantly to cling to the top of my head, gave up and slid to the floor.

"Bryan, I will tell you and Webber what I and my team have found out about the Queen Ta Ta case as soon as Beth confirms that she received my full release and grant of immunity," I said in a business-like tone, trying to retain what dignity I could in a skull cap.

"By 'your team,' I assume you're referring to Tuwanda, Sam, MJ, and Beth?" asked Bryan.

"Yes; they're my team *and* my friends," I said, my lower lip quivering despite instructions from my brain to remain calm.

"Fine. I'll be waiting in the lobby," said Bryan, standing to leave.

"Don't you have anything better to do?" I sniped.

His eyes seared into mine. "No," he said.

After the door closed behind him, Tuwanda let out a long, slow breath, and said, "He still cares about you, Katie."

I doubted it, but rather than argue the point, I changed the subject. "I'm going to order from room service. Do you want anything?"

We both ordered chef's salads and iced teas. I ordered a tuna sandwich for Her.

Forty minutes later, the food had been delivered, and we'd already finished eating when the phone rang.

I picked up the receiver, and Beth greeted me

ecstatically. She told me I was a free woman: Webber had sent the signed immunity documentations to the office.

After she delivered the good news, she put me on speaker phone and a chorus of congratulations sounded over the line followed by a tone-deaf albeit pronoun-appropriate rendition of "For She's a Jolly Good Woman."

"Thanks, you guys," I said humbly.

"You can go back to being you," said Sam.

"Actually," I began apologetically, "I've been thinking that maybe I'll stay in disguise a while longer. I think I can find more out as Liza than I can as Kate. The media won't bother with Liza, but they'll descend like vultures on Kate."

"Don't let the real Liza hear you say that," said Sam. "She'd be devastated."

I ignored him. "I'm going to stay here a couple more days and see what more I can find out."

"Why do you care? You're out of it now. You're free." said MJ.

I had no problem answering this one. "Because a young woman is dead and everyone including her mother only sees it as an income-making opportunity. Someone has to care how and why she died."

A collective groan floated out of the phone.

I heard Sam mutter, "All she needs is a donkey and a windmill."

"Since no one's paying you to do this, does that mean …" MJ started to ask.

"No, your salaries will not be affected," I interrupted, not bothering to keep the annoyance out of my voice. "Let's assume that's always the case unless I say differently, so you don't have to ask every time."

Before ending the call, I asked Beth to send Max a copy of the documents that Webber sent over.

I headed to the bathroom to fix my hair and nose. When I re-emerged, Liza's disguise was back in place.

Tuwanda was uncharacteristically quiet. She hadn't moved from her chair and was distractedly braiding and unbraiding her long Cher hair. Her expression was contemplative.

"You want me to call Bryan an' tell him you ready to talk?" she asked, rousing herself out of whatever dream she was having.

I nodded yes, but she made no move toward the phone.

"You gonna tell him you plannin' to stay undercover?" she asked.

"Yes, of course," I said, avoiding eye contact.

Tuwanda continued her pensive staring, so I called Bryan to let him know I was ready to talk.

As I hung up, I noticed that Tuwanda was still staring at me.

"What?" I asked defensively.

"It seems you want to dig into the truth about everythin' and everyone 'cept you," she said.

"That's not fair," I countered. "That I don't want to

talk about certain matters doesn't mean I'm not aware of them."

"You don' trust your friends enough to tell us about what went into makin' Kate. How's we s'posed to trust you if you don' let us in on who you are?"

"I have no idea what you just said," I said truthfully.

Tuwanda didn't have a chance to clarify, because a knock sounded at the door.

I greeted Bryan at the door. He was armed with a handheld recorder and a legal pad.

He sat on the couch and waited politely for me to take a seat. Then we got down to business. A half hour later Bryan had run out of questions and Tuwanda and I had exhausted our supply of information.

After he turned off the recorder, Tuwanda looked at me meaningfully and said, "I think Kate's got somethin' more to tell you."

Darn it. I was hoping she'd forgotten about that.

I cleared my throat. "Bryan, I plan to stay undercover for a couple more days. I think I have a better chance of getting information out of some of the employees and Queen Ta Ta's concert staff than the police do, and I want to give it a shot."

Bryan showed no surprise at this announcement.

"Webber only agreed to no charges of obstruction of justice as to your *previous* activities," he said. "Anything you do from here on in will expose you to arrest."

"I am aware of that," I said. "I'm only going to talk

to witnesses the police have either already interviewed or have no interest in interviewing. I will, of course, notify the police of anything I learn that may help them in their investigation."

"What about the part where you get kidnapped, maimed, or killed?" he asked.

I searched his face for signs that he was joking. I didn't see any.

"That's not going to happen," I asserted.

Bryan did not look convinced. "Please call me if you need help. Just because we're not dating doesn't mean I don't care anymore, Kate."

Chapter Eighteen

After Bryan left, Tuwanda gave me one of her "I told you so" looks.

"If he *really* cared about me, we'd still be a couple," I said. "We'd probably be in therapy, but we'd be together."

Tuwanda shook her head and tsk-tsked.

"I'm gonna take a nap before we meet Peacemaker an' Flyer in the bar," she said, reminding me that we had a drink date with them later. "You gonna come by my room an' pick me up, or do you wanna meet downstairs?"

"I'll meet you at the bar," I said. "I'll try to get there a few minutes early to save some seats. The bar fills up as soon as the seminars are over."

"Tha's because with this damn heat there ain't nothin' to do 'cept drink and eat. I bet anythin' the rate of alcoholism jumps way up in the summer."

I nodded in agreement. "The murder rate too; the heat makes people testy."

After Tuwanda left I was too wired to relax, so I pulled out my laptop, which Sam had thoughtfully packed in my suitcase, to find out what I could about Peacemaker and Flyer. Sam and MJ had already sent over basic profiles for both: names (Milton Fagerberg and Lenny Schlaughterhaus, respectively, which led me to believe that their stage names were adopted as protective coloring rather than a manifestation of the generation of love), ages (midfifties), addresses (Las Vegas), and prior criminal records, (Milton had three DUIs and Flyer had two DIPs [an apropos acronym for Drugs in Possession]). Prior employment histories indicated that the two moved in tandem from one light-and-sound production company to another, until five years ago when they became the co-owners and sole employees of Hot Sh__ Productions.

I found the firm's website and hit the *Skip Intro* icon to bypass a video of blinding pyrotechnics and eardrum-breaking audio. (It could have been a song, but then it could just as easily have been the sound of a jet engine superimposed over the sound of a pneumatic drill with randomly dispersed obscenities.) I discovered that Hot Sh__ Productions was a Nevada corporation and operated two subsidiaries: T&A Productions and Dandy Pool Services. If the intro was any indication of their abilities, I put my money on Dandy Pool Services as being the profit center.

A list of clients of the production subsidiary included Wayne Newten, Shar, and the Beetles; likely show business wannabes who depended on name confusion to attract an audience. Queen Ta Ta was by far the biggest name they had worked with, and I wondered why she or her manager, whoever was responsible for hiring decisions, had not chosen a firm with better credentials.

I searched Milton and Lenny by their birth names and aliases and found that both had been married several times but were currently single. I also found photos of them working on various concert setups. From their mullet hairstyles, I guessed the photos were at least twenty years old. Milton sported a beard consisting of two long braids on either side of a clean-shaved midline. Hopefully, this too was an affectation of an earlier time and had not carried over into the present decade. Lenny had a goatee and sported a tattoo of a naked woman on his arm, but otherwise the men were nearly identical in appearance.

In most of the photos, they were adjusting speakers or wires with cigarettes hanging from the corners of their mouths and beer bottles within reach. Their outfits remained the same—cowboy boots, jeans and T-shirts—except the logos on the T-shirts changed to reflect whatever band they were working with.

The only thing of interest reflected in the short biographies I found on a music industry website was that both came from Tucson. But due to the difference in age,

Milton and Lenny had likely left Tucson before Queen Ta Ta was born.

Milton and Lenny's life histories succeeded in making me sleepy, so I set the alarm for 4:30 p.m., slid the arcadia door open about six inches in case Her needed a potty break, and took a nap. I underestimated the time it took to freshen my disguise, though, so even with a half an hour lead time, I was late getting to the bar.

I spotted Tuwanda in profile as I came down the stairs. Lenny and Milton were facing in my direction, so I got the full-on effect. They still wore mullets, except now Lenny's was streaked with gray and Milton's was dyed red on one side and blue on the other. Both bore a striking resemblance to Keith Richards.

Their weird beards were gone but had been replaced by equally weird Fu Manchu mustaches. Lenny had decorated his with blue bows, which undid any inference of normalcy derived from his decision to keep his natural hair color. Their lower bodies were hidden by the table, but each wore a shiny, silk cowboy shirt: Milton's was red and Lenny's was blue—to match his mustache ribbons of course. I looked down at my own silk blouse and considered changing but then rationalized that my champagne-colored Donna Karan was different enough to distinguish Lenny and Milton's wardrobe choices from my own.

Tuwanda caught sight of me and waved as I made my way toward them, slipping around fully occupied couches and chairs and groups of people huddled in conversation interspersed with giggling.

Milton and Lenny stood politely as I approached the table, and Tuwanda introduced them to me as Peacemaker and Flyer.

"But you can call us Milton and Lenny," interjected Milton. "Peacemaker an' Flyer are our roadie names. I got tagged Peacemaker 'cuz I'm always tryin' to keep the calm, an' Lenny here's called Flyer 'cuz he flies off the handle a lot. We balance each other out."

Both men were wearing jeans and blue leather cowboy chaps.

I briefly shook hands with each of them and then slid onto the couch next to Tuwanda. Thankfully the chaps disappeared under the table when they sat.

"So Tuwanda here tells me you're a doctor," said Milton.

"Yes. I specialize in treatment of venereal diseases," I said.

Both men produced little bottles of hand sanitizer, squirted, and scrubbed.

"That sounds, um, rewarding," commented Lenny.

I nodded. "It is. You wouldn't believe the nasty infections women come in with. It's nice to be able to send them home with clean vaginas."

The hand sanitizer came out again.

"What would you like to drink?" asked Tuwanda, raising her hand to get the waitress's attention.

"The usual," I answered.

She ordered a chardonnay for me and another round of gin and tonics for her and the men.

"So you two have known each other a while, huh?" asked Lenny.

"Yes. In fact, Tuwanda is one of my best clients." This comment earned me a dig in the ribs.

I didn't care. I wanted to get information out of these two, not marry them.

"Jus' before you came, Miltie was tellin' me 'bout the sound and lightin' bid'ness," she said.

Miltie? No way was I going there.

"Go on. Tell Kate what you tol' me," she encouraged.

Milton explained how he and Lenny met in high school where they handled all the lighting and special effects for the drama club's productions.

In other words they were nerds, I thought unkindly. Not too unkindly, though, since I too had been a nerd, and still was.

He proceeded to go into great detail about the highs and lows of their careers in the music industry, with frequent interruptions by Lenny to clarify or correct certain points. Fortunately, our drinks arrived quickly, so I was feeling more beneficent by the time he finally wrapped things up.

"I got a nephew who wants to get into the music bid'ness," said Tuwanda. "He'll be thrilled to hear that

I met the guys who worked with Queen Ta Ta. That's pretty big shit."

Lenny and Milton nodded, appearing to agree with her "pretty big shit" assessment.

"How'd you get that kinda gig?" asked Tuwanda. "Did you know her well? I mean, I'm sure you guys is real good at what you do, but there's lotsa competition out there, an' everyone needs an edge. What's your edge?"

Milton and Lenny looked at each other.

"I guess it's okay to tell them. I mean, the article in *Bottom Feeders* will be out tomorrow, so we ain't hurting their deal," said Milton.

"Okay by me," said Lenny.

They turned back to us.

"We're good friends with Queen Ta Ta's mom, Muffy," said Lenny. "Though Milton knows her better than I do. He used to date her in high school."

I quickly did the math. Muffy would have been in her late twenties when the two men were in high school.

Tuwanda shot me a meaningful glance. She had done the math too.

"Was you in the same class with her?" she asked with feigned innocence.

Milton visibly puffed up with remembered adolescent pride. "Naw," he said. "She was the drama teacher."

In my opinion that deserved a big *ick*, but I managed to maintain superficial neutrality.

"I wasn't aware that Queen Ta Ta's mother—Muffy,

you said her name is?—had that much influence over her," I commented. "In fact, I thought she and her mother didn't get along."

Milton looked at me suspiciously.

"Or at least that's what I read in the *National Irritant*," I added hastily.

Milton seemed to relax. "Oh, them tabloids tend to exaggerate," he said. "Gladys—that's Ta-Ta's real name, you know—went through some adolescent stuff, but the last two years she's been sendin' her mom money. She even bought her a nice house in Sun City."

Once again, the love-equals-money equation figured into Queen Ta Ta's relationship with her mother.

"Gee. She must be devastated by her daughter's death," I said, hoping my expression passed for sincere. "Have you been out to see Muffy since the murder?"

"Yeah. I was out there last night. I didn't get to talk to her much, though, 'cuz some bloodsucker lawyer was running interference." Milton drained his drink and slammed the glass down in disgust. "He was sittin' right there in her livin' room in his robe, actin' like he owned the place. If anyone had a right to be there it was ... ouf. Damn. Lenny, what the hell ..."

"Sorry," Lenny apologized, fixing Milton with a stare and not sounding at all sorry. "There's not much foot-room under these tables."

Tuwanda put her hand on Lenny's arm and signaled the waitress for another round of drinks with her free hand. "Why don't you slide closer to me? I don' need much space," she said.

Lenny seemed to like that idea and scooched his chair as close to her as he could, impeded from sitting in her lap by the arm of the couch.

"You the closest I ever been to a superstar rock band. I bet you got some great stories to tell," she said, flipping her Cher hair flirtatiously.

I shot her a pleading look. I'd just sat through the lengthy, unedited version of their life stories. Now she was inviting them to add footnotes and addenda.

"Did you work a lot with Queen Ta Ta's manager, Joey Perroni?" I jumped in, trying to narrow the focus of the discussion. "I've seen him at the hotel and, to be honest," I paused to look anxiously over my shoulder and lowered my voice when I continued, "he doesn't seem real broken up."

This time it was Lenny who answered. "He's an asshole," he said simply. "Gladys got mixed up with him in high school. He stuck to her like a remora. He'd be nothin' without her."

"Was they, uhm, a couple in high school?" asked Tuwanda. She'd oozed over the sofa arm and was pressing up against Lenny. The distance between them became a matter of theoretical physics.

Milton looked at me encouragingly. I pretended not to notice.

"Maybe at first. Me and Milton were having kind of a

dry spell about that time. We went to Tucson and crashed at Muffy's when we got kicked out of our apartment in Vegas. Muffy was divorced by then, and I think she missed havin' a man around. Joey had already graduated from high school but hung around the school selling grass and trying to impress girls with how cool he was."

Lenny snorted and one of his mustache ribbons flew off, landing in his gin and tonic. We waited politely while he fished it out and retied it in a soggy bow.

"He'd come to the house with Glad and they'd listen to music and … stuff. He acted real uppity, braggin' about his job at the Best Buy and his in-depth knowledge of audio and video equipment.

"I 'member one time when we was all watchin' TV and I told him to get his damn feet off the coffee table. He told me I was a loser and to go to hell. Me! If you ask me, *he's* the loser."

I thought it was a draw.

"By the time they left for LA," continued Milton, "Joey was gettin' it on with someone else, though, and it was purely business between him and Glad."

"Glad was cool," said Lenny, looking misty-eyed the way drunk people who have suddenly seized on an emotion do. "She helped us get gigs in LA and later helped us set up our company. Joey wouldn't give us the time of day."

"The boot's on the other foot now though," snickered

Milton a bit drunkenly as he tried to high five Lenny and missed.

"Why's that?" asked Tuwanda.

"He don't got the story," said Milton, becoming morose as his emotions swung in the other direction. "It ain't his to tell."

"What story?" asked Tuwanda.

"It ain't yours to hear," said Lenny, eying the ice in his empty glass. "At least not yet."

Tuwanda motioned the waitress, who was weaving toward us through the crowded bar, to hurry up with the drinks.

"Sorry it took so long, it's just been crazy busy," she said when she made it to our table. "Doctors sure drink a lot. That group over there has been doing tequila shots for over an hour."

I looked in the direction of her head-jerk and saw a giggling group of women and men holding each other up like stones in a Roman arch, the keystone of which was a tall, red-faced man wearing a foam rubber saguaro on his head.

After the waitress left, Tuwanda tried to bring the discussion back to Lenny's story.

"Does what you talkin' about have anything to do with Queen Ta Ta's murder?" she asked.

But the boys had apparently sobered up enough between drinks to think twice about saying anything more and took the conversation in a different direction.

"Would you girls like to come up to our room and party?" asked Lenny.

"We'd love that," said Tuwanda enthusiastically. "Le's just finish our drinks an' then we'll head over."

I kicked her under the table and smiled frozenly. I had no intention of going along with this plan and plotted my escape.

"Sounds great, you guys. I've already finished my wine, so I'll just go visit the little girl's room while you all drink up. I've got really bad diarrhea, so give me a few minutes."

Milton looked at me sympathetically. "I've been there," he said. "I had the squirts all last week."

This was not the reaction I was looking for. I was hoping for revulsion, not bonding.

"I'll go with you Lottie," said Tuwanda hurriedly. "I'm feelin' a little gassy myself."

"We'll escort you two to the ladies room," said Lenny gallantly. "Me an' Milton can take a piss in the men's room while you deal with your lady problems."

I was too dismayed over having to abort my escape plan to point out that gas and diarrhea were hardly exclusive to women.

When we got to the restrooms, we went our separate ways with the men politely wishing us good luck.

Chapter Nineteen

As soon as the door to the ladies room closed behind us I grabbed Tuwanda by the shoulders. "Why did you tell them we'd go back to their room?" I hissed. "I don't want to spend the rest of the night fending off advances from some urban cowboy. They're wearing *chaps,* for God's sake."

"Don't you wanna know more about this 'story' of theirs?" countered Tuwanda. "It could help us find out who strangled Queen Ta Ta.

"Besides, we don't gotta go to bed with 'em. We just gotta get 'em to that man-point where they tell you anythin' to get in your pants, an' then we leave 'em high and dry. Or dry, anyway. They already pretty high."

A stall door opened and a woman hurried out, glancing at us nervously as she exited the ladies room.

"You see that?" said Tuwanda disgustedly. "She din't

wash her hands. Tha's why I never touch nothin' in these public restrooms."

I just hoped the woman wasn't reporting us to management.

"I can't do it," I pleaded, returning to the point of our discussion. "I can't lead those guys on like that. I'm not good at that kind of thing."

"Are you sayin' I am?" said Tuwanda, jutting her jaw out. "What, 'cuz I'm a ho you think that kinda thing is easy for me?"

"Well, yes."

A toilet flushed, and another restroom patron fled sans hand washing.

Tuwanda raised her fists and stepped toward me threateningly but stopped before delivering a physical comeback. Letting her arms fall to her sides, she laughed ruefully. "I guess you right. At least as to all but the leavin' high an' dry part; I ain't done much of that."

I immediately regretted what I'd said. Tuwanda had only discussed the business side of her profession with me. We'd never before discussed her experience with the service side of the industry. Now that I had crossed that line, my usually confident, no-apologies-for-nothing friend seemed deflated and uncertain.

"Tuwanda, I'm sorry," I said, putting my arm around her shoulders and giving her a squeeze. "What you do or don't do is none of my business."

She shook her head slowly. "I ain't ashamed of what I

do and what I did. I'm not a service provider no more, but I hire people who are, and I sure as hell got a lot of field experience before I got into management. It's jus' that when I'm aroun' you I feel like I'm someone different. I ain't schizophrenic. It's more like I compartment'lize."

"You don't need to compartmentalize around me," I said. "I accept you 'as is.' I hope you feel the same way about me, but I realize that I may be more of a challenge."

Tuwanda pulled back and looked at me in surprise. "You? You ain't no challenge at all. Hell, my momma used to get drunk an' dress up in old formals an' weddin' dresses a couple sizes too small an' then put on geisha makeup, which ain't at all attractive on a black woman. She'd pick me up at school like that."

I was oddly comforted by the fact that I was not as embarrassing as an alcoholic playing dress-up in white face. Admittedly the bar was low, but that's okay; pardon my mixed metaphors, but I needed a handicap.

"Now that we've reaffirmed our membership in the mutual admiration society, what do you propose we do? Those two yahoos are probably outside waiting for us," I said, gesturing to the door.

Just then a woman entered, smiling and waving with the bonhomie of a happy drunk. I recognized her as one of the AMA conventioneers.

"Excuse me, ma'am," said Tuwanda, "but did you see two men waitin' outside the ladies room?"

"You mean the ones in the chaps?" she answered.

I nodded.

"Yup. What'd they do, lose their horses?" We waited until she finished her business and left before resuming our conversation.

"You awfully hard on them guys, Kate," admonished Tuwanda. "They don't seem all that bad to me. Actually, they kinda sweet. You gotta get over them chaps."

"I can't help it. There's something disingenuous about wearing chaps in an upscale hotel where the closest horse is twenty miles away, and the closest steer, excluding the ones served in the restaurant, is in … Colorado, probably."

"Maybe the chaps is jus' somethin' that makes 'em feel better. You know, like how you wear them St. John's knits all the time. It wouldn't hurt you to add a bit of flash once in a while. Look at what you got on now. Where the hell did you find them pants and shirt anyway? You look like Hillary Clinton."

"The gift shop; I feel comfortable in these clothes … Back to the point, neither one of us wants to go to Lenny and Milton's room. So what do we do? I mean, these guys weren't turned off by VD, diarrhea, and gas, for God's sake."

"Maybe they jus' need a more concrete kinda' rejection."

"You want me to go into the hallway and defecate?" I asked, horrified at both the prospect of public humiliation and the actual mechanics of pooping on demand.

"No. I mean like standing 'em up. We can sneak out of here an' go back to our rooms."

I much preferred this approach, but then there was the problem of how we could leave without them seeing us. I pointed out this difficulty to Tuwanda.

"Maybe there's another way out of here."

We undertook a quick search of each of the six stalls and a nicely appointed lounge area but found no door. A civilized escape was not possible. Our only hope was a small, opaque window in the third stall.

I eyed the window doubtfully.

In the meantime, Tuwanda was reinspecting the lounge. "Even if we gotta stay in here it ain't too bad. We got couches to lie on, water, an lotsa bathrooms. I bet we can get room service in here too."

"I am *not* sleeping in a bathroom," I said. After all, one must hold to certain standards in life.

Tuwanda came to stand next to me and looked toward the window. "That leaves the window. Climbin' out could be painful with the crank stickin' out an' all, an' even if it opens all the way, that don't give but a small space to crawl through. I don' think I got a problem, but you might not fit."

I took issue with her inference. "I can get through," I said testily. "I bet you dinner I can."

Tuwanda shrugged and made a "go ahead" gesture.

"I'll stand guard while you get the window open," she said.

I closed the stall door and then put down the toilet lid and tested it with my foot before I put my full weight on it. The lid was loose and slid sideways. I dealt with this little idiosyncrasy by avoiding sudden, lateral movements. The window proved to be more of a challenge. I had to pull down with my full weight to get the crank to move, and when it did, it did so suddenly, causing me to lose my balance. I grabbed for the toilet paper roll to keep from falling, but toilet paper has very little tensile strength and proved to be of no help at all. Amazingly, I wasn't hurt, but one of the lid hinges had broken so I had to reset the lid before climbing up again.

"What the hell you doin' in there?" hissed Tuwanda.

"The crank was stuck," I hissed back.

I opened the window as wide as it would go, grabbed the sill, and pulled myself up. The window, frame and all, came out in my hands. I fell back and down, the lid slid sideways, and I landed in the toilet.

"Is everything all right in here?" a woman asked.

"Is jus' fine," said Tuwanda. "My friend in there is a plumber, an' she just can't leave the job at home. You might wanta use the ladies room off the dining room, though, 'cuz once she starts, no tellin' how far she gonna take it."

I heard the door open and close as yet another patron fled the women's room.

Tuwanda demanded that I open the stall door, which I accomplished by kicking it. After a few beats of shocked silence, she narrowed her eyes and said, "You cheatin'. You was supposed to climb through the window, not take out the damn wall."

"Come on. Let's get out of here," I said grumpily. I was sitting in a toilet covered with drywall; I was in no mood for criticism.

Tuwanda helped me out of the toilet. While I tried to dry off with paper towels, she crawled out the gaping hole I'd made with room to spare.

After I exhausted the supply of paper towels, I followed suit, but not exactly. Even with the widened space, I still had difficulty squeezing through. I'd managed to get my upper body out but was having problems with the rest of me.

"Come on," Tuwanda whispered urgently.

"I can't. It must be my pants. The fabric's too thick," I whispered back

"You mean your ass is too thick," countered Tuwanda.

She grabbed me under the shoulders and pulled, throwing her weight into it. I didn't budge.

"Hello, ladies," said a male voice. "Do you need some help?"

Our heads jerked in the direction of the voice, and we strained to see through the dark to identify the speaker.

He came closer, and I recognized Mark in the faint light from the bathroom.

"Hi, Mark." I greeted him with a weak wave.

Chapter Twenty

Tuwanda let go of my shoulders and straightened out her dress. "I don't believe we've met," she said, extending her hand. "I'm Lottie's friend, Marge."

Mark shook her hand and introduced himself, after which we stood awkwardly (actually, they stood; I hung), searching for a polite direction to take the conversation.

Mark cleared his throat. "Um, can I help you out there, Lottie?"

"Why, thank you. The fabric of my pants is unfortunately quite thick, and I seem to be stuck," I said.

"It ain't that, it's …" started Tuwanda.

I poked her hard in the back, interrupting her before she could explain her theory.

Mark came closer and looked the situation over.

"Bad date, huh," he remarked.

"Yes," I said, relieved that I was released from the burden of telling the uncomfortable truth.

"Yeah, that happens here more than you'd think," he said, nodding his head understandingly. "In fact, management plans to put a back door in the ladies room right about here. It's impossible to keep the landscaping looking nice when you've got ladies crashing onto it every night."

He grabbed me under the shoulders. "Ready?"

I sucked myself in as much as possible and squeaked, "Ready."

He pulled up and out and I started to move. Unfortunately, my pants liked where they were and did not come with. I popped out with nothing on but a pair of thong panties. I bought panties on sale at Victoria's Secret. This pair had "Make My Day" printed on the crotch.

Mark chivalrously removed his shirt and gave it to me to wrap around my waist.

Tuwanda stared unabashedly at his chest. "Holy Jesus."

I yelped as someone grabbed me from behind.

Batting the hands away, I whirled around to find the slightly inebriated—and if smell was any indication, now completely inebriated—woman who visited the bathroom before the demolition process. She'd grabbed onto me to pull herself through the hole in the wall.

"Wow. It is so *nice* the hotel provides an escape hatch," she said, slurring her words and sagging back against the building once she was outside. "That asshole from Tennessee was *not* going to leave me alone." She giggled drunkenly. "He's probably still outside the ladies room with those two cowboys."

"Did you happen to see a pair of slacks on your way out?" I asked coldly.

"I saw a pair in the toilet. I thought that was weird, but, hey, whatever floats your boat."

I silently apologized to St. John.

The woman caught sight of Mark. "Wow. I'm Dr. Ruth Wilkins, and right now I'm thinking I made a mistake going into gynecology. Sports medicine would have been a better choice," she said, staring at his abs. Succumbing to temptation, she reached out to touch them.

Mark neatly caught the offending extremity in a handshake.

I figured he had lots of practice with this sort of thing.

Looking apologetically at me and Tuwanda, he said, "I think I'd better escort Dr. Wilkins to her room."

"Oh God, yes," said Ruth.

Ignoring her, he continued to address us. "Will you two ladies be okay?"

"Define 'okay'?" I asked wryly.

"So you got any openin's in your schedule?" asked Tuwanda.

He pulled back in surprise.

"She means she wants a personal training session." *I think.* I was doing my best to keep things clean.

"A private one," she added unhelpfully.

"I'm sure I do," said Mark with admirable professionalism. "Just call the gym and they can make an appointment for you, Marge. Take care, ladies."

He firmly grasped Dr. Wilkins's elbow, whether to support her or keep her at arm's length wasn't clear.

Sticking close to the shrubs and mesquite trees, Tuwanda and I made our way back to my casita.

"Drat," I said when we got to the door. "My key card is in my pants pocket. We'll have to go to your room."

The door opened, and Bryan stuck his head out. "It's about time. I've been waiting here for over an hour."

I was about to ask what the hell he was doing in my room when two other guests strolled around the corner. Tuwanda stepped into the room, pulling me with her, and slammed the door behind us.

"What are you wearing?" asked Bryan, pointing to Mark's shirt.

"I lost my pants, and a friend lent me his shirt. What are you doing here?"

"What friend? And I'm here because you promised to cooperate with the police."

"None of your business. And you're not the police; you're the sheriff."

"Should I call Webber over to replace me?"

"This is interestin' an' all, but I'm hungry," Tuwanda

interjected, marching toward the small sitting room. "I'm gonna call room service an' order everthin' on the menu."

Bryan and I continued to glare at each other in a standoff while Tuwanda placed a lengthy order with room service.

When she was through, she sat on the couch, ordered both of us to join her, and directed me to "cooperate with the damn police."

I demurred and disappeared into the bedroom to put on a pair of jeans. When I came out, Tuwanda and Bryan were sharing a bottle of red wine from the minibar and diving into a twenty-dollar package of peanuts. I'd had enough alcohol for the night, so I declined Bryan's offer of a glass of wine.

"Proceed to cooperate," he directed.

I dutifully relayed our conversation with Milton and Lenny, leaving out our escape from the bathroom.

"What do you think Milton meant when he said Perroni didn't have the story?" asked Bryan after I finished.

"I don't know. Maybe it's part of what he and Lenny told *Bottom Feeders,* and we'll find out when the magazine hits the stands tomorrow."

"I don' know. They din't have any problem spoutin' off on everythin' they said they tol' that magazine," said Tuwanda. "I think they was holdin' somethin' back from us *and* the media. Maybe they's like everyone else and is waitin' for a higher offer."

"You said they met Burton at Muffy's house. Do you think they're working with him?" asked Bryan.

"No. They made no bones about the fact that they strongly dislike both Dick and Joey," I said.

The food arrived, pushed in by hotel employees on three carts. It looked like the spread in *Babette's Feast*.

After they left, Tuwanda pulled one of the carts in front of her and said, "Just grab a cart and we'll roll 'em around family style."

Not any family I've met.

I started to nibble delicately on a raw carrot. "Have the police discovered anything new, or are you guys just waiting to hear what I find?"

Bryan didn't take the bait. "The hotel verified that Queen Ta Ta had attended a private party in one of the smaller banquet rooms the night before she died. Her mother, Dick Burton, Perroni, and Che Che were among the attendees."

"If that's true, then Muffy lied to me," I said through a bite of a Reuben sandwich. (I'd bagged the rabbit food in favor of more substantial fare, reasoning that I deserved it after my morning workout with Mark.) "Muffy told me the last time she spoke with her daughter was when she called from her limousine on the way to the hotel."

"Wow. A witness lied. There's a first," said Bryan in mock surprise.

I stared at him stonily.

"It looks like we'll have to interview Muffy again," said Bryan, dropping the sarcasm.

"She didn't mention the party to the police either?" I asked.

Bryan shook his head no. "She didn't tell us much of anything. She was very distraught when we interviewed her."

"Over her daughter's death?" Maybe she had a heart after all.

"No. She heard Perroni was interviewed by *People*. Burton was there, and she was giving him hell between meltdowns."

"She seems awful close to Burton," commented Tuwanda.

"According to Burton," said Bryan, "he took her home after the party. He was still there the next morning."

"When did the party end?" I asked.

"The hotel staff said it was over by midnight. No one saw Queen Ta Ta after that until you found her body. Perroni verified that she was wearing the same clothes she wore to the party.

"Before you ask, everyone we've interviewed says Queen Ta Ta wasn't acting any different from the way she normally did. Che Che is, of course, unavailable for comment, but everyone else swears she and Queen Ta Ta seemed to be on friendly terms, and neither one appeared to be overly under the influence. The hotel bartender working the party said Queen Ta Ta only had one glass of wine. She could have taken something before the party, but she wasn't visibly impaired."

"What does 'actin' the same as always' mean when you're talkin' about a rock 'n' roll diva?" asked Tuwanda as she switched her empty cart for my half-full one.

Bryan pulled his cart closer and possessively held on with one hand. "Philosophical. She apparently treated everyone to a monologue on what makes some people great, and other people … not."

"I take it she placed herself in the former category?" I asked cynically.

He nodded yes. "She compared herself to Madonna, Billie Holiday, and Eleanor Roosevelt."

"I can kinda see the first two, but Eleanor Roosevelt? Tha's delusional," said Tuwanda.

"You're not the only one who thinks so. Joey, likely fueled by alcohol, confronted her on that particular comparison. She explained that she intended it as a reference to a category of people for whom greatness was a birthright."

"So she sayin' she got a birthright …" Tuwanda was interrupted by a knock at the door.

I answered, assuming the wait staff had come to retrieve their carts. Instead, I found Mark standing in the hallway.

Chapter Twenty-One

"After such an eventful night, I thought you might like this," said Mark, holding out a single rose.

Bryan loudly cleared his throat.

Taking the rose, I stepped back and invited Mark in.

"This is Bryan Turner, and you remember Tu … Marge," I said.

"Hey, Mark," said Tuwanda, distracted from the piece of chocolate cake she'd been in the process of shoveling into her mouth during the hiatus between Mark's arrival and the introductions. "Why don't you sit down an' join us?"

He started to pull over a dining chair, but Tuwanda scooted over and patted the seat cushion next to her. "Come on over here. Make yourself comf'table. Take off your shirt if you want."

Mark laughed good-humoredly and sat next to her.

Brave man.

"Speaking of shirts," I said hurriedly. "I'll get the one you lent me."

Bryan, who had not said a word since Mark came in, stiffened and looked at me accusingly. I ignored him and went to the bedroom to retrieve Mark's shirt. When I returned, Tuwanda and Mark were discussing the personal trainer business and Bryan was sulkily sipping his wine. I handed Mark his shirt and sat in the chair I'd just vacated.

"Before you got here we were discussing the hot topic around here: Queen Ta Ta's death," I said, pouring myself a glass of wine. "Have you heard any new gossip?"

"No, but do you remember I told you one of the housekeeping staff saw someone near the spa about the time Queen Ta Ta was murdered? Well, she quit. Didn't even bother to show up; just called it in."

"Does anyone know why?" I asked.

"One of her coworkers stopped by her house to see her and said she was acting like she'd won the lottery … By the way, are you ladies in trouble?"

Bryan looked up quickly from his wine at this abrupt change of subject.

"Why do you ask?" I inquired with forced casualness.

Addressing Bryan, he said, "Because you're the Maricopa County sheriff. I recognize you from your campaign posters."

After a few beats of uncomfortable silence, Tuwanda turned to Bryan in mock horror. "You the sheriff? You tol' me you was in waste management."

Bryan looked nonplussed.

"Yeah, and that you were from El Paso," I said, picking up on Tuwanda's thread.

"I didn't, I …" sputtered Bryan.

"I think you should leave, mister *sheriff*," said Tuwanda. "I don' know what kinda shit you tryin' to pull, but I bet your constituents would be real interested to hear you been pretendin' to be someone else an' pickin' up women."

"I've had about enough …" Bryan started to protest but then thought better of it. "I'll leave, then. But you ladies shouldn't lead men on if you're not going to follow through."

Touché, I thought.

After Bryan left, Mark said, "That guy is weird. No way will I vote for him."

"You don't think he's undercover, do you?" I asked, feeling weirdly bad that Bryan had lost a vote because of me.

Mark gave a short laugh. "If he is, he's a bad choice for that job. He's pretty recognizable."

"Maybe the law-enforcement guys are getting desperate," I said. "No one has been arrested for Queen Ta Ta's murder, and the media is giving them a lot of flak about it.

"Do you remember anything more about the man *you* saw skulking around about the time of her murder?"

"No, but I've done some investigating of my own, and none of the maintenance guys say they gave anyone, man or woman, a ride that morning. One of them, a gardener named Jose Lopez, said he thought someone used his cart, though, because when he went to get it from the employee lot that morning, it had been moved and was lower on gas than he remembered."

I tried to maintain an expression of mild curiosity, even though my brain cells were doing a high kick; this was good information. I'd been assuming the murderer was on foot and acted alone. But what if two people were involved, and one of them was driving a maintenance cart? Access to a cart could shave a couple of minutes off the time it took to get from the hotel to the canal and back again.

"How good did you see the driver of the cart?" I asked.

"About as good as I saw the other guy; just a shadow."

"But you saw enough to identify that the driver was a man?" I asked.

"Like with the stockinged guy, the way he held himself and moved seemed typical of a man. He steered one-handed and draped his other arm over the back of the seat. He seemed pretty relaxed and casual."

I took issue with Mark's characterization of "relaxed

and casual" as male qualities but excused his chauvinism because the majority of the women he ran into were probably nervous and self-conscious with a tendency toward excessive giggling, present company included.

Mark looked at his watch and stood to leave. "I've got a six o'clock class tomorrow morning, so I'd better turn in early," he said.

"Do you live far from here?" I asked, standing as well.

"Not far at all: about a block away on the other side of the canal."

I was about to say I didn't live that far either but then remembered who I was, or rather who I was supposed to be.

I walked him to the door and thanked him again for lending me his shirt and for the rose. He took my hand before leaving and said he hoped I would come in for another session, and this time it would be gratis.

After the door closed behind him, Tuwanda let out a whoop. "Whooo-eeee, I think you got an admirer, and he is *cute*."

"Right. And as with all of the men interested in me, facts will emerge showing him to be seriously defective."

"C'mon, that ain't fair. Bryan's not so bad."

"Right. Except for the part where he cheated on me, things were going pretty good," I sniped.

"Yeah, you right. Mark's pro'bly got a Liza Minnelli obsession, an' he ain't interested in you at all."

"True. And speaking of Liza, I'm sick of this disguise. I want to go back to being little old drab, uninteresting me."

"Well, you ain't on the lam no more, an' I don't think we're gonna get anything more out of Joey, Lenny, or Milton. So we might as well go back to bein' ourselves. To be honest, I'm tired of lookin' like a black version of Cher, even though a black version of any white person is an improvement."

"You missed that whole repression of the blacks thing, didn't you?" I kidded.

"Tha's one of the blessin's of havin' an alcoholic mother; you don't notice the other crap that's goin' on 'cuz you're so busy dealin' with your own crap."

"I vote we check out of here and resume our lives," I said.

"I'm with you, but we might as well wait until tomorrow mornin' since we gotta pay for tonight anyway."

I winced at the thought of the bill and prayed that I had enough credit left on my Visa to cover it. Tuwanda headed to her room, and I, resolving to make the best of it, took a long, luxurious bath and stuffed my suitcase with tiny bottles of shampoo, conditioner, body cream, sewing kits, bars of soap, and towels before retiring to bed and the comfort of the Egyptian cotton sheets and down quilt (which I couldn't cram into my suitcase despite much effort expended with regard to the same). It was only ten o'clock, so I settled in to read a mystery I'd picked up in the gift shop.

I was just dozing off when a knock sounded at the door, and a second later the door opened.

"Katie?" whispered Tuwanda.

I wasn't surprised— Tuwanda had an uncanny ability to open any lock, a fact I found both admirable and annoying.

"I'm in bed," I called out.

"You gotta get up, now!" she said, barging into the bedroom. She grabbed a pair of jeans and a T-shirt from my suitcase and threw them to me.

"What the hell. Look at all that shit you got in your suitcase. I'm surprised you din't take the toilet paper too."

"I haven't finished packing," I said. I shoved my legs into the jeans and pulled the T-shirt over my head, not bothering to take off the lacy pink baby-doll nightie I was wearing. (Another one of Sam's purchases. He took the Justin Bieber jammies for himself.)

"Why am I doing this?" I asked as I searched the floor for tennis shoes (another gift-shop acquisition).

"'Cuz I just saw Dick an' Joey goin' into Joey's room together," said Tuwanda.

This was interesting news. But then the logical cells in my brain (a minority presence), raised a valid concern. "What are we going to do? Crash their party?" I asked.

"No. Joey's got one of them little cottages near the

adult pool all to hisself. We gonna stand outside the window an' listen."

Fair enough. How much trouble could listening get us into?

I followed close behind Tuwanda as we negotiated the now-familiar pathways, stopping every so often when we ran into other guests, pretending to admire a plant in the yard lights. As we neared Joey's cottage, we stayed close to the buildings, keeping down and as quiet as possible. The staying quiet part proved the bigger challenge. We wound our way through a cactus garden filled with what I am sure were rare species, several of which became rarer when I stepped on them. Run-ins with cacti by necessity require a certain amount of cursing, and after each of my outbursts, Tuwanda loudly shushed me.

Tuwanda stopped next to a pink stucco cottage at the edge of the hotel property. "You take the bedroom window, an' I'll take the one in the livin' room."

The bedroom was around the side of the cottage, which had the same layout as my casita. The ubiquitous bougainvillea shrubs covered the window. With stoic teeth clenching, I worked my way through the thorny plants to a six-inch gap next to the building.

No lights were on in the bedroom, which meant nothing as to its occupancy status, but I didn't hear any sounds either.

I stayed in position for what seemed a long time but was probably only five minutes in real time. I was considering joining Tuwanda when the bedroom lights came on. Startled, I stepped back into the protective but painful foliage.

Except for a few areas where the bushes blocked my view, I could see most of the room. I watched as Joey entered the room and turned to speak to someone still in the hallway. He then lifted a curled index finger and made an inviting gesture. Dick entered the room, and the two men kissed. Intense groping followed.

Since the noises they made were unintelligible, I sat on the ground under the window and resigned myself to waiting it out for the pillow talk.

The boys were getting raucous, if the increased tempo of the bumps, thumps, and cries were any indication. Being an inexperienced, not to mention unwilling, voyeur, I didn't know if this was normal.

"You fucker!" one of them—I think it was Joey—screamed.

Again, due to inexperience, I had no idea whether this was a man-on-man form of verbal foreplay.

"Asshole!" I was fairly sure Dick was the speaker—or rather shouter—this time.

Again, I considered whether this was the male version of coyness.

"You are gonna die, Burton."

Some sort of S & M thing maybe? I got quietly to my feet and peered through the window. Joey had his hands wrapped around Dick's throat, and Dick was struggling to break his grip. Both men were fully clothed.

There are times when instinct is stronger than the need for self-protection, and this was one of them. I banged on the window and yelled, "Stoppit!"

Joey released Dick, and both men looked angrily toward the window.

I plowed through the bougainvillea and ran, directing Tuwanda to do the same as I shot by the front of the cottage. She ran after me, and I could hear Joey and Dick behind us. I figured that I could outrun Dick, but I wasn't sure about Joey. He looked as if he was in good shape.

I ran toward the canal path because that was the shortest route to the hotel's main building. The meandering paths were pleasant for strolling but got in the way when you wanted to go from point A to point B.

"I got one!" yelled Joey.

They had Tuwanda! I couldn't desert her.

I stopped and allowed Dick to catch up to me.

"Hello, Mr. Burton," I greeted him calmly.

"Who the hell do you think you are? How do you know me? What are you doing here?" he asked between gasps while he tried to catch his breath.

I decided to only answer his last question. "I was out jogging and saw Joey through the window. Then I saw you guys, um, fighting."

"Ah, yes. I see," he said, seeming to relax a bit.

Burton brought his face close to mine. "I recognize

you; you're the jogger who found Queen Ta Ta's body. I would think you'd stop jogging after that experience."

"Sometimes I can't sleep, so I exercise to tire myself out," I said, hoping this would also explain why pink lace was sticking out under my T-shirt.

"I take it your friend was out jogging too," he said.

I nodded yes, hoping like heck that Tuwanda hadn't said anything contradictory to Joey.

"I guess we should go rescue her. Joey isn't too happy with either of you," he said.

We retraced our steps to where Joey and Tuwanda stood. Joey had the beginning of an impressive shiner. He kept a firm grip on Tuwanda's shoulder but kept her at arm's length.

Dick repeated what I had told him, and since Tuwanda had refused to talk, I guess you could say our stories were consistent.

A small crowd of guests and a security guard had collected to see what the excitement was about. The latter asked if everything was all right. The four of us said we were fine, and Joey explained that it was simply a game of tag that got out of hand. I guess the guard had heard worse, since he accepted this explanation with an expression or relief.

After the crowd dispersed, I turned to Joey and asked, "Why were you trying to kill Mr. Burton?"

He and Dick exchanged nervous glances. "I think

you should come back to my room so we can have some privacy," he said.

I wasn't sure I liked that plan, but Tuwanda accepted before I could object.

Chapter Twenty-Two

We returned to Joey's cottage, except this time we entered through the front door instead of crouching in the bushes. We took seats in the small living room area, and Joey, playing the part of the host, asked if anyone wanted a drink. Tuwanda and I declined, but both he and Dick took beers out of the minibar.

"I guess first we should go around and introduce ourselves," said Dick.

I felt odd introducing myself to Joey and Dick again. At least I remembered what my real name was.

Dick took control of the conversation once introductions were finished.

"Katie …"

"Kate," I corrected.

"All right then; Kate it is.

"I am chief counsel for the sole beneficiary of Queen Ta Ta's estate."

"That would be Muffy," I clarified.

"Yes; that would be she. In that regard, Mr. Perroni and I have entered into negotiations concerning ownership rights to certain personal papers. Mr. Perroni and I were discussing the matter, and things got heated."

"It looked like things were pretty hot before the argument," I commented.

Dick lost some of his aplomb. "How long were you outside the window?" he asked, his voice breaking. "I thought you looked in *after* you heard screaming."

I didn't answer but continued to stare at him.

"Let's just say our personal relationship is also in dispute," said Joey.

"Are you guys an, um, item?" I asked.

"We were until this bitch started making deals behind my back," sputtered Joey.

I caught a whiff of alcohol-laced breath. The beer was likely not his first drink of the night.

"That's bullshit. You started it," countered Dick.

"I'm not the one who set up housekeeping with Norma Desmond and cornered the market on cheesy childhood stories," Joey lashed back.

"Norma Desmond?" asked Tuwanda.

"He means Muffy," Dick clarified.

"Have either of you talked to Milton or Lenny lately?" I asked.

"Those losers? Why the hell would we?" asked Joey contemptuously.

This time Dick was out of the loop. "Who?" he asked, nonplussed.

"Milton Fagerberg and Lenny Schlaughterhaus, a.k.a. Peacemaker and Flyer," said Joey. "They're a couple of hangers-on Queen Ta Ta threw a few bones to once in a while. They hold themselves out as light-and-sound men, but they couldn't flick on a light switch without fucking up."

I thought that Joey's dislike for Lenny and Milton was a bit extreme. Except for their poor fashion sense, they seemed fairly harmless. "I thought you were old friends."

"Who told you that?" asked Joey, sounding genuinely surprised.

"I dunno," I said, shrugging. "I think I read it in *Us*; something about you all coming from Tucson and Lenny and Milton being good friends with Muffy."

"Those losers have been talking to the media? About what? They have nothing to tell. All they did was hang around the house sponging off Muffy. They cared about what was in the refrigerator. Period. They were a joke."

"I heard they've got an interview in *Bottom Feeder* coming out tomorrow," I said, throwing kerosene on the fire.

Joey turned unsteadily and pointed an accusing finger at Dick. "Did you get a piece of that?"

"Of course not. I didn't even know who these guys were until now," sputtered Dick.

Joey's expression turned pensive. "We need to talk to them; you know, rein in all the information and control its release. That was the plan, right?"

"Until you got greedy," spat Dick.

"God, you're beautiful when you talk like that," murmured Joey, taking a step toward Dick.

The lovebirds finally noticed that Tuwanda and I were still there.

"I concur," said Dick officiously. "It is imperative that we preserve Queen Ta Ta's reputation as well as the assets of the estate."

I cleared my throat. "Do either of you care at all whether Queen Ta Ta's murderer is caught?"

They seemed genuinely confused.

"That's an issue for the police, not us," said Dick. "Our job is to protect Queen Ta Ta's legacy."

"C'mon, Dick," said Joey. "Let's go rein in those two yahoos. I saw them standing outside the ladies room in the lobby. They're wearing chaps, for God's sake."

Tuwanda and I were no longer a priority, which was fine by me.

"One more thing," I said. "Joey, why did you say I killed Queen Ta Ta? Did you really witness her murder? Or did you just see me discover the body?"

"I was mistaken. I saw you finding the body."

"But you told the police you saw a struggle between Queen Ta Ta and a woman. Are you now saying you lied?"

"I didn't lie. It was hard to see. For all I knew you were strangling her," he said defensively.

"You almost got me arrested for murder because of a groundless supposition?"

"Get over it," snapped Joey. "Groundless supposition is as close as we get to the truth in this business."

"You a perfect asshole," said Tuwanda. "An' I don't mean that in a flirty way, neither."

Joey waved dismissively. "C'mon, Dick. We've got work to do. Perhaps you ladies should leave too, or would you prefer to hang out in my closet for a while?"

"Can't see nothin' from the closet," said Tuwanda. "Kate, let's go outside and get some fresh air; air that ain't been tainted by these two."

Tuwanda and I followed Dick and Joey outside and waited until they disappeared down the path.

"Let's follow 'em," hissed Tuwanda.

"What's the use? We're not going to get information out of any of these people unless we come up with a big check."

"Look, they might work a deal with Milton an' Lenny to share profits from the sale of whatever information they holdin' back. If they do, I wanna hear what them cowboys have to say."

"What if they see us?"

"They won't. We gonna wear disguises."

"How? We've run out of disguises. Plus, I've been so

many different people over the past few days, I've forgotten who I really am."

"This time it'll be easy. You just gotta look the part; you don't gotta say nothin'. Stay here. I'll be right back."

She trotted into the darkness and a short time later returned with two sets of the hotel's trademark chino pants, blue golf shirts, and logo baseball caps.

"Where did you get those?"

"The laundry. We passed by it on the way to Joey's cottage. By the way, if anyone asks, we on break," she said, handing me a pile of clothes.

"From what?" I asked.

"See, this is one of your problems; you can't improvise. You always gotta' work off a script. Jus' pretend you a janitor. Get into the head of a janitor. *Be* a janitor."

"Character acting?"

"If you need a label, then okay; it's character actin'."

We hid in a breezeway and hurriedly changed into the uniforms, hiding our own clothes under a yucca.

"You all ready?" Tuwanda asked as she belted her pants. Her pair was about twice the size she needed, so the belt was essential. My pants, however, fit a bit snug.

"Do you want to switch pants?" I asked. "I think you got the larger pair."

"They the same size."

Had I let myself go that much?

"Let's get this show on the road," she said impatiently.

"Tuck your hair up under your cap and keep your head down."

We checked the hall outside the ladies room first. The only person we saw was a short, rotund man with a comb-over pacing back and forth, checking his watch every few seconds, and repeatedly glancing at the ladies room door. I sensed that the rear exit we'd created had been put to use again.

We spotted our quarry in the bar area. The four men sat around a low table, huddled in an intense conversation.

Dan the bellhop—the same young man who had escorted me to my room upon my arrival—passed by and then stopped and backed up.

"Hi. I'm Dan. I haven't seen you two around here before," he said with a friendly smile. "Are you new hires?"

"We're on break," I said.

"Sorry," apologized Tuwanda. "She's nervous. It's our first day on the job. I'm Rose and this here's Hilda. We was jus' lookin' aroun' durin' our break. It's a real pretty place."

"Wait until you've been here for a while. It loses its allure over time," he said.

Fortunately, our getting-to-know-you session was cut short when he was summoned by the efficient hotel-management major working the registration desk.

"Good luck, ladies. I'll see you around," he said over his shoulder as he trotted off.

"Hilda?" I hissed once he was out of earshot.

"You don't make up a name, I'm gonna make one up for you."

I gave her an eye roll and then refocused on the quartet in the bar, trying to figure out how we could get close enough to hear them without raising their suspicions.

"I'll get us some supplies," I said to Tuwanda and then hurried back to the ladies room, nodding to the hair-wrap guy as I passed him.

Fortunately, the hotel staff had restocked the paper towels after I'd used up the last batch to dry my pants. I unrolled a stack of them. Before leaving, I checked the third stall on the off chance my pants were still there. An *Out of Order* sign was hanging from the closed stall door, but all it took was a hard push with my hip to open it. My pants were gone, but a skirt and purse lay on the floor next to the toilet.

The hair-wrap guy looked up hopefully as I left the bathroom. I took pity on him.

"There's no one in there," I said.

Chapter Twenty-Three

I thrust half the paper towels at Tuwanda when I reached her and directed her to "dust."

I casually worked my way toward the bar area, dusting, straightening, and picking up imaginary pieces of trash (the hotel was disappointingly immaculate). I took special care to dust and buff a brass lamp sitting on a table not far from where the men sat. Out of the corner of my eye, I saw Tuwanda approaching from the other direction. She stopped to polish the heck out of the intricately carved wood legs of a banquette.

"You don't have any creds in this business," said Joey. "I do. You assign us 50 percent of the rights to your story, Dick calls *Bottom Feeders* and tells him the deal is off because Dick and I have an ownership interest, and then I make a few calls and start a bidding war that will get you top price."

"I'd rather give it away than give you a piece of the profit," growled Milton.

"What have we ever done to you?" asked Dick. "I'm offended."

"Then be offended," said Milton bitterly. "You wouldn't let us get near Muffy after Glad died. You treated us like trash. And Joey here ain't done nothin' for us ever. If we got any work, it was because of Glad."

Dick leaned into Milton's face. All pretexts of blossoming friendship flew out the window. "What the hell could you have done for Muffy? The way I understand it, you've been mooching off her for years. What were you gonna do—offer her the chance to support you permanently?"

"He's got a right to see his wife, you dick, Dick," said Lenny, not wanting to be left out of what was building up to be one doozy of an argument.

Everyone became quiet, and the three who were not Lenny stared at him open-mouthed.

Milton spoke first. "Why the hell did you tell him that, Lenny?"

"You're Muffy's husband?" asked Dick exhibiting the level of horror of someone learning that the person seated next to him on a twelve-hour flight has swine flu.

"Yes, I guess so," admitted Milton. "At least we never got around to a divorce that I know of."

As far as I was concerned this left the issue open; I got

the feeling Milton was fuzzy about the last twenty years, and the twenty years before that were iffy too.

"Do you even remember *when* you were married?" asked Joey, echoing my thoughts.

"I think I told you enough already," said Milton. "And we ain't changin' our minds about not hiring you guys as our agents."

Lenny grunted his concurrence.

Milton stood to leave, and Lenny followed his lead.

"To tell you the truth," said Milton, "I feel dirty just talkin' to the two of you. Two young women are dead— Glad and Che Che—and I ain't picked up on a smidgen of sadness from either of you. I'd think you, Joey, knowin' them as long as you did, would feel somethin'. You're just a damn user."

Joey jumped to his feet and punched Lenny in the stomach, which hardly seemed fair since Milton was the one who had spoken.

"I made Gladys into a superstar. Without me she would have been nothing, and Che Che would have been less than nothing. Gladys wasn't strong enough to make in on her own, and Che Che's only function was to supply Gladys with drugs, but not until she took a hefty share for personal use. I'm surprised those two lasted as long as they did."

Milton launched himself at Joey's throat. "Why don't you tell us all who got them hooked on that shit?"

Joey flailed at Milton and attempted a snappy retort that came out like a croak.

Dick came to Joey's rescue after an unduly long period of consideration, but Lenny cut the rescue effort short with a well-placed punch to Dick's temple.

I was so fascinated with the fight that I didn't notice Mark until he launched himself into the vortex of the action and emerged holding Milton and Joey by the scruffs of their respective necks. I caught Tuwanda's attention and gave her a let's-get-out-of-here head jerk. She shook her head slightly and stared appreciatively at Mark, who had changed into shorts and a tight T-shirt since we'd seen him last.

Chapter Twenty-Four

"Why don't you gentlemen go back to your rooms?" said Mark, sounding like the sheriff of Dodge.

Dan appeared on the scene now that everything was under control and offered to escort Milton and Lenny to their room.

Lenny ratted out Dick as to the fact that Dick was not a hotel guest, so Mark escorted the latter to the hotel entrance. Tuwanda started to follow Mark, but Dan called out and asked that we see Joey to his room. Since he used our most recent names—Rose and Hilda—and, as is bound to happen when you have too many aliases, neither Tuwanda nor I recognized us, he had to repeat himself before we responded.

"We really should finish our dusting," I said. "We'll have hell to pay if we don't finish by the end of our shift."

"Don't worry. I'll explain what happened to anyone who needs to know," said Dan. "Now please escort this man to his room. I doubt he will give you any trouble."

I was pretty sure Dan was wrong, especially when Joey realized who we were.

Keeping my head down, I gestured for Joey to take the lead. It was a good thing he was too occupied massaging his throat and testing his vocal chords to take much notice of us. Regrettably, he regained the ability to form words and sentences as we neared his casita and made the most of it.

"I'm going to sue those assholes, the hotel, and that muscle-bound cretin."

You mean the muscle-bound cretin who saved your life? I thought disgustedly. I figured Joey was mad because Mark made him look like a wimp. Whoever said, "Vanity thy name is woman," hadn't met the Guido generation.

Fortunately, hotel employees were invisible to people like Joey, so he continued to pay us little attention.

We waited politely for him to open the door to his room as he continued to list potential defendants in his lawsuit. (Starbucks? Really? Because they threw his day out of sync by screwing up his double-latte order?)

He dropped his key card as the door swung open, and we all went down at the same time to retrieve it. A collision ensued.

"Damn," yelped Tuwanda, placing a hand over her injured forehead.

"God dammit to hell," yelped Joey, not to be outdone.

My problem was more serious; my hat fell off when I cracked heads with the other two. I scrambled to get it, but only succeeded in kicking it under a prickly pear cactus. As I tried to retrieve the cap, a delicate operation requiring a steady hand, Joey cried out, "You!"

The jig was up.

He yelled for a security guard and was revving up for another try when Tuwanda grabbed his arm and gave a twist. She placed her free hand over his mouth and frog-marched him into the cottage. I followed, closing the door behind us.

Giving him a shake, she said, "I ain't gonna take my hand away unless you promise you ain't gonna scream."

He nodded his head yes.

"Now if you lyin', I'm gonna call a security guard myself an' tell 'em you tried to molest me an' my friend, an' we took offense. It's gonna be your word against ours."

Joey cast us a narrow-eyed "you wouldn't dare" look.

"Just try us," said Tuwanda through gritted teeth.

After a few beats, Joey shrugged and nodded again.

"Why are you two following me?" he hissed as soon as Tuwanda released him.

"Don't get all conceited. We followin' lots of people besides you," said Tuwanda.

"Why?" he insisted.

I fielded that one. "Because a young woman is dead and you tried to finger me for her murder."

"Finger you? Who are you, Sam Spade?"

"You know what I mean," I said defensively. The fact that I adored Sam Spade was none of his business. "We want to find out who killed her."

"Well, I certainly don't kn—wait a minute, are you trying to scoop the police so you can make a bundle on the deal?"

I wound up to deliver a detailed description of what an asshole he was, but Tuwanda stopped me with a slight shake of her head.

"Maybe," said Tuwanda.

Joey clapped his hands. "Brilliant. Absolutely brilliant. What do we do next?"

Things had taken an unexpected turn. Our main primary suspect wanted to go into business with us.

"Why do we need you? We been doin' jus' fine detectin' on our own," said Tuwanda suspiciously.

Joey launched into much the same presentation he and Dick had delivered to Milton and Lenny.

"So, how much do you get out of the deal for settin' up this biddin' war thing?" asked Tuwanda.

"The standard agent's fee; 20 percent of the proceeds."

That sounded high to me. "I was thinking more in the neighborhood of 3 percent," I said.

"What if, in addition to my negotiating services, I help you find out who the bad guy is?" countered Joey.

"I don't see how you gonna be much help. What's to keep you from sellin' information you get and cuttin' us out?"

"We'll put it in writing. If I screw you, you can sue me, and vice versa. Hell, Kate, according to the newspaper you're an attorney. You should know how this stuff works."

My contracts professor had drilled into our heads that a contract is only as good as the parties signing it. Applying this principle to the present circumstances, any agreement with Joey was worthless.

"What about Dick? Isn't he your partner?" I asked.

"Dick is a *noodge*. He tried to cut me out of his deal with Muffy. We keep him out of this deal."

I pretended to give it some thought.

"Then let's get started," I said. "Get me a pen and some paper."

I wrote the agreement on hotel stationary, which was a step up from a cocktail napkin.

I wandered around the room while Tuwanda and Joey read the agreement and noticed that Joey had a pile of correspondence from media companies, including several contracts for exclusive interviews. Business was good for Joey.

Joey made a few minor modifications to the agreement. We signed it and then got down to business.

"What have you found out so far?" asked Joey.

"You first," said Tuwanda.

"How about we trade information item by item? So you tell us something and then we tell you something," I suggested.

Tuwanda and Joey murmured their consent. The ground rules having been established, Joey made his first offering.

"Dick was at the hotel the morning Queen Ta Ta died," he said.

"I thought he went home with Muffy?" I asked, surprised.

"He did. But he came back about one in the morning to see me."

"How long were you with him?" I asked.

"I don't know. When I woke up at five a.m., he was gone. I can only alibi him from one to two. I fell asleep after that. And in case you're wondering, I didn't leave my room until six, *after* I saw Queen Ta Ta lying on the path with you leaning over her. One of the housekeepers vouched for me to the police.

"Now it's your turn."

"Queen Ta Ta used drugs," I said.

"Duh. That doesn't count," scoffed Joey. "Everyone knows that."

"Do you know what drugs were found in her system after she died?"

I thought I saw a flash of fear in his eyes. He recovered

quickly, though, and the trademark Joey smirk was back in place. "You'd have to have access to the toxicology report to know that, and after the leak of the initial autopsy report, the police clamped down big time. I've heard only two members of law enforcement have access to the evidence in the case."

Three, actually. I thought. *And Bryan is one of them.* I suddenly realized the importance of being nice to Bryan.

"I have connections," I simply said.

"She got *lotsa* connections," emphasized Tuwanda. "She so connected she like a substation."

"A what?" asked Joey.

"A substation. You know, them places where all the electrical lines go into."

"I'm not sure that's an apt simile," commented Joey. "I think those are electrical boosters, so it only works if she embellishes the information as it goes through. I'd compare her to a power strip, maybe."

"I feel like I'm in a creative writing class," grumbled Tuwanda.

"You feel 'as if' you were in a creative writing class, you mean," corrected Joey.

"Cut that out or you gonna feel like you in a wrestlin' class," said Tuwanda.

"Stop it, you two," I interjected. "You're wasting time. The police are on this case twenty-four-seven. We've got to get moving if we're going to beat them to the punch."

"So get me a copy of the toxicology report," said Joey. "Until then, I don't have an obligation to tell you anything more."

"She had a lot of drugs in her system. Did they come from you?" I asked.

"What the hell? That's not a question; that's an accusation," said Joey indignantly.

"Why you so big on semantics?" asked Tuwanda. "A clue is a clue. Don't matter if it's incriminatin'. I don't remember our agreement excludin' anything incriminatin'."

"I didn't give Queen Ta Ta any drugs," he said.

"Did you *sell* them to her?" I asked. Don't ever engage a lawyer in a game of semantics. We live for that stuff.

Joey's silence was as good as a yes.

I continued to press. "Isn't that how you first met Gladys? You sold drugs to the kids in your hometown high school."

"It's not as if I was the big bad dealer introducing young innocents to the world of drugs. Both Che Che and Gladys were into the stuff way before I came along."

"What 'stuff' did they use?" I asked, remembering that most of the drugs in her system were prescription.

"Meth. That's it, as far as I know."

"Was she still using meth?" I asked.

"I don't know. You're the one with the toxicology report. You tell me," snapped Joey. "All I know is that Queen Ta Ta made enough money to buy whatever she wanted. Meth is a cheap street drug. Maybe she upgraded to something classier, like cocaine."

"I thought you two were close. You were her manager. Wouldn't you know something like that?" I asked.

Joey looked at me suspiciously. "Why are you so interested in what drugs she used, anyway? She didn't OD; she was strangled."

The police had done a good job of keeping that piece of information out from the press.

I thought fast. "It could be relevant if the person who strangled her is the one who gave her the drugs."

Joey appeared to consider this possibility and nodded. "I see your point, but so far as I know, Che Che was her only supplier—except for the occasional gifts from fans—and Che Che was on the way back to Tucson when Queen Ta Ta died; or so says Muffy."

I went in with another question since Joey seemed to have lost count. "Did Queen Ta Ta leave with anyone after her birthday party?"

"How did you know about the party? It was supposed to be hush-hush. Queen Ta Ta didn't want to make a big deal of her age. Most of her fans are tweens, and twenty-four is ancient to them."

Wow. Over the hill at twenty-four. In tween years, I'd qualify for Willard Scott's birthday segment.

"One of the hotel staff members mentioned it to me," I lied.

"I didn't see her leave with anyone. I did see her get into a real pissing match with Muffy, though."

"What about?"

"Dick talked Muffy into writing a book about her daughter, offering his services as book agent, of course. The working title was something like *How to Raise a Rock Star*. From what I know about Muffy's child-raising skills, it would be a short book: 'Ignore your kid, stay drunk, and bring a different man home every night.' That about covers it."

"Was Queen Ta Ta afraid her mother would write a tell-all that put her in a bad light?" I asked.

"Hah. Hardly. Queen Ta Ta thrived on being weird both on and off stage. She adored any sort of scandal."

"Maybe she was afraid her mom would say she had a normal childhood," commented Tuwanda.

Joey laughed. "That would be great; like it turns out the queen of weird was a young Republican and head of the church youth group." Then he sobered. "Actually, they were arguing over royalties. Muffy wasn't going to give Queen Ta Ta a percentage even though her daughter's star power was the only reason the book would sell. As Queen Ta Ta put it—loudly, I might add—she became famous 'in spite of' her mother, not because of her."

"But Queen Ta Ta was worth millions. Why would she care about book royalties? It's not like her fans are big readers. I doubt the book would make much money," I said.

"You can bet the book is going to make a lot now that she's dead, though," said Tuwanda. "It's like when a artist dies; his paintings is all of a sudden worth more. Same thing with biographies. If a guy is still around to answer questions it ain't as good as when he's gone an' writers can make things up. I always think people seem smarter after they dead. It's like once you die it's easier to figure out what your life was about. Before you're dead the point ain't clear."

"Is your friend a heavy drinker?" asked Joey.

He should talk. "She's got a point. Let's look at who would benefit the most from Queen Ta Ta's death."

"Queen Ta Ta," answered Joey promptly. "Michael Jackson made more after …"

"I know, I know," I interrupted. I didn't want to hear about the financial genius of Michael Jackson's corpse any more.

"But a scheme like that would be too weird, even for her," continued Joey. "I mean, once you're dead …"

"Who did she leave her estate to?" I interrupted, trying to focus on rational conjecture.

"I don't know," he said. "What I do know is that Queen Ta Ta was convinced she'd die young and dramatically, which would add value to an already valuable commodity: her life story. She made a game of changing the beneficiary to whoever was most pleasing to her at the moment. At one point it was a chimpanzee named Daisy she used in her music video for 'High Strung Bitch.'"

Against my will I was intrigued. "What did Daisy do in the video?"

"Queen Ta Ta refused to bring in a trained chimp because she wanted what she called 'raw, animal emotion.' Daisy was the pet of a friend who had kind of a Montessori approach to chimp raising: she encouraged Daisy to discover and develop her inner strengths, and those strengths were making and throwing poop.

"For the first twenty or so takes, she threw ape shit on the stage. We had dancers sliding all over."

"And Queen Ta Ta made this chimp her primary beneficiary?" I asked.

"More like her primate beneficiary," guffawed Joey.

I groaned, which was all that joke deserved.

"She claimed she bonded with the chimp on a very primal level. None of us wanted to know what she meant by that," said Joey with a wry twist of his mouth.

"Could Daisy still be the beneficiary?"

"Daisy was killed in an unfortunate water-skiing accident less than a week ago. According to Dick, that means Queen Ta Ta died intestate, and by statute, Muffy's the sole beneficiary."

I thought the timing of Daisy's death was suspicious. *Was she a victim of foul play?*

"I'm surprised she didn't name you as beneficiary," I needled. "After all, you were her manager and she'd known you a while."

"Queen Ta Ta needed to control everyone around her,

but I couldn't be controlled. She found that out when I took up with Che Che without her permission."

"She ran your personal life?" I asked.

"No, she *tried*. She had more success with Che Che. She fired Che Che because of our relationship. Che Che was about to cut if off with me to get back into Queen Ta Ta's good graces. But then Queen Ta Ta died; they both did."

I noticed Joey's voice held no sign of regret or bitterness. It was as if he was discussing a business deal gone bad.

"I consider myself to be an expert in relationships, especially superficial ones," said Tuwanda, "and it seems to me you play on both teams at the same time. Maybe *that's* why Che Che wanted to break up with you. Most women don't like it when whoever walks in the room is potential competition."

"You mean Dick? There's nothing serious going on between us. I just toy with him once in a while to soften him up. It's a negotiating tool.

"Anyway, Che Che was no innocent either. She and I both had relationships with Queen Ta Ta before we got together, and Daisy was no casual bystander either."

I have always prided myself on being open minded. But by now my "open mind" was screaming, *Ick, ick, ick ick*, and I was playing whack-a-mole with the picture pop-ups in my head.

"Do you think her impending breakup with you was the reason Che Che killed herself?"

Joey shook his head and barked a cynic's laugh. "I doubt it. I can't think of anything that would make Che Che kill herself. Che Che was as self-involved as Queen Ta Ta. She didn't do anything unless there was something in it for her."

Joey suddenly turned pale underneath his tan, and the hand he raised to his brow was shaking.

"You doing okay, Joey?" I asked.

"I'm tired. Maybe we should wrap this up."

"Okay by me," said Tuwanda. "We gotta plan a strategy before we call it a night, though."

"We should talk to Muffy, Milton, and Lenny again," I said. "I also think we ought to take a trip to Tucson to talk to Che Che's parents. Che Che's suicide was too much of a coincidence. It's possible she was involved in the murder somehow and killed herself in remorse."

"Sounds good to me," said Joey with complete lack of enthusiasm. His excitement for our mutual project was waning.

"Tuwanda and I will take the Tucson trip," I said. To remind Joey that this was a joint endeavor, I added, "Your job is to keep an eye on Dick and find out anything he knows that you don't."

"Sure, sure. Whatever." Not a strong reassurance by any means. Joey was fading fast. He probably needed another hit of something.

"What about Muffy?" I asked.

"Won't talk to me. She hates me," said Joey. His

eyelids were drooping, and his body sagged in the chair. He would be comatose before we got out the door.

I didn't press the issue. Bryan would tell me anything Muffy said of interest during the police's follow-up interview.

Although our plans to team up with Joey were fake, I was irked that he was already proving to be worthless. But if everything went right, Muffy and Dick would join the fake team as another resource.

We left Joey nodding off on the couch and headed back to our casitas, too tired to rehash the events of the evening. But the night wasn't over for us.

Chapter Twenty-Five

"So who are you for real?" asked a masculine voice from close behind.

I turned around and was nose to nose with Mark.

"What do you mean?" I asked, trying to cover my surprise.

"The first time we met you were Lottie. Now you're a hotel employee," he pointed out, unfortunately, correctly.

How could he possibly know? No one else had recognized me in my Lottie getup.

Mark must have understood the question in my silence. "I'm a personal trainer. I watch how people move. You and Lottie move the same way, and your friend here moves like the person you introduced to me as Marge."

"I thought you were going home," I said, consistent with the theory that a good offense is a good defense.

He wasn't biting. "I told *Lottie* I was going home."

I groaned and looked at Tuwanda for help but was

dismayed to see that she seemed to be enjoying the exchange.

"Let's start again," said Mark. "Who are you?"

"I'm Kate Williams. I'm a local attorney."

Mark removed my hat and peered at me closely. "You're the jogger they thought killed Queen Ta Ta. Why did you do that lipstick thing on TV?"

"I thought it was ChapStick," I muttered, snatching my hat back.

"I get it. You want to figure out who killed Queen Ta Ta so you can get yourself off the hook." As soon as he said it he realized the defect in his reasoning. "But according to the paper you're not a suspect anymore. So why are you still spying on people?"

"She got no personal life," said Tuwanda. "This is kind of a hobby for her."

It saddened me how much truth there was to this.

"I can't explain it," I said. "I guess maybe I'm tired of hearing Queen Ta Ta's life reduced to a profit-loss statement, and I thought someone should care."

Mark gave Tuwanda an "is she for real?" look.

"She got this need to figure things out," provided Tuwanda. "This ain't nothin' compared to some of the other stuff she's done. If you got a spare hour or two I could go into it."

Mark looked at me thoughtfully for a few seconds and then said, "I figured you were like everyone else, trying to get a story to sell."

I shook my head. "No. In fact, I've lost money over this thing. I'll probably have to file bankruptcy after I get the hotel bill." Remembering the expensive Scotch Tuwanda and Joey charged to my account, I estimated that the bar tab alone would be close to a thousand dollars.

"What about you?" I asked. "Are you telling me you wouldn't jump on the gravy train if given the opportunity?"

"I never did understand that term, 'gravy train.' It sounds disgustin' to me," commented Tuwanda irrelevantly. "Think about it: train cars full of meat juice."

"She's tired," I explained.

"In answer to your question, no, I gave the police all the information I had, and I'm not writing a book or fishing for interviews. You can believe me or not; I don't care."

I sensed something in his tone, a sadness that indicated a personal involvement. "Did you know Queen Ta Ta?" I asked.

"I used to," he said. "Listen, it's getting late. Let's say I walk you two back to your rooms, which I assume are the same ones Marge and Lottie occupy."

I was not going to let the matter drop that easily. As I trotted to keep up with him, I continued to press. "What do mean you *used* to know her?"

Mark shook his head slightly. "I doubt it matters, but Queen Ta Ta and I went together for two years in high school."

"You?" I blurted out. I had a hard time picturing clean-cut Mark and a wild, rocker diva as a couple.

He laughed ruefully. "I know. Hard to picture, right?" he said, reading my mind. "It was different then. Gladys was captain of the cheer squad and I was the star quarterback. The high school handbook requires that people in those positions date."

Here was another challenge to my ability to visualize: Queen Ta Ta as a cheerleader? I wasn't too far off when I joked to Joey about Muffy threatening to write a tell-all about her daughter's normal childhood.

"She was funny, bright, energetic, kind—the perfect girlfriend. Then Joey entered the picture. She dropped cheer the second half of her junior year and dropped me not long after that. She started hanging around with Che Che and developed an attitude about school, Tucson, and middle-class life in general. Since Joey was a dealer and Che Che had been busted a couple of times for meth possession, we figured that Gladys had gotten into drugs. I hadn't spoken to her in five years."

"You ran into her at the hotel?" I asked.

"Yeah. At the pool. She pretended she didn't recognize me but later tracked me down at the gym. She said her manager and the local media were with her before, and every time she so much as said 'hi' to a man, the rumor mill started; by evening the tabloids would have us married, divorced, and locked in a dramatic custody battle over Daisy. Daisy is a …"

"I know who—or what—Daisy is," I interrupted. *Or rather was.* "What did you talk about after so many years?"

"I told her I did a four-year stint with the marines after high school, and my plan now was to work here long enough to save enough money to start my own personal training business. She didn't need to tell me what she'd been doing—anyone who breathes knows that."

Except, apparently, me.

"So I asked how she was handling all the fame," he continued. "She looked at me kind of weird and said, 'You think it's going to be wonderful, but it's not. The people around you write the story, and you become the story. You let go of the parts of you that don't fit the story, and that means letting go of people you care about. Then all of a sudden she got all narrow-eyed and suspicious-looking and said, 'You can quote me for cash, you know; maybe get that business of yours off the ground.' Like I was only using her. I cut the conversation short after that. I wished her good luck on her concert and walked away.

"She was so nice when I dated her in high school, but she'd become someone else, and not a nice someone else. Still, I felt sorry for her. She sure as hell didn't deserve to die."

We had dropped Tuwanda off at her room and were now standing in front of my casita. When he stepped into the halo of light from the porch lamp, I could see the strain and exhaustion on his face.

I felt a wave of sympathy for him and decided, perhaps too hastily, to recruit him as an ally.

Rushing my words, I said, "I'm not going to stop looking for Queen Ta Ta's murderer, you know." I explained that Tuwanda and I entered into a practical (as opposed to ideological) partnership with Joey and intended to do the same with Dick and Muffy. With all of them thinking they would scoop the police on solving the murder and sell the story for big dollars, we could access information not available to law enforcement.

"That sounds like a dangerous plan," said Mark. "What if they find out you're playing them against each other? I don't know Dick, but I know Joey and Muffy, and I wouldn't put it past either of them to use whatever means available, including violence, to get what they want."

Interesting: so maybe they weren't the nonviolent, albeit litigious, types Tuwanda thought they were.

"Does that mean you won't help?" I asked.

"Hell, no. It just means I have to beef up my medical coverage and maybe get a life insurance policy."

"Are you worried about leaving something for your wife and kids?" I asked.

"No. My parents. And Ralph, my Great Dane."

"No way. You have a dog named Ralph? *I* have a dog named Ralph."

We gaped at each other over this astounding coincidence.

"What kind of dog is your Ralph?" asked Mark, breaking the silence.

"I don't know." I said. "He's big and hairy, though. If shedding was an Olympic sport, he'd win gold."

I felt awkward, as though our joint revelations put us on new, personal ground.

"Well, I guess I should get some sleep," I said.

Mark nodded but did not move away. Instead, he brushed his hand against my cheek and said, "I was right. You do look better without makeup. In fact, you look beautiful."

My stomach and parts below shivered in delight.

"Um, would you like to come in for a while?" I asked and immediately gave myself a mental head slap for exhibiting the sophistication of a middle schooler. A second later, though, Mark had me in his arms, and after a few sweet, tentative kisses, we were tongue-exploring each other's throats.

I managed to get the door open (no mean feat when you're locked in a passionate embrace), and we left a trail of clothes to the bedroom as we competed to see who could get naked faster. (He won, by the way. I blame the extent and complexity of women's underwear for my loss.)

I could not account for Mark's explosive energy, but I had not been with anyone since Bryan and I broke up; think of a bottle of champagne carried cross-country in a pogo-stick jumper's backpack.

Chapter Twenty-Six

When I woke up the sun was shining through the window, Mark was snoring, Her was sitting on my stomach, and someone was knocking on the door.

I carefully moved Her onto Mark's stomach and then grabbed a hotel robe and headed for the front door, closing the bedroom door softly behind me.

I looked through the peephole as a precaution and saw Tuwanda standing in the hallway. She was fully dressed but looked as sleep deprived as I felt.

I barely had the door open when she pushed by me, muttering, "Coffee," and made a beeline to the coffee maker. She did not speak again until the brewing process was completed and she'd taken a few sips of liquid speed.

"Good for you."

"Why?" I asked as I poured myself a cup of coffee.

"You got some last night."

I looked toward the bedroom to see if Mark had emerged, but the door was still closed.

Tuwanda chuckled. "You forget; I'm a pro. You can blindfold me an' I still know what's what. So who's the lucky man?"

I felt a blush creep up my neck and cursed the pale skin inherited from my Scottish ancestors.

"Mark."

"Whoa, I take it back. *You* is the lucky one," said Tuwanda, clearly impressed. "That man is goooood lookin'. 'Course, that don't mean he's good."

"In this case it does," I said and wondered if excessive blushing could make your hair fall out.

Another knock sounded at the door.

"It's pro'bly the housekeepin' folks," said Tuwanda. "It's already ten, an' they need to get the room cleaned."

"Well, they'll have to wait a little longer," I said, going to the door. "Checkout isn't until noon, and I'm going to take advantage of my last two hours of luxury."

But it wasn't housekeeping. It was Bryan.

My first reactions were panic and guilt, but then the part of my brain still capable of rational thought pointed out that, after all, Bryan had dumped me and hadn't even waited until the official announcement before moving on.

I needn't have been concerned about his reaction, though, because he was preoccupied with news of his own.

"Dick's dead," he said.

"How? When?" I asked, shocked and saddened despite the fact that Dick was not one of my favorite people.

"Ax. We won't know the time of death until the postmortem, but his secretary discovered his body in his office early this morning."

"Ax?"

"Yes, ax, as in the implement used to fell large trees," he confirmed. "We want you two out of the investigation. It's too dangerous."

"Why? Do you think his death is related to Queen Ta Ta's?" I asked. "I mean, I don't know for sure, but based on Dick's personality and his business methods, I think he had more than a few enemies."

"According to his secretary, since Queen Ta Ta's death, he's been tending to her estate's business twenty-four-seven. His most recent project was negotiating a percentage of tickets and T-shirt sales in connection with memorial services, street dances, and barbecues occurring simultaneously in London, Paris, Moscow, Berlin, Tokyo, Los Angeles, and New York. They've already sold millions of tickets."

"Do you got any suspects?" asked Tuwanda.

"We just picked up Joey, Milton, and Lenny for questioning. According to one of the bellhops, the four of them were involved in a fight in the hotel lobby last night. We're also looking for three hotel employees—two janitors and a personal trainer—who witnessed the fight."

I looked nervously at Tuwanda, who gave me a slight nod.

"Tuwanda and I were the janitors," I confessed.

His expression reflected surprise and then acceptance in rapid succession. "Do you even know how to be Kate anymore? Compared to you, Sybil was normal. I think she only had sixteen personalities."

"That's not fair!" I said. "Disguises are an important investigative tool."

"That's the problem, Kate; you're not an investigator," countered Bryan.

"Sometimes I am," I sputtered. "People can have more than one occupation."

"I hate to interrupt what for you two is a fascinatin' conversation an' is not at all interestin' to me," interjected Tuwanda, "but, Sheriff, do you wanta hear what we found out last night or not?"

Mark chose this moment to make his entrance wearing only a towel wrapped around his waist. If he was surprised at the size of the crowd in my hotel room, he didn't let on. "Good morning … Tuwanda, isn't it?"

"Hey, Mark," said Tuwanda.

He then extended his hand to Bryan and reintroduced himself. "I believe I met you yesterday here in Lottie-Kate's room."

Bryan shook Mark's hand woodenly but said nothing. He looked like he could have used a couple of Xanax.

"Mark also witnessed the fight last night. In fact,

he was the one who broke it up," I offered, hoping Mark's witness status would somehow make things less awkward.

Bryan remained unresponsive, so I pulled Mark off to the side, poured him a cup of coffee, and suggested that he put on a robe.

"No problem," he said, kissing me on the nose before returning to the bedroom.

Bryan glared at me. "How old is that guy?" The way he said it made it more an accusation than a question.

"I don't know; twenty-four? Twenty-five?" I guessed. "He went to school with Queen Ta Ta, so they're probably about the same age."

"I'm taking you all down to the station," said Bryan.

"Why?" I asked. "We'll tell you everything. You don't need to use intimidation to make us talk." Mark re-emerged from the bedroom wearing one of the hotel robes. "What's going on?" he asked.

"Get your clothes on, pretty boy," snarled Bryan, sucking in his stomach and placing a hand on his gun holster. "We're all going down to the station."

Mark looked at me. "Pretty boy? Is this guy for real?"

"I'm standing right here, buddy," said Bryan through clenched teeth. "If you've got something to say, say it to me."

Mark stepped toward Bryan and pushed his face into his. "Who writes your dialogue? John Hughes?"

"Who's that?" asked Tuwanda.

"He directed a bunch of teen movies in the eighties," I provided. "Did you ever see *The Breakfast Club*? That was one of his."

"Damn, I love that movie. But I woulda' said he talks more like that guy in them old *Dragnet* shows. He was always sayin' shit like, 'You goin' downtown.'"

The sheriff had clearly lost control of his audience and the conversation.

"All of you—get dressed. You're going downtown," barked Bryan.

"I'm already dressed," Tuwanda pointed out. "Do you want me to change?"

"No. I meant these two," he said, jabbing his finger toward me and Mark.

I shrugged and bent down to pick Mark's trousers up off the floor.

"Don't touch those," ordered Bryan. "They could be evidence."

Things were definitely getting weird.

"You, Mike ..." Bryan continued.

"Mark," corrected Mark.

"Pick up your clothes and get dressed."

Mark, probably realizing that he was not dealing with a mentally stable person, picked up his clothes without comment, and we headed for the bedroom.

"Kate, get your things and change in another room.

And don't let him touch you … I mean your clothes," ordered Bryan.

Tuwanda followed me into the bedroom to help me collect my clothes. Once we were out of earshot, she side-whispered, "Ain't none of that sounded like cop-talk. He so jealous he ain't makin' any damn sense."

"He's not jealous," I whispered back. "He's a domineering asshole."

"There is some of that goin' on too," said Tuwanda nodding thoughtfully. "But I still say most of it's because Mr. America was in your bedroom."

Mark and I got dressed—in separate rooms—and then we all reconvened in the sitting room for transport instructions. Bryan was on his cell phone requesting another car for Mark. Apparently, he wasn't going to let us sit in the same vehicle either.

I made a bold decision.

Chapter Twenty-Seven

"I want to talk to Webber," I said, a request falling somewhere between desperation and suicidal impulse.

Bryan, his jaw set in bulldog mode, looked like he was going to refuse, but then an expression of pure evil flashed across his face. "Certainly, Ms. Williams, if that is what you want. I feel compelled to warn you, though, that Detective Webber has been under a great deal of pressure lately and is noticeably more irate than usual."

That was like saying an atomic bomb was more explosive than usual.

I hesitated, thinking that perhaps I was making a mistake, but then Bryan made a nasty remark to Mark about steroid use, and I repeated my request to speak to Webber.

Bryan punched a number in his cell with unnecessary force. I couldn't hear the other side of the conversation but did pick up sounds evidencing annoyance, disbelief, and then annoyance again as Bryan conveyed my request.

"He's agreed to meet with you," announced Bryan, snapping his phone shut. "Tuwanda, Marky-Mark, you come with me. Webber is sending a police car for you, Kate. Do not leave this room until it arrives. I've already notified hotel security, so don't expect to make it past the lobby without a police escort."

Bryan marched Mark and Tuwanda out the door. I sat down with another cup of coffee and tried to think through what was happening. Queen Ta Ta, Dick, and Che Che were dead. Why? It didn't make any sense. And now Bryan's injured ego was getting in the way of my investigation.

I slipped out the door and, staying in the shadow of a covered walk, made it to the reception area. Bryan probably lied about hotel security being on high alert, because I spotted nary a one of the Bermuda-shorts-clad guards.

Dan was not on duty, but another young man in hotel khakis and golf shirt helpfully summoned a taxi for me and deposited me in the backseat.

The driver, whose posted permit identified him as Hamid Naviti, asked me where I wanted to go. Without giving the matter the thoughtful consideration it deserved, I said, "Tucson."

Hamid turned to study me. Apparently he decided I was both sober and sincere and in a heavily accented voice agreed to take me to Tucson, with the caveat that he would need to charge me for a round trip.

"That's fine with me, because you're taking me back too," I said.

"You have to buy me lunch then, and you gotta pay me for the time I wait for you in Tucson. If it is a long time, you will also pay for a movie and snacks."

"What, no clothing allowance?" I asked sarcastically.

"You pay for that however much you think is right," he answered seriously. "Enough money for shoes is usual. I will charge you only half fare for cat."

"Cat? What cat. I ..." I stopped in midsentence when I realized that Her was curled up next to me.

I thought of taking issue with Hamid's billing practices, but then a squad car pulled up under the porte-cochere next to us. I ducked down in the backseat and told Hamid to get moving.

"Passengers running from police must pay additional 10 percent of fare and must pay all lawyer fees if I am arrested," said Hamid.

"Fine. Move!" I ordered. It's not like I had a strong negotiating position.

Hamid complied, and we took off down the road at a fairly good clip. When I voiced a concern that we might be stopped by the police for speeding, Hamid replied, "I go five miles over limit. Police never stop you for five miles over limit. Now stay down. Guidelines require that you stay down until we are outside city limits."

"Guidelines?"

"Yes. I was driver in Iraq where escape requests are common. The other drivers and I came up with a list of passenger guidelines to increase efficiency and cut down on hysteria. It is hard enough to drive under such circumstances without someone screaming in your ear.

"Here; I have copy."

He tossed a sheet of paper into the backseat. Sure enough, it was a typed list of dos and don'ts for the *passenger on the go*. Except for the prohibition against firing automatic weapons inside the vehicle, I found its content helpful. Per instructions, I snuggled closer to the floor and avoided making sounds that might distract the driver. Her remained comfortably situated on the seat.

When the car accelerated and maintained a steady speed, I knew we had made it to the freeway. Still, I waited until Hamid gave me the all clear before sitting up (Rule Four).

We passed the airport and shot diagonally across three crowded lanes of traffic to make the I-10 exit. I had to hand it to Hamid; he knew his stuff.

"How long were you in Iraq?" I asked conversationally.

"All my life, until last year. A captain in your army helped me get a visa because many people wanted me dead."

"Because you were a driver for the Americans?"

"Partly that and partly because I was member of

Saddam Hussein's regime before the occupation, and after that I worked for the Sons of Iraq, a pro-American anti-insurgency group. There may have been a couple of weeks where I worked for an oil company. It's hard to know. Things change very fast there."

"Do you favor any particular ideology?"

"My ideology is survival. Most Iraqis are fervent believers in survival."

"It must be a relief living here," I said.

"I like that you have no IEDs in your roadways. It takes the edge off driving. But you have different problems here. I watch the reality TV shows, and it is terrible how people—even women and children—treat each other. Everyone is angry."

"It's still better than daily gun battles," I pointed out.

"I don't know; sometimes quick death is preferable to such rudeness and anger."

I hoped the Iraqis never got around to producing reality shows.

We drove in silence down I-10 South, which, according to the general consensus, is the dullest stretch of highway in the country. The temptation to speed and get it over with quickly is held in check by roaming hordes of highway patrolmen with low job satisfaction.

When we were near the outskirts of Tucson, Hamid asked if I had an address more specific than "Tucson" for where we were going. Sadly, I did not. I knew where

Gladys's childhood home was, and I assumed that Che Che's parents lived in the same area, but that wasn't the level of specificity Hamid was looking for. I texted MJ to find out if she had an address for Che Che; she texted back immediately with Che Che's real name, Rosario Herrera, and the names and address of her mother and stepfather, Isabel and Renaldo Ramirez. She also ordered me to dispose of my phone immediately because the police were looking for me and could triangulate my location based on the signal. I had no idea what that meant, but I tossed my phone out the window anyway.

I'd recognized Ramirez as one of the names on the contact list of Joey's phone.

"You should not have kept your phone so long," commented Hamid.

"Maybe you should add mobile phone disposal to your passenger guidelines," I grumbled.

"That is good suggestion. Here," he said, handing me a pencil. "Please add."

I gave Che Che's address to Hamid and then went about supplementing the guidelines. In addition to mobile phone disposal, I added my own helpful hints: avoid facial expressions resembling Munch's *The Scream* that might tip off other drivers or scare their kids; no hymn singing; and don't hyperventilate or hold your breath—keep it somewhere in the middle.

It took us another forty-five minutes to negotiate Tucson's interminable road construction zones (during which time Hamid voiced a preference for IEDs) and find the right exit. Another twenty minutes later, we turned into a subdivision with row upon row of identical beige stucco homes with gravel, postage-stamp-sized front yards. The only break in the monotonous landscape was an occasional dispirited palo verde. Although the subdivision couldn't have been more than a few years old, cracked pavement, curbs, and driveways indicated lack of enthusiasm or concern on either the part of the developer or the homeowners' association. The ambiance was one of decay and failure.

"There it is. It's the next one on the right," I said.

"The beige house?" asked Hamid, rolling his eyes in the rearview mirror.

"Funny. Are you going to wait here for me? This shouldn't take long. They may not even be home."

Hamid pointedly looked at his watch. "It is after lunchtime already. I will only wait half an hour. Then we eat. Also, you pay extra fifteen dollars for pet-sitting," he said, head jerking toward Her.

I didn't see how it could take longer than a half an hour, so I agreed.

Chapter Twenty-Eight

The doorbell was at the end of a long wire hanging out of a hole next to the door. I bent down and picked it up and then noticed that the button was missing.

I knocked on the door and dislodged a couple of patches of peeling paint. I was trying to plaster them back on the door with spit when the door opened. A stout woman stared warily at me from the dark interior of the house.

"What you want?" she asked in low, sandpapery voice.

"I am a friend of your daughter," I lied without batting an eye. "I heard she passed away. I was, er, in the area and wanted to offer my condolences."

The woman looked over my shoulder at Hamid, who had gotten out of the car for a cigarette.

"That's my driver, Hamid."

She shook her head slowly, and I thought she was

going to turn me away. But then she stepped back to let me in.

Inside, I was enveloped by the smell of stale and fresh cigarette smoke, and when the door closed behind me the house's interior darkened yet more. Thin lines of daylight at the edges of the windows indicated blackout shutters. Due to the poor economy and high energy costs, these window coverings had become popular.

She turned on a table lamp that emitted the soft white glow of an energy-efficient bulb and gestured for me to take a seat on a plastic-covered couch of indeterminate color. The introduction of light had the unfortunate effect of showcasing her enlarged pores, blackheads, and broken capillaries. She sat across from me in a gold-upholstered La-Z-Boy that looked as if it had passed the lazy stage and into the dead and decaying stage.

"You're a reporter," she said. "How much will you pay?"

Oh, for crying out loud.

I tried to look offended, doing that movie-thing where the offendee places her hand over her throat and performs a short intake of breath.

"We don't accept checks. Only cash and Visa," she said, obviously unimpressed with my performance. "You would be surprised how many people cheat you in this business."

What business? Talking about your dead child is a business?

"Just this week a friend of mine got a check for twenty thousand dollars for her story, and it bounced," she continued.

I thought I knew whom she was referring to.

I decided to drop the act and play along, figuring that even if I convinced her that I was a grieving friend, she'd probably throw me out because the profit margin on grieving friends is thin. "I will not pay you anything until you tell me who you've talked to and what you've already said. Your information is worth very little unless it is exclusive."

She laughed unpleasantly, and I noticed that oral hygiene was not one of her priorities.

"You're in luck. I had a deal lined up, but then my representative got axed."

"Dick was your agent?" I asked in surprise.

"Yeah. I just got a call from his secretary about his passing. Bastard has fifty thousand dollars of my money."

"You mean he collected the money for your story but was holding it until you delivered the goods?"

"Of course. The buyer was supposed to come by today, but he called and said he got held up in Phoenix."

"Do you know the buyer's name?"

"Yeah. He's that little piece of shit Joey Perroni. He was pissed because we signed on with Dick, but I'm glad I did because I got a lot more money than if I'd dealt with Perroni directly. Or at least I was supposed to."

I thought it interesting that Joey hadn't mentioned anything about the Ramirezes last night. But I couldn't claim the high road either; I wasn't entirely forthcoming with him.

"Twenty-five thousand," I said, pulling out my billfold and handing her my Visa.

"That's half of what I was supposed to get from Perroni," she answered. She grabbed my card, though.

"Twenty-five thousand in your pocket is better than an offer ten times more from Perroni."

"You know him?" she asked.

"Yes. He's trying to horn in ahead of me on the Butoff interview."

"Muffy Butoff?"

"Yes. Do you know her?"

"Yeah, she's the one who got the bounced check. She didn't tell me she was talking to Joey."

"She was, but it's my understanding that Joey and Dick were working together."

"I didn't know that either. If Dick and Joey were partners, Joey probably made a low-ball offer for my information, and Dick, as my supposed agent, talked me into it. That way they could make profit on the resale. So what I got to sell is probably worth more than $50,000."

"Fine," I said, holding my hand out for my credit card. "Talk to Perroni then. You'll have to wait until the police are through with him, though, and there's a good chance he'll stay clear of Dick's deals until the police's murder investigation is over."

Mrs. Ramirez's eyes widened. "The police are talking to him? About Dick?"

"That's why he canceled your appointment this morning. I believe he's a person of interest in both Gladys's and Dick's deaths."

I let her mull over this new information and checked my watch. I didn't want to exceed my half-hour limit; I didn't want to be stuck in this house with Mrs. Ramirez until Hamid decided to come back from lunch.

After wasting three precious minutes mulling, she reached under the sofa and pulled out a manual credit card machine. She then opened the drawer of a small side table and found a blank credit card receipt and a pen. She hummed to herself as she made an imprint of my card and filled out the payment information.

She handed the pen and receipt to me.

"Sales tax?" I asked after scanning the receipt.

"Hey, I run a legit operation here. By the way, the tip is optional, but 20 percent is usual."

I gave her 15 percent. I found the service lacking.

After I signed, she checked the signature on the charge slip against that on my card and handed me my card and the carbon copy.

I kept the pen and found an AT&T bill in my replacement purse to write on.

"Please state your full name," I said.

"Isabel María Veracruz López Hidalgo García Hershowitz Mendoza Ramírez."

I wrote down "Isabel Ramirez" and fought the urge to waste precious minutes asking about the Hershowitz connection.

"Marital status?"

"Divorced."

The newspaper said the parents found Che Che's body.

"Was your divorce recent?" *As in yesterday?*

"No, but my ex-husband and I still live together."

"I understand you and your ex-husband found your daughter's body when you returned from a trip to Las Vegas."

"In the garage. Yes. The police told us it was carbon monoxide poisoning, but the car was not running and it had a half a tank of gas left. Maybe the car overheated and quit running, but I didn't smell any burning smells."

"Did your daughter leave a note?"

"No, but then she was never big on communication."

"Had she changed since you saw her last?"

"Yeah. She was dead."

"I mean, was she thinner or, assuming for a minute she wasn't dead, look ill?"

"She wasn't recognizable. You ever see a body after it's been sitting in a hot garage for three days?"

Not yet. But with my luck, it was only a matter of time.

"We knew it was her because of the hair—she always wore it long—and the bracelet she was wearing; it was the one we gave her for her *quinceañera*."

"Do you know if she and Gladys were getting along?"

"She talked about Gladys during her annual Christmas calls, but only to say how wonderful she was doing and how famous she was. She and Gladys were in love in high school. I'm not stupid; I know about these things."

"She never said anything about a breakup."

"I heard she and Joey were dating. I also heard Gladys fired her as her assistant."

Isabel shook her head adamantly. "She hated Joey. Joey tried to get between her and Gladys before. I think Joey made up that stuff about Rosario being fired and leaked it to the press. Maybe he hoped Rosario would hear about it and think it was true. My daughter was not a strong person. Something like that would destroy her."

"Do you think Che Che—er, Rosario—heard that Gladys was letting her go and took her own life?"

She shrugged. "It could be."

A knock sounded at the door. Isabel went to answer it and returned with Hamid, who had Her cradled in his arms.

"You are late for your luncheon engagement," he announced.

"Five more minutes," I said. "Then we will leave for El Norte."

El Norte was a five-star restaurant in the Catalina foothills in north Tucson. Hamid must have recognized the name, because he smiled broadly and sat on the couch next to me without complaint.

"Why do you have an Arab driver?" asked Isabel suspiciously.

"Do not worry," said Hamid. "We prefer high-profile targets, and I doubt anyone would notice if Tucson was missing."

Isabel accepted the sagacity of this reasoning with a thoughtful nod.

I continued with my questioning. "Isabel, were drugs found in your daughter's system?"

"Yes, but not in high levels. The drugs aren't what killed her."

"Did anyone in the neighborhood notice when she arrived at your house?" asked Hamid.

I looked at Hamid in surprise and annoyance, but Isabel neither questioned Hamid's knowledge about her daughter's death nor his right to take part in the interview.

"Our only neighbor lives at the end of the street, and he saw nothing. The other houses are empty, foreclosed on by the banks. We'll lose this house at the end of the month," continued Isabel. "The money you gave me today is all we have."

"Didn't you inherit anything from your daughter?" I asked.

"We don't know, and it will take too long to find out. A lawyer called us the day after we found Rosario's body and said that if Rosario died before Queen Ta Ta everything goes to Queen Ta Ta. If she died after, it goes to us."

"Why is that? Did she leave a will?" asked Hamid.

"I haven't seen it, but it must exist. How else could that happen?"

I could think of one way but didn't say anything.

I heard the front door open, and a rich, low voice called out, "Izzy! What's that cab doing out in front?"

"In here," Isabel yelled. Since the front door was less than five feet away, I thought yelling was excessive.

A handsome man with dark skin, crinkly blue eyes, and a thick mane of white hair brushed back from his forehead entered the room.

"My ex-husband, Renaldo," Isabel introduced.

"Hi. I'm Natalie Funkerhaus," I said. I was running out of names. "And this is Hamid Naviti."

Neither Hamid nor I extended our hands because Renaldo didn't have any, and that's something Miss Manners didn't address. In place of hands were metal devices with more attachments than a Swiss Army knife.

Feeling something was required, I gave him a little wave.

"They're here asking about Rosario. Natalie here paid

twenty-five thousand for an interview with me," explained Isabel.

Renaldo threw back his head contemptuously and said with bravado, "My interview will cost more. I have a contract with Joey Perroni for one hundred thousand dollars …"

Isabel reared back and let loose with a string of obscenities. "You lying bastard. You told me you never talked to Perroni. And what the hell; no way is your story worth more than mine. I know the same things you do."

I delivered the same speech I gave Isabel about the unlikelihood of Perroni making good on his agreement. Isabel, arms tightly crossed over her chest, chimed in every so often with a Greek chorus of "Uh-huhs" and "I told you sos."

"You pay me fifty thousand then," said Renaldo.

Negotiations were cut off when the front window shattered. Light streamed into the room through the shredded remains of the black-out shade.

I didn't see much more because Hamid pulled me onto the floor and lay on top of me.

Chapter Twenty-Nine

"Keep down!" he yelled unnecessarily. It's not like I had a choice—Hamid was a big man.

The bullets came faster. Sounds of glass shattering, wood splintering, and plaster falling filled the room. Ominously, there were no human noises, though; no calling out, screaming, or moaning. Nothing.

"We need to move to back of house," Hamid whispered loudly into my ear.

"What about Isabel and Renaldo?" I whispered back, a feat made difficult because my face was smashed against his chest.

"Dead," he stated bluntly.

I started to shake uncontrollably.

"I will crawl. Hold onto me like baby monkey holds on to its mother," ordered Hamid.

I did as I was told, throwing my legs and arms around Hamid's waist and neck, respectively. He crawled through the debris into a kitchen at the back of the house where he pried me off and deposited me on the floor.

"They will come to check the body count soon, so we must go quickly," he said.

"But they've seen the cab outside. They know someone was here with the Ramirezes. If they don't find another body they'll come looking for us."

"So you choose to wait here and be shot? You give up just like that? Your survival skills are very bad."

He belly-crawled to an arcadia door leading out to the back patio and, with my choices limited to die now or die soon, I followed close behind.

Just as he slid the door open the firing stopped. We got to our feet and ran like the very devil was after us. Hamid, despite his well-fed appearance, was fast, and he took the lead. We jumped the low walls dividing each backyard from the next as if we were Olympic hurdlers; adrenaline has that effect.

None of the houses looked inhabited, and abandoned swing sets and plastic toys from a happier time littered the yards. At one point Hamid stopped at a sandbox and filled his pockets with fistfuls of sand.

"Sand? You're picking up sand? They've got bullets," I said, breathing hard.

"You have poor attitude," he hissed back.

At the end of the block was a house showing signs of occupation. A neat vegetable garden filled half the small yard, and a barbecue smelled as if it had been used recently.

I heard yelling from the direction of the Ramirez house. Hamid grabbed one of the large river rocks used as a garden border and threw it into a sliding glass door. Neither of us worried about being met by a gun-wielding homeowner, because if anyone had been there, they would have called the police back when the shooting started.

Hamid reached through the broken door and opened it from the inside.

I got to the phone first and hit 9-1-1. I managed to explain the emergency and give the Ramirezes' address but drew a blank on my name. I looked at Hamid for help.

"Natalie Funkerhaus," he whispered.

I repeated my name for the benefit of the 9-1-1 operator and hung up.

"What is your real name?" asked Hamid.

I told him.

"In my car's glove box I have a list of aliases recommended for people on the lam. It is better to use a more common name, like Mary Smith. Easier to remember, and harder to trace."

"Have you ever thought of publishing a *How to …* guide?"

"As matter of fact, yes. I am working on the chapter about safe houses now. You would be surprised how many people underestimate the complexity and extent of the topic."

I heard voices outside and made a slicing motion across my throat to halt Hamid's enthusiastic lecture on the ins and outs of safe-house selection.

"Here!" someone yelled. "They're in here. The back door's busted open."

I fully expected a redux of the attack on the Ramirez house, but instead of a rapid-fire barrage of bullets, a man I had never seen before entered through the broken door, weapon raised.

Hamid shoved me under a dining table and approached the shooter with his hands held out to show he had no weapon.

"If you are selling something, I cannot afford it. If you are planning to rob me, go ahead; I have nothing to rob." This was true, since nothing in the house belonged to him.

"You live here?" the man asked. Without waiting for an answer, he raised the gun and said, "Why don't you fix your door?"

In one fluid motion, Hamid reached into his pockets and flung sand into the eyes of his would-be shooter, who managed to squeeze off a few shots that went wild before he dropped his weapon and clutched his eyes.

I heard running footsteps coming from the front of the house as Hamid dragged me out from under the table and pushed me outside. A second man, also a stranger, emerged and took dead aim at Hamid. I grabbed a river rock and hurled it at his head as the gun fired. Hamid and his shooter sank to the ground.

I didn't hear the sirens because I was on the ground with Hamid, simultaneously trying to stop the flow of blood from his chest and administer CPR.

The shooter and his sandy-eyed colleague recovered sufficiently enough to make their escape before the police burst in.

The EMTs arrived soon after that, and I stayed with Hamid until they loaded him into the ambulance.

"I have to go with him," I said to the officer assigned to making sure I didn't leave. "I'm the reason he got shot."

"I'm sorry, ma'am, but we need to interview you first," he said in cop-monotone.

"Here's an idea: why don't you find the guy who shot him first?"

"We have several cars looking for him right now, ma'am."

"Cars? Cars? How about sending some people?" My voice was high and squeaky, which is how it sounds when I am closing in fast on grand-mal hysteria.

"This will go a lot faster if you calm down, ma'am."

Another officer approached us. "Is she giving you problems, McCarthy?"

"No, sir. She's upset, and, under the circumstances, she should be."

I shot McCarthy a look of thanks.

"Why don't you get a box of Kleenex, McCarthy, and maybe dab her cheek while you hold her hand."

Who is this guy? Webber's Tucson twin?

Chapter Thirty

M cCarthy ignored the sarcasm and left, presumably to get the Kleenex.

I had to give McCarthy high grades for emotional control. I would have socked the asshole in the puss.

Realizing that I may still have that opportunity, I balled my hand into a fist.

"I know who you are, missy," said Officer Asshole.

"Then you have the advantage. I don't know who you are," I snapped.

"Officer Phillips, at your service. And you are the infamous Kate Williams. Every police department and sheriff's office in Arizona is looking for you."

He produced plastic cuffs and directed me to hold my hands behind me.

"Cuffs? You're kidding. I'm not the bad guy here," I protested.

"You have been identified by the Maricopa County sheriff's office as a flight risk, ma'am."

Damn Bryan.

I folded my arms stubbornly. "I'm not going anywhere until I find my cat. For all I know she could be dead." The lump in my throat, there since Hamid was shot, got bigger, and tears were not far off.

"Ma'am, make it easier on both of us and cooperate. I understand that you may be a bit hysterical under the circumstances, but you need to settle down so we can get this over with."

"I am not hysterical! I am angry! I know the difference—believe me. When I'm hysterical I throw up and …"

I proceeded to barf old coffee and bile on the front of his shirt.

"A little help here," yelled Phillips.

Officer McCarthy trotted in with a box of Kleenex and handed Phillips a wad of tissues. He and I watched Phillips scrub ineffectually at his shirt with disintegrating tissues. The front of his uniform looked like an exploded papier mâché project.

"Paper towels would have worked better, sir," commented McCarthy.

Another officer came over and handed Phillips a T-shirt. The crowd of onlookers had grown to three. We stood and watched as Phillips changed. Unfortunately, the T-shirt was a couple of sizes too small and did not quite cover his bulging gut. It was hard to take someone who looked this way seriously.

Phillips looked unhappy. "I'm going to take you to our southwest substation for questioning, Ms. Williams. Officer McCarthy will find you a paper bag, and if at any time you feel a bout of hysteria coming on, please use it."

I followed McCarthy to a squad car where, after scrounging under the front seat, he held a greasy fast-food bag out to me. I declined the offer because the smell of old fried food alone would induce barfing.

With McCarthy at the wheel, Phillips riding gunshot, and me sitting in the back behind a wire partition, we rode without speaking for about fifteen minutes until McCarthy pulled into a parking lot behind a squat, windowless, brick building that looked as if it was built by a kid whose parents wouldn't buy him the Lego expansion kit.

Phillips opened my door and ordered me to get out.

"What the hell!" he said, talking a step back. "Where did that come from?"

I looked in the direction he was staring and saw Her sitting on the floor of the backseat.

"My cat!" I lifted her into my arms and cuddled her, burying my face in her matted fur.

Phillips made a move toward me and held out his hands.

"She goes where I go," I said, moving Her outside the grab zone.

"But, where did she come from? I didn't see ..." Phillips's voice trailed off and he withdrew his hands. He probably realized that the matter wasn't worth pursuing.

The "complete lack of imagination" theme of the building's exterior was carried throughout its interior. The walls were painted off-white, and beige-specked, off-white linoleum covered the floor. Photographs depicting Tucson circa 1910 lined the walls except where they were interrupted by a hand-printed poster upon which was written, "Thought for the Day: Age kills more people than guns. Don't even the odds." Someone had crossed out "Don't," and so the message, already of ambiguous value, had a decidedly negative effect.

We passed a series of desks occupied by officers of both sexes busy at computer monitors. Each looked up as we walked by, and Phillips garnered wolf whistles from the female officers and guffaws from the male officers.

Phillips opened a door at the end of a short hall and gestured for me to go in. "Take a seat, Ms. Williams. McCarthy, bring us a couple of waters." He followed me into the room and waited for me to sit in a gray metal chair next to an equally unexciting gray metal table before he sat in an identical chair across from me. He stared at me wordlessly until McCarthy arrived and set bottles of water on the table. I opened mine, poured some into an empty ashtray for Her, and then drank thirstily. When

I was through I set the empty bottle on the table and thanked him.

McCarthy volunteered to bring more water, but Phillips ordered him to stay and take notes. Since there was a recorder on the table, I thought notes were redundant. Maybe it was just that Phillips didn't want to be alone with me. He was probably afraid I would throw up again and needed McCarthy to shield him.

After McCarthy got situated with pen and paper, I was subjected to another spate of Phillips's wordless staring. As interviewing techniques go, his was not effective.

A third man entered the room. He wore a gray, pinstriped business suit, a white shirt, and a red tie. Bland brown hair cut short and parted on the side, gray eyes, and a slightly pink complexion combined to create a completely forgettable visage. For me to be able to pick this guy out of a lineup the other participants would have to be black women.

He placed a nondescript briefcase on the floor and extended his hand. "Agent Kenneth Black, CIA."

Another man who could have been Kenneth's twin entered the room. Placing his identical nondescript briefcase next to Kenneth's, he introduced himself as Don Johanson, FBI.

Ken and Don then greeted each other, avoiding eye contact like acquaintances who didn't much care for each other.

McCarthy brought in two more folding chairs, and Ken and Don sat on either side of Phillips.

"Shall we get started, gentlemen?" asked Don.

"What about NSA?" said Phillips. "Shouldn't we wait for their guy?"

Don turned to Ken. "Who are they sending?"

Ken snickered. "Carter Freeman. He's probably still trying to find Arizona on the map."

Don added his own layer of snickering. "God no. That man can't communicate with anything that doesn't have a keyboard."

"Do you know what NSA stands for?" said Ken. "Nerd Spy Agency."

The giggling died down when the men finally realized that I wasn't joining in the hilarity but was staring pointedly at my empty water bottle.

Ken cleared his throat uncomfortably. "Let's get going, Phillips."

Phillips turned on the recorder and got down to business. He gave the time and date and asked me to recite my name and spell it. Her hissed at him after each question.

The preliminaries having been dispensed with, he asked, "When and where did you first meet Hamid Naviti?"

That wasn't the question I expected.

"I met Hamid today. I'm staying at the Biltmore Hotel in Phoenix. I requested a cab this morning, and Hamid was driving the cab that came. I've known him all of four hours," I said.

Kenneth jumped in. "Did you specifically request that Mr. Naviti be your driver?"

"No."

"Do you know the men who were shooting at you and Mr. Naviti?"

"No."

"Have you ever heard of the LA Enforcers?"

"Is that a basketball team?"

I was not being facetious, but apparently Ken and Don thought so. Both stood and paced menacingly around the room, which was unfortunate because as long as they kept their assigned seats I could tell which was which. Now I had no idea how to tell them apart.

Ken/Don frowned. "I think you know damned well who they are. We have a witness placing one of them in your hotel room—all night."

"Was I there too?"

"Yesssss," hissed Ken/Don.

Well, that certainly narrowed the possibilities. They were talking about Mark.

I still didn't get the connection, though. "What's an LA Enforcer?"

Ken/Don leaned over the table toward me. "Don't play dumb, sister."

"Can I Google it?"

Ken/Don sneered. "Sure. Go ahead. You won't find anything."

He took a laptop out of his briefcase, fired it up, and pushed it across the table. I rapidly typed in *LA Enforcers* and hit search.

> *An organization largely made up of ex-marines who offer themselves for hire to enforce contractual agreements through intimidation and, in some cases, bodily harm. The majority of its clients are drawn from the media and entertainment industries.*

"What the hell," Ken/Don exploded as he grabbed the computer. "Jesus, she's right. We've been working twenty-four-seven for months to track down the organization, and it's right here on Wikipedia. There's even an e-mail address and a page for donations."

"You guys should take advantage of the seminars we offer on electronic investigations."

I looked up to see Brad Pitt's twin standing in the doorway. Now this was more like it.

Ken/Don, Phillips, and McCarthy turned to greet the newcomer with varying levels of civility.

"Hey, Carter. I almost didn't recognize you. I've never seen you this far away from your desktop," said Ken/Don.

Carter introduced himself to me and Phillips and then found a chair and joined the others. Their side of the table was getting crowded.

"Would one of you like to sit next to me? There's more room over here," I offered politely.

Carter started to get up, but Phillips put a hand on his arm.

"Don't trust her. She puked on me earlier."

Carter freed his arm. "I take it that's why you're wearing a midriff-baring T-shirt?"

Carter relocated to my side of the table, and Phillips resumed the interrogation.

"Now that we've established who the LA Enforcers are, perhaps you can explain your connection to them."

"I have no connection to them. Mark, the gentleman in my room last night, is a personal trainer at the hotel. We became friends during my stay."

"You slept with him; isn't that correct?"

"How is that relevant?" I countered.

"Because your so-called friend is an associate of the men who were shooting at you today."

"Did you and Mr. Ramos ever discuss an entertainer with the stage name of Queen Ta Ta?" asked Carter.

Another name I did not know. "Who is Mr. Ramos?"

"He's the guy you shacked up with," provided Phillips.

My face felt hot, and I knew I was blushing bright red; Mark and I had never gotten around to formal introductions.

"Why were they shooting at me?"

"Why are you asking the questions?" interjected Phillips.

I fixed him with a stare and with feigned patience explained, "Because I am one of the victims. They were shooting at me. I was not shooting at them. You seem to know who they are; I do not. You must have an idea why they were shooting at the Ramirezes, Hamid, and me or you all wouldn't be here. The CIA, FBI, and NSA aren't brought in on random local shootings."

Phillips ground his teeth. "Look at it from our point of view; you just happened to find Queen Ta Ta's body and then just happened to get romantically involved with a guy who intimidates businessmen for a living, including Queen Ta Ta's manager. Then you get in the car of a known terrorist in order to evade questioning by Phoenix law enforcement about the deaths of Queen Ta Ta and Dick Burton. Then you just happened to end up in Tucson at the house of Rosario Herrera's parents, whom we know have information about Queen Ta Ta that is of great interest to clients of the LA Enforcers.

"You and your terrorist friend probably led the shooters to the Ramirez house on purpose, but then you spotted an opportunity: you got the information from the Ramirezes, thinking you could make a bundle selling it once the Ramirezes were out of the way. But the Enforcers figured you were double-crossing their client and went after you."

I was stunned. "I have no idea what you just said."

"Bullshit!" yelled Phillips, slamming the flat of his hand on the table top.

I don't like bullies. I was the victim of childhood bullying. I got out of the situation as soon as I was old enough and vowed to never submit to a bully again.

I remained still as a hard, cold, calm settled over me. Phillips must have seen something in my eyes, because he stopped pounding and looked nervously at Ken/Don.

Carter spoke next, which was a good strategy, because I wasn't in the mood to cooperate with Phillips. "Maybe you can tell us your side of the story then."

"It's not a side, and it's not a story. It's the truth."

"Then tell us your truth," he said in a mollifying tone.

"It's *the* truth."

"Have it your way, then. Tell us *the* truth," snarled Phillips sarcastically.

I stared evenly at him. "I always thought fat people were jolly."

Ken/Don did a snot take and then tried to regain his composure.

"Please proceed with your statement, Ms. Williams," directed Carter.

In much the same way I approach a closing argument, I took a few moments to focus my mind and collect my thoughts. Then I described everything that happened from the point of my discovery of Queen Ta Ta's body until now. With representatives from most of the federal law-enforcement agencies present, I felt that a detailed explanation was expeditious and would cut down on future reiterations.

Carter was the first to speak after I was through. "Are you trying to tell us you've never heard of the LA Enforcers much less knew Mark Ramos was one of them, and your sole motive throughout this whole thing has been to find Queen Ta Ta's murderer because you believe it's your civic duty?"

I nodded yes and then repeated myself aloud because I remembered we were on tape.

A young woman police officer stuck her head into the room. "Detective Phillips, Sheriff Turner is holding on line two."

Phillips grunted and left the room.

I had no idea what Bryan was going to tell Phillips. I prayed that he'd gotten over the whole Mark thing. I needed intelligent corroboration from him, not incoherent accusations.

We waited in uncomfortable silence until Phillips returned.

"Turner says she's telling the truth."

You could almost hear sighs of disappointment.

"Also, Lieutenant Colonel Jenkins from Quantico left a message. He says you guys need to lay off Hamid. He said, 'For the last time, Hamid is one of the good guys. Give him some peace.' He said if you bother Hamid again he's sending the drones after you. He was also pretty specific about Carter needing a hobby since dating was out of the question."

Only Officer McCarthy laughed.

"Did Sheriff Turner say how the shooters knew I would be at the Ramirezes' house?" I asked.

"No idea. He said it was coincidence. They were probably after the Ramirezes and you got in the way."

"What about Mark? Has he been arrested?"

"He's been taken into federal custody in Phoenix for questioning."

None of this seemed right to me. "Is it possible the Ramirezes were shot for a reason having nothing to do with a contract for information about Queen Ta Ta?"

I could tell by the looks on their faces that this possibility had not occurred to them.

"Are you even sure the shooters are members of the Enforcers?"

Ken/Don looked at Ken/Don, who then turned to Carter. "We're here because of the Ramos connection."

"Me too," replied Carter, who then proceeded to explain, "The CIA, FBI, and NSA are part of a joint task force that has been investigating the LA Enforcers for the last six months. We knew your connection with Ramos, and when the NSA picked up the police bulletin saying you skipped your appointment with the police and headed for Tucson, we were suspicious."

Damned cell phone.

"Are you telling me your whole case hangs on the fact that I slept with Mark last night?"

The men exchanged uncomfortable looks.

I was really heating up now. "Maybe you should focus your resources on finding the two shooters instead of trying to build a case around my love life. You haven't even asked me to describe them. Isn't that what you're supposed to ask first?"

Carter shifted in his seat and stared at his hands. Ken/Don found something on the ceiling that seemed to fascinate them.

Phillips finally spoke.

"They're dead," he said flatly. "My guys cornered them in one of the vacant houses, and they tried to exit Butch Cassidy–Sundance Kid style. My guys shot back—a lot."

I made a mental note to ask the IRS for a tax credit equal to that portion of my taxes that went to pay these guys.

"Assuming the shooters were Enforcers, who were they working for?" I asked.

"We have information indicating that Max Goldstein, the CEO of Mass Media Communications, is the client."

I'd heard that name before. But where? A few beats later it came to me: Max Goldstein was one of the names Tuwanda saw on Joey's caller list during her enthusiastic exploration of his beloved cell phone.

I hazarded a guess. "Is Joey Perroni your stooge?"

Ken/Dan smirked. "He may be a stooge, but he's not our stooge. Our undercover guy is a hotel staff member."

Dan the bellhop, I thought. *He doesn't seem to work a particular shift, and I've never seen him carry any bags other than mine.*

"Are you aware that Joey has been in contact with Goldstein?" I asked.

Carter smiled. "NSA is. I don't know about the other shops, though. It's hard to keep up on phone records when you have to get a warrant first."

"Get over yourself, Freeman," snapped Ken/Don.

"However, we found no evidence of communication between Joey Perroni and any known member of the Enforcers," Carter continued evenly, "and the phone calls with Goldstein had nothing to do with the Enforcers.

"So far as we know, the first and only contact between Perroni and an Enforcer was last night when Ramos intervened in a fight among Joey, Dick Burton, and two other men."

The idea that Mark was a member of a secret organization of contract enforcers for hire seemed farfetched. First, every bar association in the country would scream bloody murder about an organization that could put attorneys and the courts out of business, and this was the first I'd heard of it. Second, Mark didn't seem the type. But then, what did I know; I didn't even know his last name until today.

"Do the Enforcers hold meetings? Wear matching jackets? Charge dues? Have a secret handshake? I mean, how do you know the shooters were members of a larger group and not just a couple of entrepreneurs?"

"Because we've got an undercover man working for them," said Ken/Don.

"Who?"

"You know we can't tell you that."

I rolled my eyes. "You don't know who it is, do you?"

"That information is given out on a need-to-know basis," said Carter.

I tapped my finger on the table. "And you don't need to know."

Ken/Don grinned. "Carter hasn't even been told where the men's room in his office building is. His security clearance isn't high enough."

"Can it, Ken," Carter shot back.

At last, clarification of the Ken/Don identity crisis.

"My security clearance status is higher than yours, and you know it," continued Carter.

They were like kids arguing about who had more crayons.

As far as I could determine, the joint task force was not concerned with finding Queen Ta Ta's murderer, and they weren't particularly concerned about the Ramirezes either.

"Gentlemen, I don't know how I can help you with your investigation. I don't know anything about the Enforcers or their operations."

Phillips took a poll, and they agreed that they didn't have any further use for me.

"May I leave then?"

"Sheriff Turner is sending transportation to pick you up. You are to remain here until it arrives," said Phillips.

I was afraid of that. "Will someone at least let me know how Hamid is doing?"

"Why do you care? I thought you said you only met him today," said Carter.

I looked at him stonily.

"I'm funny that way. When someone saves my life, I like to keep track of them."

Phillips, showing a heretofore uncharacteristic sense of decency, ordered McCarthy to call on Hamid's status and let me know. He continued to amaze me by also asking McCarthy to scrounge up a sandwich for me.

The men filed out. Carter, who was last in line, stopped before going through the door and turned to face me. "So, what do you do when you're not being shot at? Do you like movies?"

I couldn't believe it. He was hitting on me. Was it possible that I'd met someone with fewer social opportunities than I?

"I don't get out much," I answered truthfully. "But I do like movies, provided there's no violence."

"So you don't see very many movies, then."

I smiled wryly.

"Is it okay if I look you up sometime when I'm in Phoenix?" he asked.

"Sure. My phone number is …"

"No need to tell me. I can find it."

"Oh, yeah, um, right. I forgot."

He saluted and left.

First Mark and now Carter; at least some men were attracted to women who used aliases, wore disguises, and got shot at.

Chapter Thirty-One

I laid my head on the table and was close to dozing off when McCarthy returned. He softly nudged me on the shoulder and, when I raised my head, placed a sandwich and a Diet Coke in front of me.

I looked at him inquiringly.

"Hamid is in surgery. He had a collapsed lung. The nurse said that just before he went under he asked them to tell someone named Natalie that the meter was still running. I take it he was referring to you."

I nodded miserably. "Will he be okay?"

"The nurse seemed to think so."

This, at least, was good news. Knowing Hamid's billing practices, though, he would not only charge me for his time but would tack on his medical expenses and related miscellaneous charges as well.

Pointing to the sandwich, McCarthy said, "It's peanut butter. I hope that's okay. It's all I could find."

I smiled my thanks. Peanut butter was okay by me; I was starved and in no position to be picky. Before digging in, though, I tore one-half the sandwich into small pieces and laid them on the floor for Her.

McCarthy sat across the table from me and settled in as though he was there for the long haul. I figured he pulled the short straw and got guard duty.

I finished my half sandwich and sat back.

"Did you guys consider the theory that whoever killed Queen Ta Ta—or watched her die—killed the Ramirezes because they knew too much?" I asked.

"Could be. But you need to talk about that to Sheriff Turner. He's in charge of the Queen Ta Ta investigation. All other agencies are on 'don't need to know' status."

"Sheriff Turner? I thought the Phoenix Police Department was handling the case."

"As of the interdepartmental memo de jure, the sheriff's got it. The Phoenix PD retained jurisdiction of the Burton ax-murder, though."

This was bad news. I was hoping that Webber could serve as a buffer between me and Bryan, absurd as that theory would have sounded to me as little as a week ago.

The sound of a helicopter, a distant stutter at first, grew deafening.

"That would be the MCS helicopter," said McCarthy, rising to his feet. "You must be an important witness to get this kind of treatment."

He left the room, locking the door behind him. (I

checked to make sure. Escape from a police facility was a long shot, but my flight or fight instincts kicked in on the side of flight; a fight was out of the question.)

Bryan burst into the interrogation room like a Nazi storm trooper, although admittedly this characterization might be biased in light of my perspective at the time.

"What the hell are you trying to pull? Do you have any idea what you've put me—I mean my office—through? The Phoenix police and my deputies were forced to redirect valuable resources to track you down. Webber is fit to be tied. This afternoon he handed the whole mess to me because he said he is 'no longer capable of the detachment required of an officer of the law.'"

"And you are?" I said sarcastically.

"Do you also know your boyfriend is a knee-breaker and is being questioned by the feds as we speak? And that your driver is on the national terrorist watch list? Are you aware that two more people are dead because of you?"

My face grew hot with anger.

"How dare you! I left to escape your adolescent fury over my social life. I didn't have time to do a background search on Hamid before I jumped in his cab, and as I recall I wasn't the one shooting at people at the Ramirezes. What are you going to do next? Blame me for the US involvement in Iraq?"

Phillips and McCarthy, who had followed Bryan into the room, hastily backed out. Bryan, however, stepped toward me, his face flushed and jaw clenched. His left eye twitched, and his eyes darted around the room as he appeared to struggle to find words. I crossed my arms and glared at him.

He reached out and laid his hand on my arm. I jerked it away.

Her hissed.

"Touch me again and I'll claim police brutality," I growled.

He let his hand fall to his side, and his shoulders sagged. He looked like a parade balloon with a leak. "Why are you doing this to me?" he asked quietly.

I couldn't believe it. "Wait. Let me get this straight. You think my only reason for getting up in the morning is to figure out how to screw up your life? Copernicus had it wrong; the world revolves around *you*. Who knew?"

Bryan ran his hand over his eyes.

"Kate, you know that's not what I meant. I'm the acting sheriff … I'm trying to be the elected sheriff. I'm in a sensitive position …"

"You put yourself in that position. If you'd left the Queen Ta Ta murder in Webber's hands, you wouldn't have to deal with me at all. You're just trying to inject yourself into a high-profile investigation for the publicity."

"How can you say that, Kate, after all I've been through for you? Did it ever occur to you that I stick my neck out time and time again because I care about you? Because I don't trust anyone else to protect your best interests the way I can?"

In fact, that possibility *had* never occurred to me.

"I don't believe you," I said stubbornly, even though inside I was wavering.

"You've been through a lot, Kate, but you've got me, other good friends, and a loyal staff who have always had your back. Despite all that, you don't trust anyone, even the people on your side. What happened to make you so distrustful?"

"For starters, your love affair with Miss Normal."

"Uh-uh. You can't lay it all on me. You held a part of yourself back from me and everyone else who cares about you long before Michele came along."

So Miss Normal's name was Michele. I started to run through the list of the Micheles I knew.

"I know what you're thinking, Kate, and stop it. Who I had an affair with is not the point. The point is you push away anyone who gets too close to you."

I felt unfairly targeted and wanted to cry. I was not the bad guy here. He was.

Still, a long ago memory nagged at me from a dark place in my mind; a place guarded by barbed wire surrounded by a moat and covered in a mound of cement and posted with No Trespassing signs, hazmat warnings, and tow-away zones.

My mother, a dedicated Calvinist, taught me that the only way to deal with trauma was to ignore it and move on. What she failed to mention was that ignoring some situations requires an incredible amount of energy and a lifetime commitment. Moreover, while Mom's advice might have been helpful to an adult with fully developed coping skills, it did no good for a child too young to have learned such skills. But Mom covered that issue as well; only the weak and undisciplined were unable to overcome adversity through exercise of will, regardless of age or experience.

Mom's training won out; I ignored the nagging.

"You have no right to judge me," I sputtered.

Bryan set his jaw and glared at me squinty-eyed. It looked like a standoff, but after a few seconds his features relaxed.

"Have it your way, Kate. I'm through trying to convince you of anything. So let's go with your assumption that I'm a publicity-grabbing politician with the morals of a slug."

"An immoral slug," I spat back.

"Whatever," he shrugged. "I'm going to sign you out of here. Then we'll leave for Phoenix."

"I want to see Hamid first."

"The terrorist?"

"He's not a terrorist, and he got shot because of me. I was an innocent bystander, but he was a more-innocent bystander."

Chapter Thirty-Two

Bryan, having lost the will to fight, merely nodded.

"I demand my right to make two phone calls, because technically, I have been taken into custody twice; once by you and once by Phillips."

He waved weakly and exited the room. A few seconds later McCarthy came in and handed me a cell phone.

I waited until he left before punching in Beth's number. I brought her up to speed and assured her that I was okay. Then I asked her to patch me as a conference call and contact the FBI's field office. (I didn't want McCarthy or anyone else to see this number on the phone's call record.) After three transfers, Beth got the right person.

"Agent Fagerberg." The voice was gruff and self-important sounding.

I took over from there.

"I understand from one of your men that you have Mark Ramos in custody."

"Who is this?" he asked suspiciously.

"Kate Williams, counsel for Mr. Ramos. You are to stop all questioning of Mr. Ramos until I get there."

"And when will that be?"

"I am presently out of town but will be flying up by helicopter shortly. I will notify you when I arrive."

I saw no reason to mention that I was still in custody and the helicopter belonged to the MSO.

Bryan came back a few minutes after I'd hung up with Fagerberg. He led me out the back door of the station to the waiting helicopter. He seemed to perk up at the sight of it.

"A Bell JetRanger," he announced proudly, as if he'd made it all by himself in his basement.

I shrugged. It didn't mean anything to me. But I was impressed later when we landed on Tucson General's rooftop heliport after mere seconds of flight. Her handled the trip with equanimity. Maybe she'd been a pilot's pet in one of her nine lives.

Hamid had emerged from surgery and was in post-op. The floor nurse cautioned us to limit our visit to no more than ten minutes and warned us that Hamid would likely be groggy and nonresponsive.

He was neither groggy nor nonresponsive. As soon as I pushed the curtain aside, his eyes flew open and his gaze locked on my face.

"You are okay," he said. "That is good."

I was touched that after all he'd been through, he was concerned about me.

"It is hard to collect payment from dead lady," he added. "Not impossible, though."

So much for the touching moment.

"I'm surprised to see you alert and doing so well," I said. "We were told you'd be out of it for a while. You had a serious operation."

He raised an eyebrow and snorted. "This? This is nothing. It is no worse than stubbing a toe. I suffered worse injuries in check-out line at al-Ashaar market."

The nurse accompanying us nodded. "His X-rays look like a mini munitions dump. The surgeon wouldn't go near him until a member of the bomb squad assured him Mr. Naviti was nonexplosive."

"You mean you still have bullets in your body?" I asked, aghast.

"Some, yes, but mostly shrapnel. You get used to it," said Hamid.

I shook my head in disagreement. "And yet, I think I wouldn't."

Bryan pushed in front of me. "Did you recognize either of the men who shot at you? Did they say anything?"

"And you are?" Hamid asked, his eyes turning cold and distrustful.

Bryan introduced himself and described his current purpose in life; to wit, investigating the death of Queen Ta Ta. Then he repeated his questions.

"No as to both. But based upon years of experience with such matters, I concluded that they were not open to introductions," Hamid said, not bothering to disguise the sarcastic bite in his voice. "They shot Ramirezes first. They were clearly their primary targets. Natalie and I were at wrong place at wrong time."

Bryan looked at me questioningly and mouthed, "Natalie?"

"It's okay to use my real name, Hamid. He knows," I said, ignoring Bryan's eye-roll.

"Did police catch shooters?" asked Hamid.

"In a manner of speaking," provided Bryan. "There was an exchange of gunfire, and the shooters were killed. We haven't been able to identify them yet."

"Check with Los Angeles police. One of them—the one who came into Ramirezes' house first—has Crips tattoo on his arm."

Bryan looked surprised. It wasn't clear whether his reaction was caused by the substance or the source of the information. He left the room, pulling out his cell phone en route.

"How do you know about that kind of stuff?" I asked. "I mean about American gangs and tattoos."

"The American culture is dominant even in places like Iraq. We know all about your cowboys, gangsters, and gangs, and how you love guns. Your Constitution protects your right to have weapons but says nothing about rights to medical care, food, or education."

"The Second Amendment notwithstanding," I said huffily, "I hate guns and do not own one."

"You people lack intelligent consistency," said Hamid. His bravado was undermined by his weakening voice, however.

The nurse touched my arm and motioned that I should leave. I brushed Hamid's hair back and planted a kiss on his forehead. "Thank you for saving my life, Hamid."

He looked surprised and then pursed his lips. "You still owe me money."

It was difficult to tell in the room's harsh, bluish-white light, but I think he was blushing.

Before we left, I gave my phone number to the nurse and asked that she call me when Hamid was ready to go home. I didn't know much about his personal life, but it was a safe bet that he didn't have a lot of family and friends in the area.

The flight to Phoenix was quick. In no time Her and I were sitting in an interview room nearly identical to the one in Tucson. I was given another Diet Coke and settled in for another round of questions.

Bryan took me through the events of the past two days, wisely skirting the Mark issue, mention of which was unlikely to buy him cooperation from the witness. It was I who finally raised the issue when Bryan finished his questions.

"Why is Mark being held by the FBI?" I asked.

"We transferred him to their local branch office at

the request of the agent in charge for questioning in another matter. He lawyered up, though, and isn't saying anything."

Good boy, Mark, I thought.

"Is the 'other matter' the FBI's investigation of the LA Enforcers?"

Bryan looked surprised. "How do you know about that?"

"Because in Tucson I was questioned by FBI, CIA, and NSA agents who are part of a task force investigating the Enforcers."

Bryan muttered a string of obscenities under his breath. "Those guys are out of control. They're supposed to notify local law enforcement agencies of investigations in their jurisdictions. As far as I know, the Enforcers' activities have been limited to California. I have to hear it from you that they may have expanded their territory."

I was tired of hearing about the Enforcers. Neither the fact nor the nature of their operation made sense to me. I wanted to get back to the Queen Ta Ta and Burton murders.

"Did Webber get any information out of Joey about Burton's murder?" I asked.

Bryan shook his head. "He says that after you and Tuwanda left his room he fell asleep and didn't wake up until one of Webber's men pounded on his door this morning. We can't find anyone at the hotel who saw him leave or, conversely, can vouch that he never left. The ax used to kill Burton was a fire ax from the hallway outside his office, so it's possible that it was a last-minute choice, indicating that it was unplanned.

"Unfortunately, none of this narrows the field of suspects. Dick had lots of enemies, including two angry ex-wives, an ex–male lover, and a list of burned colleagues longer than the Phoenix phone book."

"Are your guys looking into a possible connection with the Queen Ta Ta murder?"

He shook his head no. "It looks like the Queen Ta Ta matter may be back-burnered for a while."

"What?" I said in an overloud voice. "You just took a helicopter to Tucson at public expense to pick up a material witness despite the fact the case is not a priority?"

"It's looking more and more like a drug overdose. She was strangled just after she died or contemporaneously with death from overdose. It's not clear whether the strangling could cause her death, but it's crystal clear that the amount of drugs in her system could. The most the strangler could be charged with based on what we know now is desecration of a corpse. We're close to making a public statement to that effect."

"What's holding you back?"

"What *was* holding us back was her manager, who, after dropping the murdering jogger theory, insisted that she was force-fed drugs and then strangled when whoever gave her the drugs thought she wasn't dying fast enough. He claims that she used meth and marijuana exclusively, but the cocktail of drugs in her system were largely prescription. Until his death, Burton was also pushing the murder theory, as were the myriad attorneys representing her estate."

"Have they given up on that tack?"

"No. But we have. There's not enough evidence to support their version of Queen Ta Ta's death."

I wasn't ready to give up either, but I was a minority of one on the investigation team. "But you're going to try to find the strangler, right? He or she may not have known Queen Ta Ta was already dead when she was strangled. That makes him or her a killer—at least by intent."

"We'll continue the investigation, but with her death solved, the matter drops in priority. We've got too many other fish to fry, and with all the budget cuts, we're shorthanded."

"I doubt the press will let up. Queen Ta Ta's postdeath strangling, plus the murder of the attorney for her estate and the suicide of a childhood friend, all make for great stories."

Bryan shook his head slightly. "I don't know about that. The public has a short attention span, and Joey thinks once the funeral and the pre- and postfuneral events are over, interest will die down."

"Joey?"

"Yeah. Joey's in charge of the barbecues and street dances planned for the day of Queen Ta Ta's burial. Webber's people had to confiscate Joey's cell phone before

Webber interviewed him because the thing was going off nonstop. Did you know his ringtone is 'You my bitch'?"

I nodded. "Unfortunately, yes."

I'd had fantasies about shoving that phone up a certain part of Joey's anatomy.

"I take it from what you're saying that Joey isn't paralyzed by grief over Dick's death."

"Not at all. If anything it's energized him," said Bryan.

"Did Webber release Joey after he questioned him?"

"He had to. There's not enough evidence to hold him."

He was right, but I wished they could have locked him up for a while based on the general principal that jerks *should* be locked up once in a while.

"So, Joey's free, Mark's still in the feds' custody, and … wait … where's Tuwanda?"

"After I finished talking to her, Webber's guys picked her up for questioning about the Burton murder."

"Have they released her?"

Bryan tried to hide a smile. "Webber released her less than a half hour into the interview. She left behind a host of traumatized police officers who are rethinking their commitment to a career in law enforcement."

I had to smile too. "I shouldn't be so cooperative. Maybe I'd get to go home early if I used Tuwanda's approach."

Bryan shook his head in disbelief. "Cooperative is not

a word I would use to describe you—ever. But you're not under arrest. You can leave at any time."

"I can? That's a surprise. I guess all the armed deputies outside had me fooled." I immediately stood to take my leave.

"Out of curiosity, though, where are you going to go?" asked Bryan.

I shot him a piercing look and prepared to tell him where *he* could go and how fast but thought better of it; there was no harm in telling him my plans. I had hit a dead end as far as leads go, so my plans were limited.

"I'm going to go back to the hotel to pack and check out; then I will pick up my dog at Macy's and go home." I didn't think it worth adding that I would have to stop off at a pet store to buy Ralph a bribe first. Ralph did not handle abandonment well, even though he'd spent his period of abandonment with a doting caretaker. (Macy made him roast beef and peanut butter cookies.)

The thought of Ralph reminded me of Mark. I couldn't believe that anyone who named their dog Ralph could be a criminal, and I refused to entertain the possibility that I might be projecting in this regard.

Bryan approved of my plan overall but insisted on driving me and Her to the hotel and waiting while I checked out, after which he would take us home. Maybe he was afraid I'd pick up another personal trainer if left to my own devices. Whatever his reason, the cat and I needed a ride, so I didn't object.

When we walked into the hotel a short time later, I was surprised to see Tuwanda at the front desk. I had assumed she was already back home or at work.

Upon catching sight of me, she trotted over and gave me a bear hug, being careful not to crush Her. "Thank God, you okay. What the hell you think you doin' takin' off without ol' Tuwanda here an' gettin' shot at?" Then she caught sight of Bryan and, without waiting for me to respond, said, "What the hell is *he* doin' here?"

"*He* is Kate's ride," said Bryan.

Tuwanda pursed her lips in disapproval. "You be better off findin' another terrorist cabbie, Katie."

"How did you know about that?" I asked.

"The officer who drove me here after my interview with Webber was one of them nervous babblers. I never seen anybody flinch that much. I guess they lettin' anyone into the police force these days.

"Hey, before I forget; looka this." She pulled a newspaper out of her purse, opened it with a flourish, and handed it to me.

There I was, staring out from the front page of the Society and Fashion section. And I looked *good*; I was fully clothed, and no dogs appeared in the photo with me. The picture was one taken of me at a bar presentation a couple of weeks ago. The article accompanying the picture was a fluff piece about fashion-forward professional ladies.

"Where did this come from?" I asked.

"Max. She got the picture from Beth, an' one of her

newspaper contacts wrote the article. It gets better; Max signed you up for a bunch of society charity balls too. You about to become well known, but in a good way this time."

Bryan, who had been reading the article over my shoulder, looked pleased. This annoyed me, so I shoved him away.

"Are you heading home now?" I asked Tuwanda, gesturing toward the pile of suitcases at the front desk.

"Uh-huh. Then I'm goin' to work. I've had enough of bein' here. Luxury resorts ain't all they cracked up to be."

"Well, if you two could stop meddling in—" Bryan started to say.

I cut him off. "Why don't you wait a bit and Bryan will give you a ride too?"

Bryan looked unhappy at this suggestion, but Tuwanda readily agreed.

"Tha's great," she said. "I'll go an' help you pack. The two-timin' asshole can wait in the lobby."

The two-timing asshole mumbled something under his breath and headed for the bar.

Chapter Thirty-Three

Tuwanda and I made short work of packing my things. After we finished we decided to share a bottle of wine in farewell to the lifestyle of the rich and famous.

It was too hot to sit outside, so we pulled a couple of chairs up to the arcadia door overlooking the patio.

I gave Her a bowl of water and a couple of cream cups before sitting down. Tuwanda had already opened the wine and filled two glasses.

"What you gonna do with that cat?" she asked.

"I don't want to leave Her at the hotel to fend for herself. We've bonded. Or at least I've bonded with her."

It's hard to know if a cat likes you back.

"An' Ralph?"

"Ralph—well, Ralph will have to get used to it."

We sipped our wine contemplatively.

Tuwanda spoke first.

"We din't find out who strangled Queen Ta Ta, but we sure as hell gave it our best shot."

I explained what Bryan had told me about Queen Ta Ta's drug overdose and how the murder theory was out as far as the police were concerned. Then I concluded with my own opinion. "I don't see it that way, though. The strangler had intent to kill, which still means we have a murderer running around."

"I agree with that. You think Bryan tol' you they was backin' off the investigation to throw us off?"

This theory had not occurred to me. I gave Bryan another black mark.

"It don't make sense," Tuwanda continued. "This ain't no average case. Maybe if it was to happen to one of us they could shuffle it under the rug an' move on. But Queen Ta Ta was a superstar."

I told her that Bryan was dismissive when I said the same thing.

"What about Goldstein?" I asked, getting back on the track of finding a murderer. "The one who was on Joey's list of phone contacts. The feds said Goldstein had a connection to the group they were investigating. Maybe we've been going about this all wrong: it wasn't a crime of passion. It was a business deal between Goldstein and Joey."

"Knockin' off the goose that lays the golden eggs is dumb bid'ness. Why the hell would they do that?"

"Maybe she was planning to quit or change managers

or production companies and one of them put a hit out on her, but the hit man didn't get around to killing her until after she was dead. It makes sense. The companies in charge of her before she died would still retain rights after her death, so they'd profit more from her death than if she lived."

"That could be it. We need to talk to this Goldstein guy."

I agreed, but there was a hitch to this plan. "The problem is, we don't know where in Los Angeles he is, and I doubt he'll talk to us on the phone."

"I think it's time you ladies went home."

We hadn't heard anyone come in, and we both jerked around to identify the speaker. It was Dan.

He looked different today. Instead of khakis and a collared sports shirt he wore a gray suit with a white dress shirt and red tie; the standard uniform of FBI agents.

I'd guessed right; Dan was the plant. "You've been undercover all this time? Why? Were you assigned to keep tabs on Mark?"

Dan smiled grimly. "At first, yes. But complications arose when you came on the scene. You stuck your nose into the Queen Ta Ta murder and got the local sheriff interested in our target before we had sufficient evidence against him. Mark's in custody now, but I doubt we have enough to hold him. We would like to observe him without you getting in the way."

"The agents I met with in Tucson mentioned the name Goldstein," I persisted. "Are you following up on him?"

"Unless Mark breaks his silence and tells us something, we have no direct evidence to tie Goldstein in."

"So why are you still here?"

"To make sure you leave. You have a way of showing up at the wrong place and the wrong time and screwing up our operations."

I had heard similar sentiments from several other law enforcement organizations over the last year.

"You in luck, then," said Tuwanda. "We about to leave. We was just havin' a good-bye drink. You want to join us?"

"I can't drink while I'm on duty," he said prissily.

"You guys might do a better job if you was to lubricate some and loosen them creative juices. You lack imagination."

Dan stared at her in stony silence.

Her chose this moment to climb up Dan's pant leg and introduce Herself.

"What the hell is that?" he yelped.

"That's Her," I said, unhelpfully.

"Her who? It looks like a giant gray rat."

"What a mean thing to say about Her!"

"What is her name?"

"Her."

"Yes, her. What is her name?"

"Stop it," said Tuwanda. "It's like a bad version of

'Who's on First.' Dan, or whatever the hell your name is, Her is the name of the cat."

"My name *is* Dan. Now please get Her off my pants."

"I bet that's the first time you ever said that," chortled Tuwanda.

I unsnagged Her's claws and lifted her into my arms.

Tuwanda and I finished our wine and then poured another glass and eventually finished the bottle, ignoring the impatient noises coming from Dan's direction.

I didn't hear the shot, only the sound of Dan's body hitting the floor. Tuwanda and I whirled around. Our wineglasses shattered on the floor. A man walked in and positioned himself between us and the door. He was muscular, with a ponytail and a bald pate. Diamond earrings the size of dimes adorned his ears, and another diamond was imbedded in a front tooth. The latter was visible because he was grinning happily, which I found in very poor taste under the circumstances.

Two more men followed closely behind Diamond Tooth. They were best described as goons and, in fact, fit the stereotype so closely that they could have come out of central casting in a gangster movie. One of them held a gun and swung it in an arc around the room in case Dan had friends with him.

I couldn't see Dan from the waist up from where I

sat, but since the part of him I could see wasn't moving, I feared the worst.

One of the goons pointed his weapon toward me and looked questioningly at Diamond Tooth. Before Diamond Tooth could respond, though, we heard a commotion outside and then Bryan yelling, "We've got you surrounded, Goldstein."

Surrounded with what? Air?

They must teach trite phrases in cop school. I would have appreciated something more personal—like, "You touch a hair on either of those ladies' heads and you are dead."

Goldstein swore under his breath and motioned to Goon No.1, who reacted immediately by grabbing me around the throat and pressing his gun against my temple. Goon No. 2 tried to do the same with Tuwanda but, having lost the element of surprise, got a knee in the groin from her. Goldstein jumped in as a substitute goon until Goon No. 2 was through writhing and muttering something about God, revenge, and cheap employers who refused to provide athletic cups.

Goldstein resumed the position of he-who-issues-commands as soon as Goon No. 2 was able to stand upright and hold a gun. Tuwanda's goon did not hold her by the neck but stood a good three feet away and pointed his gun at her head.

"Let us go peacefully or we will shoot these two lovely ladies," Goldstein intoned loudly.

"You mean one lady and one bitch," growled Goon No. 2.

"Get over it," hissed Tuwanda.

There was an uncomfortable silence, and I could picture Bryan scowling and mentally running through his options, which were few and shouldn't have taken long to consider.

"Release the women and take me!" he yelled.

"No," Goldstein responded without hesitation.

Goldstein was not likely to exchange two female civilians for a highly trained male law-enforcement officer, but it was sweet of Bryan to offer.

Another period of silence ensued.

"All right," yelled Bryan. "We will stand down and allow you to leave. But if you do not release the hostages alive and well prior to embarkation, we will shoot you down before you're three feet off the ground."

Chapter Thirty-Four

It wasn't long before I knew what Bryan meant. With Goldstein and his two goons using Tuwanda and me for shields, we walked out of the room and across the lawn to a waiting helicopter. I guess this was my week for helicopter travel.

The only members of the law-enforcement community I saw on the way were Bryan and a nervous-looking security guard. A gardener defiantly waving a rake stood near Bryan, but he seemed to be more concerned about the lawn than the hostage situation; in exclamatory Spanish, he loudly protested the use of his grass as an impromptu landing pad.

Goon No. 1, the last in line, shoved Tuwanda and me on board and then climbed in after us. The security guard shot his Taser, which landed yards away in the opposite direction. A single shot ricocheted ineffectually against the side of the helicopter.

Goldstein's helicopter was not equipped with turbo engines, but it traveled fast nonetheless. Tuwanda, Tweedle-Dee and Tweedle-Dum, and I crammed into the two facing passenger seats while Goldstein took the controls. There weren't enough headsets to go around, so Tuwanda and I could not hear what the others were saying. We rose straight into the air and headed south.

I caught Tuwanda's eye and mouthed, *Mexico?* She nodded somberly. Despite her stoic expression, I saw fear in her eyes. My stomach sank, and because it had already taken a plunge when we took off, it was running out of vertical movement options.

Why was Goldstein doing this? I thought. *What could possibly be so important that he would shoot Dan and then kill Tuwanda and me?*

I'd already told the police everything I knew, and the only information I had about the LA Enforcers was what the police told *me*. I wasn't a threat to anyone.

I felt a prick of anger. I believed very strongly that one should know why one is going to be killed prior to said killing. I did not want my post-death spirit to have to wander the earth seeking answers; I wanted it to be able to proceed directly to the revenge-haunting stage.

Placing my mouth close to my goon's ear, I yelled, "Why are you doing this?"

He shook his head to indicate incomprehension, lifted the side of his headset closest to me, and gestured for me to try again.

I repeated my query.

He looked sharply at Goldstein and said something into the mike attached to his earphones. Goldstein guffawed. He was such a jolly person. Kind of like an evil Santa.

He answered my goon between residual giggles. My goon respectfully giggled back.

Goldstein dug under his seat and produced another headset. I panicked when he took his hands off the controls and turned to hand it to me. I knew very little about flying helicopters, but I didn't think the pilot should take his eyes off the sky.

We had left the city behind and were flying low through rock-strewn canyons. The mountains towered above us, a situation I found disconcerting. When airborne, I prefer that all large land masses be far below.

Goldstein's voice floated through the headphones. "Ms. Williams?"

"Good guess," I said. I got sarcastic when I was nervous.

"Bob here indicated that you want to know why you're going to die," continued Goldstein, ignoring the barb. "Because I'm a reasonable man, I've decided to tell you."

"If you think you're reasonable you need a new analyst, because you suffer from a serious lack of self-awareness."

"Shouldn't you be nicer to me? Most people in this situation try to convince me that they're my friends and don't deserve to die."

"Did it help?" I asked.

"The end result was the same, but I was persuaded to be more—efficient, shall we say."

I stared at him contemptuously.

His expression changed. He no longer looked jolly, and his eyes were hard.

Much to my relief he faced forward again like a proper pilot.

"You spoke to the Ramirezes before we had a chance to silence them. Your death would be unnecessary but for that. I still don't know how you got to them before we did. I had you watched during your stay at the Biltmore, and despite our very thorough surveillance efforts, you slipped out. Then, of all things, you went to see the Ramirezes the very day they were to die."

"I have a history of that kind of thing happening. My lousy karma aside, why did you kill the Ramirezes?"

"I believe you know the answer to that."

"I really don't. Why would I waste the last minutes of my life asking you something I already know the answer to?"

Goldstein turned and scrutinized my face carefully. Then, shrugging, he faced forward again.

"We may be making a mistake by killing you and your friend, but these things happen. It's the cost of doing business," he said matter-of-factly, as if discussing an increase in the price of paper clips.

"Wait, I'm going to die because of management error? That's it? I'm a line item in the cost column?"

My goon, Bob, no doubt alarmed at the level of my agitation, placed a restraining hand on my arm. Tuwanda looked at me questioningly.

"Give my friend a set of headphones and tell both us *right now* what's going on," I demanded.

Goldstein ignored me, but Bob removed his headphones and handed them to Tuwanda. I don't know whether this was an act of kindness or he was sick of my yelling.

Tuwanda wasted no time in contributing her input. "What the hell is goin' on?"

Goldstein still didn't say anything, so I filled Tuwanda in on our prior conversation.

"So we dyin' for no reason an' he won't say what the reason woulda been if there was one?" she asked.

"You realize, of course, that I can hear every word you're saying," said Goldstein.

Tuwanda harrumphed. "Damn right."

Goldstein's shoulders shook with laughter. His jolly nature had reasserted itself.

"I will tell you ladies, if you ask me politely," Goldstein said finally.

I caught Tuwanda's eye and shook my head stubbornly.

Her microphone picked up the sound of her sigh. "Please, Mr. Goldstein, sir, could you enlighten us as to the reasonin' underlyin' your actions?" she asked in a sugary voice.

"Your friend seems to have all the manners you lack, Ms. Williams. Would you please provide a similarly worded request?"

I gritted my teeth and fought the urge to tell him to sit down hard on the joystick.

"Sir, if you could be so kind; I, too, wish for an explanation as to why you want to kill us." I got the words out, but my sugary tone needed work. Goldstein seemed satisfied, though.

"Let me start by filling you in on the back story," he began. "I'm in the advertising and public relations business. In fact, my company operates internationally with offices in twenty-one countries including Colombia."

"Is that where you're heading now?" I asked.

Tuwanda looked at me questioningly.

"No extradition," I provided.

"Ms. Williams is correct," said Goldstein, doing a reasonably good imitation of Alex Trebek.

"I have been in the process of purchasing all the rights to Queen Ta Ta's name, music, and legacy. Perroni came on board immediately, and now that Dick is out of the way, we should have no problem getting Mrs. Butoff's cooperation. The Ramirezes were another loose end we needed to tie up for two reasons. First, they were intent upon proving that Queen Ta Ta predeceased Che Che. If that was the case, Queen Ta Ta's estate would have gone to Che Che and then through intestacy to her parents, because, you see, Queen Ta Ta and Che Che were married last year in a civil ceremony in Iowa."

"But Joey said he had a thing going with Che Che," I interjected.

"Yes. We needed to create the impression that Che Che and Queen Ta Ta were no more than employer-employee so no one would bother to look for another connection. That brings us to the second reason the Ramirezes were a problem. Not only did they know about the Iowa marriage, but they found a suicide note that read that with Queen Ta Ta dead, Che Che had no reason for living.

"What it boils down to, then, is another rock star dead of a drug overdose, and, quite honestly, that's been done to death—no pun intended. I mean, let's go through them: Jimmy Hendrix, Elvis Presley, Janis Joplin, Jim Morrison, Keith Moon, Michael Jackson ... and that's just off the top of my head. But we haven't had a murder in a while, and you know how well that worked for Lennon. People still worship him like he's a god."

"Didn't work so good for Sam Cooke and Marvin Gaye," muttered Tuwanda.

Goldstein ignored her.

"Her fans see Queen Ta Ta as a lady of mystery and a rebel of the first order. Her death needed to be spectacular.

"I found her that night in her room—dead—or near

dead—on the toilet. The *toilet,* for God's sake. That is so Elvis. We came up with the idea of staging a murder by strangulation, which would have kept the press going forever.

"Perroni strangled her and changed her into the clothes she'd been wearing that night at the party. He wrapped her in a robe and tossed her into the back of a golf cart. After he moved her to the jogging path, he removed the robe and placed her in a suitably dramatic pose.

"Unfortunately, he screwed up. He blamed you for the murder and was careless in letting two people see him on his way back to the hotel. The maid was easy. We scared her so bad she's probably back in Mexico by now. But Mark, the personal trainer, was as impossible as you. We couldn't shake him off our tail. So Perroni came up with this great idea: we created an Internet identity for Mark that put him directly in the sites of NSA as a homegrown terrorist. We had created a gang called the LA Enforcers some time back as a red herring in case the police caught wind of our unorthodox business practices. We set it up so that the Enforcers took responsibility for every unsolved felony assault in California during the last ten years. The feds love that kind of stuff, so they put a task force together to investigate a nonexistent organization. Perroni spread the word that Mark was a member of the Enforcers and went so far as to post a picture of Mark's tattoo on Twitter and identify it as the gang sign."

"The only tattoo Mark has is of the Marine Corp insignia," I pointed out.

"Don't get me wrong, Perroni isn't brilliant, but fortunately neither are the guys at NSA. They immediately took it to mean that the members of the LA Enforcers were all ex-marines."

Our tax dollars at work.

"Mark said the man he saw the morning of Queen Ta Ta's murder got into a golf cart that headed toward the check-in area. What about the golf cart driver? Weren't you afraid he'd identify Perroni?"

"Nope. He was one of ours. He helped Perroni clean up Queen Ta Ta's room so it looked like she never went back there after the party."

"So this whole setup, including the deaths of the Ramirezes and Dick, is because you wanted to create a more bankable legacy for your dead client?"

"Of course." Goldstein's tone implied that I was silly for asking.

"Look at poor Michael Jackson bein' killed by that doctor …" started Tuwanda.

"Enough with Michael Jackson," I broke in. "Mr. Goldstein, where are your values?"

"You put your finger on it: value. I'm all about value."

"But the police already know that Queen Ta Ta died from an overdose. Your plan didn't work," I said.

Goldstein whirled around, and the helicopter dipped and swayed.

"Watch the sky!" I screamed.

"What do you mean the police know? Perroni killed her while she was near dead but still breathing."

"They've known for a while. They were going to make the announcement today."

Goldstein spouted a string of obscenities impressive in length and originality.

"Pinky—check the news." Pinky, a.k.a. Goon No. 2, punched a couple of buttons, and Bryan Williams's voice came out of the headphones: *Fans reactions to the police announcement today were varied, but most agreed that, although Queen Ta Ta was a unique performer, the cause of her death is, sadly, all too common in her industry.*

"Common?" yelled Goldstein.

The helicopter took another dip and swung sideways.

Bob and Pinky looked at each other nervously. I caught Tuwanda's eye and then stared pointedly at Bob's gun, which was lying unattended on the floor next to him.

Tuwanda launched into a loud, steady moan, interspersed with intervals of singing. Tuwanda is tone deaf, so I wasn't clear as to her musical selection, but it sounded a little like the chorus of Aretha Franklin's "Respect."

I moved quickly for the gun and got to it just as Pinky

raised his own gun to fire at me. I fired first, and Pinky's body jerked with the impact of the bullet. I'd hit him in the chest and he wasn't moving, but Bob was.

Bob hurled himself at my gun and grabbed it before I could get off another shot. Tuwanda, who had gotten hold of Pinky's gun, smashed its butt against the back of Bob's head. The helicopter wobbled, and she lost her balance and dropped the gun, which slid back and disappeared under a luggage shelf.

During the tumult, Goldstein had deserted the pilot's seat and was coming at Tuwanda with a hunting knife. Tuwanda, who was struggling to get Pinky's gun out from under the seat, did not see him. Driven purely by protective instinct, I threw myself at Goldstein's legs and brought him down. He stabbed wildly with his knife and landed a blow to my shoulder. I screamed in pain and struck out at him with my legs, pushing him toward the exit door. In the meantime, Tuwanda had given up on the gun and came at Goldstein from his other side. He pushed her viciously, and she fell back hard against a metal armrest.

The unpiloted helicopter did as it pleased, sliding and bouncing like a disco dancer with a lousy sense of rhythm.

Her came out from under the luggage shelf, leaped at Goldstein's face, and dug her nails into his forehead and chin. He screamed and pulled her off. She took patches of his skin with her, and blood gushed into his eyes and down his face.

Despite my injury, my adrenaline was high, and the injuries inflicted by Her had given me an advantage: Goldman's vision was impaired by blood. He'd managed to get back on his feet, though, so I went in for another tackle. His body crashed against the door. Before he could right himself, I pushed the door handle down and gave him a shove. He fell through the door and would have taken me with him if Tuwanda hadn't grabbed my shirt and hauled me back in.

Chapter Thirty-Five

We lay on the floor of the passenger cabin, breathing hard.

"What'd you do that for?" gasped Tuwanda. "He was the damn pilot."

The helicopter lurched sideways as if to emphasize the point that it was indeed a free agent.

"He was trying to kill me. What was I supposed to do? Ask to take a time out and land before resuming a struggle between life and death?"

"That wasn't no struggle between life and death. It was a struggle between one way of dyin' and another way of dyin'. We gotta get to them controls an' figure out how to fly this thing before we crash."

"Do you know anything about flying helicopters?" I asked.

"No. I got lotsa skills, but that ain't one of 'em."

"Well, I don't know how to fly one either. So what exactly are we supposed to figure out?"

"Katie, you got a limited imagination."

"I was knifed in the shoulder. Bleeding slows my thinking," I muttered defensively.

"Ain't you ever seen them TV shows where the pilot gets incapacitated an' some passenger who ain't got a clue on how to fly is led through the landin' process by someone sittin' in an airport tower? We just gotta figure out how to get hold of one of them tower guys."

We stepped over Bob and Pinky and sat in the pilot and navigator seats. The helicopter was heading toward a canyon wall, and we both went for the joystick. I got there first and jabbed it to the far right, slamming my foot down on a pedal I assumed was a brake. The helicopter obligingly turned and kept on turning but did not slow.

Tuwanda took exception. "We gonna just fly around in circles?"

"It beats slamming into a wall of rock."

We had no problem finding the radio controls, which were distinguishable from the other blinking lights on the panel by the designation *Radio Controls* written above them.

I readjusted my headphones, which kept slipping due to centripetal force, and punched the button numbered "1." Loud rock music blasted out of my earphones.

"What the hell! He got the Rolling Stones as the first preset? The man's priorities was a mess!" yelled Tuwanda as she dived for the second button. It was the Playboy channel.

"That at least makes some sense," said Tuwanda as she went for the third button.

Technical chatter filled our ears as pilots announced weather and landing conditions and rattled off acronyms that meant nothing to us.

"Great," I said. "We can hear them, but how do we get them to hear us? I'm getting nauseous, by the way."

"Maybe we do it the same way as on a plane. Remember how I took them flyin' lessons?"

"As I recall, they did not end well."

"It wasn't that bad. I hear the instructor is doin' fine. He can eat solid food again an' everythin'."

Tuwanda experimented with a couple of buttons while yelling, "Hello? Hello? Is anyone out there?"

I began to view my nausea as a blessing; at this point, I didn't care if I died.

Miraculously, a voice answered her. "You don't have to scream, ma'am. We hear you loud and clear."

"Who are you?" I asked.

"I was just about to ask you that. This is Bravo Papa niner niner."

"English, please."

"Border patrol, ma'am. Are you reporting a situation 7700?"

"Seriously, stop it."

"That's code for emergency, ma'am."

"If you call a pilotless helicopter locked in a spin with two female kidnap victims, one wounded man, and one possibly dead man on board an emergency, then yes."

"You had me at kidnap victims, ma'am. What are your coordinates?"

"I told you; in the air, spinning."

Fortunately, Tuwanda stepped in and, after confirming the location of the appropriate digital displays, read off the information. Of course, the directional coordinates were a waste of time because they kept changing, but she managed to give him meaningful position coordinates. She next gave him the helicopter's model name and number.

"You are in Mexican national airspace, ma'am. We will need to contact the closest Mexican air base to help you land or move you back into US airspace. First, though, we're going to get you out of that spin."

"We're in a canyon. If we drive the wrong way we're dead," I said.

"Ma'am, even an expert can't pull off a hover-spin without drift. My guess is if you look out the window you'll see you're heading in a direction you don't want to be going in."

He was right. We were slowly moving closer to the side of the canyon.

"I want whichever one of you is sitting in the pilot seat to grab the cyclic—that's the stick that should be located between your legs."

Tuwanda guffawed. "I bet they's a lot of jokes about that in the pilotin' industry."

"Actually, ma'am, no. Now which one of you is in the pilot seat?"

"That would be me," I said, obligingly wrapping my hand around the stick. "You know, though, that this stick is the thing that got us into trouble in the first place."

"And it's going to get you out of trouble now, ma'am. Now I want you to gradually push the stick to the left, and at the same time push the left pedal on the floor next to your feet. When you are pointed east by northeast, take your foot off the pedal and ease the cyclic forward."

"What?"

"He means when you pointed forward and not headin' into a canyon wall, ease forward."

I did as he said, and the helicopter lurched and bobbed.

"We rockin', hard," said Tuwanda nervously.

"Ma'am—the lady doing the piloting—what's your name?"

"Kate Williams. My full name is Caitlin Williams, but I'd prefer to be referred to in my obituary as Kate."

"Kate—my name is David, by the way. Kate, the cyclic—that's what we call the joystick you're holding—is extremely sensitive in your particular machine. You need to handle it gently and with great care."

Tuwanda guffawed again. I gave her a warning look, which she disregarded.

"I bet men is lots better at this, havin' had all that practice with they own sticks."

I gritted my teeth and, following David's instructions, eased the cyclic slowly to the left until the nose was headed down the canyon and then took my foot off the pedal and eased it forward.

"Now one more thing: you've got to add more lift, because the canyon you're in ends in a couple of miles. Your former pilot was taking a route popular with drug runners. One of their tricks is to fly low to avoid visual detection."

"Thank you for the historical perspective. Now how do I go up?" I snapped.

"She ain't usually this mean. She got a knife wound in her shoulder, and I think it's makin' her testy," apologized Tuwanda.

"Yeah. The possibility of dying in a fiery crash has me bugged too."

"Maybe you should switch places then," said David. "You're going to need both hands to work the collective— that's the stick to the left of the pilot—and the cyclic."

"Fine with me," I said.

We crawled over each other, and I assumed the crash position in the copilot seat.

"That ain't at all reassurin'," said Tuwanda.

I ignored her and stayed rolled up like an armadillo.

"Now, what is *your* name?" asked David.

"Tuwanda Jones, spelled g-o-d-d-e-s-s."

A short pause followed. "Tuwanda? From Phoenix Tuwanda?"

"Yeah. Do I know you?"

"No, but you know a friend of mine—Derek Anderson."

"Derek? How the hell he doin'?"

"He's eating solid food now."

Tuwanda gave me an "I told you so" look.

"Tuwanda, I want you to grab that stick to the left of you and pull it back. That will cause you to lift."

"Don't I gotta give it throttle like in a plane? Where's the damn throttle?"

"Don't worry about the throttle. The model you're flying has a governor system that will automatically increase your throttle speed to whatever speed is necessary to keep you in the air."

Tuwanda pulled the collective back gradually, and miracle of all miracles, the helicopter steadily rose to where we were above the canyon.

"We did it!" Tuwanda cried.

I heard David talking to someone in the background, and then he came back on line.

"Apparently you two are being sought by the Phoenix police, the Maricopa County sheriff, the Pima County sheriff, and the FBI, CIA, and NSA," he said brusquely. "I have explained your situation and have been ordered to bring you down safely on the American side of Nogales.

The Mexican authorities are aware that we are in their airspace and are allowing us to proceed."

Tuwanda snorted. "No reason to be so snippy. We the victims here."

"We are sending a helicopter to your position to escort you to Nogales. Please verify when you have visual contact with your escort, and we will patch the pilot in."

In less than ten minutes our escort appeared, and we were transferred to US Navy pilot Captain Greer, who sounded like he'd had a bad day and needed a cup of coffee. We followed his aircraft at the distance directed. Eventually he circled a field, indicating the area in which we were to land. It took three tries for Tuwanda to master the tail rotor and land semistraight. The last try we landed on the left skid and skipped forward. Tuwanda cut the rotors, and we rocked sideways and came down hard on both skids. The helicopter engine groaned after Tuwanda turned off the engine but did not burst into flames.

We were immediately surrounded by vehicles representing every government agency with even a smidgeon of jurisdiction. The Department of Agriculture agent reached us first but backed off when we informed her that we weren't transporting produce and Tuwanda told her where she would "stick that shit" if we were.

Next on the scene were the firemen and EMTs. We pointed them toward Pinky and Bob and waited for the next wave of EMTs for our own ministrations. Most of the emergency personnel spoke Spanish, so I did my best to follow along despite frequent interruptions by Tuwanda, who kept yelling, "What he say? What he say?"

I finally reached over and removed her earphones. She listened for a while and then said, "That didn't help at all. I still don't get what they babblin' about."

Two EMTs entered the cockpit and checked us for broken bones. By this time the helicopter was getting crowded.

My EMT examined my shoulder wound and then reached into his pouch for a syringe.

"Don't give her anything until I've had a chance to talk to her," intoned a voice from outside.

The EMT turned to see who was talking, shrugged, and put the syringe away.

Now that the adrenaline had worn off, my shoulder burned like crazy. I wanted whatever was in that needle.

Satisfied that neither of us had any broken limbs, we were assisted from the cockpit. Bryan intercepted us as soon as our feet hit the ground. He looked me up and down with very unsheriff-like concern.

"You've been wounded," he said.

"Yes, and it hurts. Why did you stop them from giving me a painkiller?"

"It's important that we know what happened first. You have no idea what we've been through trying to keep track of you."

I rolled my eyes and set my jaw. "Why is it always

about you? I'm the one who got kidnapped and knifed and then crash-landed a helicopter."

"Hey," interjected Tuwanda. "*I'm* the one who crash-landed the helicopter."

"Fair enough. But I'm the one who got it out of the spin."

"You the one who put it *into* the damn spin."

Bryan gestured for the EMT to come over. "Give her some of that painkiller," he said, pointing to me. Then, pointing to Tuwanda, he added, "If you've got any extra, give some to her too."

Bryan rode with us in the ambulance to the hospital, and although I don't remember exactly what I said, apparently I told him enough about our adventures and Goldstein's confession to complete the picture for him. The next day I had to tell the same story to the CIA, FBI, NSA, and the Pima Sheriff's Department. My hospital room looked like a lecture hall at Quantico.

Max had been busy in the meantime, and an article appeared in the Tucson and Phoenix newspapers that credited me with great acts of derring-do that resulted in the deaths of two bad guys and the serious injury of a third. Tuwanda was miffed because the articles only mentioned her once, referring to her as "another victim targeted by Goldstein."

"Victim my ass," she'd grumbled. "Tuwanda ain't nobody's victim."

We spent the next day visiting with Hamid, who would

not be released until the following week. Three days after our crash landing, Bryan drove Tuwanda and me back to Phoenix. Although he offered the use of the department's helicopter, neither Tuwanda nor I was interested.

We were on I-10 and had settled into a comfortable silence when Bryan commented, "You look like you've lost a lot of weight, Kate."

Tuwanda, who, along with Her, had commandeered the backseat, guffawed. "Yeah. She went on a crash diet."

It hurt to laugh, so I had to settle for muffled giggles.

Bryan reached over and patted my thigh.

"Look, Kate, I …"

The serious tone of his voice made me nervous.

"If you want to say something personal, maybe you should wait until we're alone," I interrupted in a whisper, head-jerking toward Tuwanda.

"Don't mind me," said Tuwanda. "I don't got no interest in what you two have to say to each other. I'm just gonna put on my headphones an' get some sleep."

I turned to look at her in surprise. "You kept the headset from the helicopter?"

"Damn right. I take them little barf bags off planes an' anythin' else I can get hold of. This time I took these," she said, waving the headset in the air. "They great. I can't hear nothin' when they on. I'm gonna be wearin' these a lot. I just may buy a bunch more for my Care Bares. Some of our clients is real screamers an' …"

"I get it. No need for details," I said hurriedly.

We waited for Tuwanda and her headphones to get settled, and then Bryan started again.

Once again, his delivery was thwarted. My new cell phone rang.

I briefly considered not answering in light of the intense, personal moment Bryan and I were about to experience, but strong emotions make me uncomfortable, and at some level the distraction was a relief.

The screen indicated the caller was "unknown." I'd probably interrupted an intense conversation for a robo-call.

"Hello?"

"Hi, gorgeous."

Mark.

I glanced nervously at Bryan.

"Hi. Were you released or am I your one phone call?"

"They let me go. They claimed they had a great case against me except for one minor defect: no evidence. I heard you survived a kidnapping and a helicopter crash. I had to hear your voice to make sure you were okay. Sam at your office was nice enough to give me your new cell number."

"It's been a busy week," I said modestly. "So the FBI no longer thinks you're a member of the LA Enforcers?"

Bryan's hands tightened on the steering wheel, and the muscles in his neck bulged.

"The FBI no longer believes the LA Enforcers exist."

"Excellent. I'm glad to hear you're a free man."

"Speaking of free, are you free for dinner anytime soon?"

I didn't have a chance to answer, because Bryan grabbed the phone and ended the call.

"Kate, I want to be friends again."

"Friends? As in we can play together during recess and sit at the same table in the lunch room?"

"All right. More than friends. Being sheriff is important to me, but being with you is just as important."

I grunted sarcastically.

"More important," he corrected.

I smiled at him sweetly.

"Can't we put the past few months behind us and be a couple again? I only ask that you try not to get kidnapped, shot, stabbed, or burned until the election is over. After that you can go back to your standard routine of confusion and mayhem."

Tempting, but I was still hurt over Bryan's affair with Miss Normal and resented his implication that my behavior was the sole cause of our breakup. Plus, I wanted to get to know Mark a little better now that we'd slept together and I knew his last name.

"I need time to heal, Bryan," I said carefully.

"Sure. I understand. I'll give you a couple of days

to think about it," he said, giving my thigh a couple of pats.

"*You'll* give me a couple of days? I'll take as long as I want. In the meantime, you think about what part *you* played in our breakup." I was sputtering now. "*You* had the affair. *You* decided to run for sheriff. All I did was be Kate as consistently and honestly as I knew how." We stared straight ahead, silently, for the remainder of the trip.

I didn't know it at the time, but I wasn't through with Bryan. He would come back into my life again under strange circumstances.

Made in the USA
San Bernardino, CA
02 March 2014